I0603430

THE GHOST MOTHERS

A FUN MAGICAL REALISM FANTASY

JACKIE MCCARTHY

CURLING TEA PRESS

This book is dedicated to the intelligent, passionate and courageous amongst us…and for those who don't yet know that they are.

1

*Y*asmin Taylor-Lee strode down the main street of Sydney's CBD the day after she fake-graduated from university. Which meant it was the day she was officially, as her mother so eloquently put it, 'out on her derrière.' Which was code for, 'move out and get a job.'

Her mother didn't know about the whole 'fake' part of the graduation, although she should have guessed. Yasmin was often cavalier with the truth – bending it in ways that suited her imagination, rather than actual reality.

In any case, Yasmin had decided that today was the beginning of the realisation of the dream she'd had since she was ten years old. Today, she was going to land her dream job at Warner Williams Corporation, working with *the* Felicia Pine on *The Woman's Standard*.

Yasmin believed that she was destined to steer *The Woman's Standard* into the next decade and beyond. Who better than a super-fan? And she was the biggest super-fan of all. For as long as she could remember, she'd scoured the back issues and waited by the mailbox for the latest delivery. She held a particular obsession for the magazine and everyone in it.

Yasmin nursed a hot chocolate in a coffee shop, scoping out the building opposite. She knew that she only had to flag the notorious editor down and wheedle her way into her dream job. And she would find her idol at the offices of the Warner Williams Corporation. Somewhere inside, on one of the floors, Felicia Pine would be sitting in her office.

Yasmin absently fingered the penny on a chain that she always wore around her neck. It was an old penny, and where the Queen should have been, three women appeared instead. Three inter-locking circles graced the other side.

The steel and black marble of the WWC building reflected the sun. The windows were tinted, as if to protect the identity of the celebrities inside. Just visible behind the windows were two over-sized LED screens, stretching from floor to ceiling. They flicked from one glossy magazine cover to the next: single shots of wasting models and full-sized advertisements for luxury cars. The screen featured all of Warner Williams's magazines, from those targeted to the high-end motor industry to fashion and teenage magazines, and, of course, *The Woman's Standard*.

Yasmin flattened out her shapely fifties' frock and pulled at her auburn curls, springing them back into place. She checked her makeup in the small antique mirror she kept in her handbag, then she took a deep breath, smiled winningly, and crossed the street, heading towards the imposing glass foyer. She felt her stomach turn, as if she were approaching royalty, or a crying baby, or a small explosive device. Then she remembered her skill at telling porkies. Her heart slowed.

The people entering the building were uniformly stick-thin, head-to-toe in labels. Their made-up faces glistened with bright colours – lip glosses, eyeshadows, deep-tone mascaras. And abso-lutely everyone wore their designer sunglasses into the foyer.

Yasmin took a deep breath, slipped on her sunglasses and sluiced through the glass revolving doors, her heels clacking on the black marble floor. Beyond the swipe gates, the mirrored lifts glinted as they swished open. Every shiny surface magnified an elongated, distorted reflection. She might as well have entered a new world, and those around her were an exotic, carbon-based species.

The long concierge desk ran along the wall. A snooty receptionist languished behind it, with a severe bun and red lipstick slashed across her mouth like a surgical incision.

Yasmin took a breath. She put on her best smile and strode towards that desk, ready to start the rest of her life.

The receptionist flirted with a bicep-hearty man. He wore a suit with a white shirt and a black tie, which outlined the chiselled chest beneath. Neither one saw her approach.

"Excuse me," Yasmin said, affecting a slight English accent.

The receptionist kept talking. Yasmin noticed the coiled earpiece in the security man's ear and the walkie-talkie he lifted from his belt. He leaned over the desk casually, one arm resting beneath him.

Yasmin cleared her throat.

The receptionist peeled her attention away from the man. Yasmin saw his name tag: it read 'Buckley.'

"Yes?" the receptionist said, clearly flushed.

"I'm so sorry to interrupt, but I'm running a few minutes late for my 9:30 with Felicia. Would you be so kind as to buzz me through?" Yasmin pushed her sunglasses up her nose and feigned disdain.

The receptionist eyed Yasmin. "Haven't I seen you here before?" she asked.

"Yes, of course. I was here last week. And the week before that." Yasmin leaned in. "We're very tight, Felicia and I. We meet regularly, you know, to exchange ideas. In fact, I was the inspiration for last month's cover. It was my idea to feature Nicole Kidman."

"No, that's not it." The receptionist seemed wary and frowned. "You come here all the time. And sit over there. In that chair."

"Are we okay here?" Buckley put a hand on the hip that held the walkie-talkie.

"We most certainly are not," Yasmin huffed, her English inflection forgotten. "You're delaying my meeting with Felicia. I suggest that if you don't want to raise her wrath, you let me straight in."

3

The security man gently grabbed Yasmin's arm. "You have no business being here, *ma'am*," he said. "It's best if you leave."

Oh, my. Yasmin was being thrown out of the Warner Williams Corporation!

"Well!" Yasmin huffed. She yanked her arm free. "I can see myself out, thank you very much."

She noticed a worker passing through the security gates – which sprang open and hovered for a frozen instant in time.

She hurled herself at the gate, just as the arms clicked shut. Her chest smacked into them. She ricocheted back, into the bear-hug of the security guard.

He manhandled her through the revolving doors and pushed her out onto the street.

"Please don't come back," he said, straightening his tie and reaching for the walkie-talkie at his hip. He pressed a finger to his ear. "All clear this end, Roger. Thanks."

He watched her stalk away, waiting until she had crossed the lights at the next block.

Yasmin stumbled down Park Street towards the bus, frustration and humiliation threatening to spill over. Today was meant to be the day she finally met Felicia. She was destined to work at WWC. It was her dream. How could they turn her away?

She stood waiting at the lights, caught in her head, her surroundings a blur.

She only half-saw the black limo pull up beside her. Only half-watched the window as it slid open, revealing the tan interior. Only briefly saw a sunglass-wearing, bouffant-haired older lady, with a smooth forehead – clearly botoxed. The woman's sharp eyes seemed to check outside for signs of rain. And then the window rose again and snapped shut.

It couldn't be.

The windows were darkly tinted so that Yasmin couldn't see through. Was that—?

No. Yasmin shook her head. Now she was delusional, on top of being recently shamed in the very office in which she hoped to someday forge her career.

4

But it was. Wasn't it?

The woman in that limo looked a hell of a lot like Felicia Pine.

The pedestrian light turned green and bleeped, urging Yasmin across the road. But she stood her ground, there on the kerb. The commuters pushed around her, cursing. The lights flashed red again, then green for the limo, which turned the corner and – yes! – headed straight towards the WWC building.

Yasmin wheeled around and kept pace with the limo, which crawled in the early-morning traffic. She followed it to the next block, then the next. It cleared the traffic and turned – right on cue – at Elizabeth Street. Yasmin ran as fast as her heels would allow and watched the limo pull into the car-park entrance. The limo driver slid her window open, speaking to the man at the ticket box by the gate. He wore the same security outfit as his colleague inside.

Yasmin didn't think, didn't rationalise, and certainly didn't stop. She bent low and crouched beside the car as the gate rose. She moved with the limo. Both she and Felicia had entered the car park!

The limo's tyres squealed slightly on the polished concrete as it slipped ahead, along the ramp. Yasmin checked over her shoulder. The security man hadn't seen her. He tapped his walkie-talkie on the ticket box, lost in thought.

Yasmin followed behind the limo, but her heels wobbled on the smooth, sloping concrete. She took off her shoes and carried one in each hand. One of the heels had cracked – but what was a three-hundred-dollar pair of shoes, compared to this opportunity?

She ducked her head to see the floor below. The limo made a sharp turn into a reserved car space. Yasmin sprinted, going into a slide just as the driver opened the door. Felicia stepped out.

Yasmin jerked to a stop directly in front of a shocked Felicia Pine, editor of *The Woman's Standard* and revered media personality for the last thirty years.

"Oh." Felicia's stiffened brow wrinkled ever so slightly.

She was fifty-two, but she could pass for early forties due to the amount of work she'd had done. Her straight shoulders and squarely planted feet completely dominated the space; this was a woman used to getting her way. She flicked her earth-toned scarf back over her shoulder, regarding Yasmin with a hard set to her lips.

"I'm sorry," Yasmin said, hopping on each foot as she put her heels back on.

"Ah, ma'am?" the driver asked, moving to take Yasmin's arm, and not in a friendly way.

"It's okay, I just want to talk," Yasmin said, backing up enough that Felicia could close the car door. The driver watched, on high alert.

"What is the meaning of this?" Felicia demanded, straightening herself.

"I'm so sorry, Ms Pine. I realise this is a little forward…"

"Don't worry, it happens all the time," she said.

"Really?"

"No," Felicia said. "First time."

"Well, I tried to make an appointment, you see, but you must be awfully busy, so I thought we could, you know, walk and talk?" Yasmin said hopefully.

Felicia pushed her sunglasses to the top of her head. Her lips pursed as if to say "don't try any funny business."

"You have exactly one minute of my time, and we will stay right here," Felicia said, fussing with a collection of manila folders.

"Oh, thank you, thank you so much, Ms Pine," Yasmin gushed. "You see, I've been waiting for this moment since I was ten years old and I first discovered your magazine."

"Starting a little young, weren't we?"

"Oh no, I love your magazine. I have every issue. I've memorised all the editors – none as weighty as your good self."

"Thirty seconds." Felicia pretended to check her Cartier watch.

"So, I wanted to present myself in person because I would be the perfect head journalist on *The Woman's Standard*." Yasmin stepped back a little. She didn't want to crowd her idol.

Her breath came in little pants – granted, she wasn't in the best

6

shape, but she was also in awe of the magnificent person standing right in front of her. She reached out her hand, slowly, towards Felicia's shoulder, just to feel the silk blouse and prove that she was a real person.

"Stop that," Felicia said. "I can see you're persistent and sending you away empty-handed will only result in more of these ridiculous encounters."

"Thank you!" Yasmin said.

"That wasn't a compliment," Felicia said. "But I'll tell you something – we only accept recent graduates with outstanding grades and excellent work experience. We also like to see a healthy swathe of community service."

Yasmin mentally noted everything.

"Awards don't go astray either. We like to know you can write."

"And?"

Felicia sighed and shifted the weight of the folders. She turned from the limo, heading towards the heavy lifts that would whisk her directly to the magical world of *The Standard*.

Felicia turned back again, regarding Yasmin's earnestness.

"Gargantuan Consulting handles all our recruiting." The lift arrived, and she entered, her brusqueness returning. "And if you ever stalk me again, I'll call the police."

2

*Y*asmin couldn't wait to tell her besties about her surprise encounter with Felicia Pine. They wouldn't believe her. She glowed all the way home on the bus, nearly missing her stop in the excitement. She ran from the bus stop, rubbing blisters into the heels of her feet, and burst straight through the front door of her childhood home, up the stairs and into her bedroom.

She placed her handbag in the corner and sat on the patchwork quilt on her single bed, gazing up. Right across the ceiling, from cornice to cornice, Yasmin had created a collage of pictures carefully snipped from the pages of *The Woman's Standard*. She had pasted images from every issue, dating right back to 1933. Ads for smarter lives littered the black and white pages: cleaning products, the latest cookers and diet pills; recipes for tinned pineapple and aspic jelly – everything a woman of each era needed to live a fulfilling life. Then there were the photos of women who had lived in the times of yesteryear. And of these photos, three women featured more than others.

"You'll never guess what happened today!" Yasmin said, her face raised to the collage.

A wind gusted around the room. Yasmin wrapped her cardigan tighter against the cold. The breeze flapped at the corners of the magazine pictures. Something began to pull at the very pages, as someone from the photos came to life.

First was Audrey, hand-painted onto the yellowing cover of a magazine. She wore a brown air-force uniform with a tan under-shirt and blue tie, her face highlighted in a kind of shimmery, silver outline.

She looked stunning, in that classic, old-movie siren kind of way. Each hand-painted brushstroke reached out, the soft colours melting into each other. She was glorious.

She reminded Yasmin of her grandmother.

Audrey began to glow all around the edges of her picture. First, the outline of her skirt shimmered in silver, and then the metallic flash danced through her teeth and the whites of her eyes.

Then the whole picture pulsated. Audrey moved her arms, peering at her uniform. She gave a little shoulder shimmy.

And then she seemed to puff out, to grow out of the page itself. Her limbs inflated, and she pulled free. First, her head lifted out of the page. Then her torso, her arms, her legs. As her skin pulled free, her ancient colours came with her, her skin and clothes an imprint of the sepia tones of the magazine from 1950.

She hovered a foot below her cover, a life-sized, translucent ghost of a person. Yasmin could see straight through her to the mirrored desk behind. Audrey's form glowed faintly, from the tips of her square-heeled shoes to the ends of her dark curls.

She stepped free from the page and hovered above Yasmin's bedroom floor.

"Hi, Audrey!" Yasmin said, moving in for a hug, shivering as their skin met.

"Hi there, chickadee!" Audrey said. "How did your big day go?"

Before Yasmin could answer, a second ghost began to mate-rialise.

Deborah wore a flared jumpsuit and shaggy lambskin vest. Her hair flowed across her back, the crown of her head garlanded with flowers. Her expression was supremely blissed-out, as if nothing could ever faze her.

In her magazine picture, she sat in a circle, hands joined with a ring of other women. She looked like an angel, with such calm on her face as they sat in the grass under a large-limbed tree. The women were intoxicating – they had so many friends. They seemed so content, so utterly without issues or problems. As if they had life all figured out.

The cover of the magazine glowed, washed in a ruby light, and Deborah began to puff out, inflate, just as Audrey had done. Her limbs pulled free of the page as she filled out into a life-sized entity.

Her skin and clothes were also imprinted with the colours of her magazine: a washed-out, grainy, photographic tone, just like her cover from 1970. She looked like someone from a photograph in an old album, where someone had scrubbed at her features over the years.

She stepped from the magazine to Yasmin's bedroom floor and stood admiring herself in the mirror affixed to the front of the wardrobe.

Yasmin shivered as they pulled in for a long hug. Deborah had a lot of love to give.

"Did you stick it to the man today?" she asked.

"Well…" Yasmin thought about the day she'd had, and a smile played across her face.

"We can't forget our Nicole," Audrey said, pointing to the ceiling.

The wind blew softly this time, halfway between a breeze and a draft down the hallway. It gusted below Yasmin's bedroom door and in through the slightly open window. The curtains billowed. The soft cone of wind swirled around Yasmin, cooling her skin.

As the wind eased, she opened her eyes again, and watched as Nicole's cover radiated a soft gold around its edges. Nicole's features also shone in backlit gold. Her hair shimmered with high-lights, as if from a Pantene ad. Her skin grew luminescent, and she moved.

She put down a beaker filled with green liquid onto the bench in her magazine, and pulled free from the page, her skin retaining the glossy sheen of the paper. She morphed into a ghost of a person, her skin shiny, lacquered and translucent. She radiated a soft, less intense gold.

Her presence felt gentle, less like the fiery incarnations of Audrey and Deborah. Yasmin could also see through Nicole, as she could with the others.

"How did your little experiment go today?" Nicole asked.

"You are not going to believe this!" Yasmin said.

Yasmin's 'fairy ghost-mothers' – the war-hero, the feminist and the scientist – all gathered around.

"Guess what? Guess what? Guess WHAT!?" Yasmin squealed.

The ghost-mothers hovered translucently above Yasmin's bedroom floor.

"You got the latest issue of *The Standard* in the mail today," Deborah said, deadpan, as she waved a placard denouncing the patriarchy.

"You found out you don't have to do the dishes," Audrey said, filing a piece of metal into a key.

"You sat for your uni exams?" Nicole looked up from her paper for the Intergovernmental Panel on Climate Change.

"I talked to Felicia Pine! I actually said words to her, and I asked her for a job! Can you believe it?"

Her fairy ghost-mothers couldn't. For the next minute and a half, a barrage of quickly fired questions hit Yasmin. She felt as if her lungs were a deflated bagpipe, and she couldn't get her wind back.

"So, what did she say?" Nicole asked.

"When do you start?" Audrey said, stepping forward.

"How much are they paying you?" Deborah asked.

"Well, I have to call the recruitment agency first," she said.

"So you don't have the job," Deborah said, frowning.

"Well, no." Yasmin thought for a moment. "But I've as good as got it, once I call the agency."

"Pull back for a second," Audrey said, holding her key up to the light, blowing away a stray metal filing. "You can't just call the agency without an infiltration plan."

"She's right," Deborah said. "We need to prepare you for the call."

"But I'm good at making things up. Everyone fudges their resumes. Nobody tells the truth."

"Yes, but you'll have to remember the fibs you've told to the recruitment company because you'll have to tell the same elaborate tales to Felicia."

"She's right," Audrey said. "Your falsehoods don't always add up."

"But stretching the truth is my best strength!" Yasmin said.

"Parking fine; court ten days later," Deborah reminded her.

"That wasn't my fault," Yasmin said. "The judge deliberately misled me in the way she phrased her questions."

"I didn't see the sign," Nicole prompted. "All you had to remember was, 'I didn't see the sign.' And instead, you deflected into a tale of misplaced feather boas and sun-faded paint."

"Good point. I don't want to mess this up," Yasmin said. "It's too important."

"And you'll need supporting documentation."

Nicole unfurled a piece of paper, which folded out from an inch across, to napkin size, then A4 size, then into an A3 sheet. It was crisscrossed with lists, thought bubbles and colour-coded lines. She laid it on Yasmin's desk and began checking things off.

"You'll need references, work experience and a strong social-media and LinkedIn presence. Exemplary high school and university grades, awards, community service, dedication to journalism in general and *The Standard* in particular. Drive and determination. Something that implies you're good with people and have an outstanding work ethic. Finally, something that flatters Felicia's ego. Everyone loves a little flattery."

Yasmin, Deborah and Audrey stared at Nicole, their mouths agape like skewered fish on a grill.

"What?" Nicole said. "Clearly I'm the career woman of the group."

"Yes, that's great," Yasmin said. "Thank you. Now, how the heck am I going to get all that?"

Deborah set her placard aside, a slyness to her smirk.

"Ladies? Let's get to work."

SNAP!

The SLR shutter *clicked* as Yasmin stood in front of a glossy, marble background, beaming in a mortarboard and gown. Her auburn curls cascaded over one bronzed shoulder, oh so perfectly.

However, the person behind the camera was not the university photographer, and the marbled background was an A3 sheet of paper tacked to her bedroom wall.

Audrey put the digital camera down on the desk, admiring the electronics.

"We could have used this type of thing to spy on the Germans," she said.

Yasmin took off the mortarboard and gown. She felt a thrill prickle her scalp as she began downloading the photos onto her laptop.

"It feels like I really did graduate from uni, instead of just pretending to go to class…" Yasmin said.

"Yeah, and taking a whole five years just to fail to graduate," Deborah said, grinning.

"So, let's think about this strategically," Nicole said, shifting a strand of hair behind her ear.

Deborah stepped forward. "You've never written anything."

"I pen a pretty mean birthday card," Yasmin said.

"You don't have any work experience."

Yasmin screwed up her face. "I'm only interested in working at *The Standard*. I can't waste my time anywhere else."

"And your grades are pretty much shot."

"Don't worry," Nicole said. "We'll build you anew, from the ground up, create the ultimate worthy job applicant."

"That sounds perfect," Yasmin said.

Deborah nodded to Nicole, who settled in front of the laptop. The others watched over her shoulder as she typed out a LinkedIn profile, citing impressive work experience at the university news-paper and various roles at local rags, culminating in the position of journalist at *The Guardian*. She outlined Yasmin's high-achieving results at high school, then university. She waxed lyrical about her passion for charity work.

Once the fake Yasmin had been brought to life online, Nicole posted the 'graduation' photo they'd just taken as her profile picture.

Next, Deborah created a carefully curated public Facebook profile. Yasmin had never bothered with social media. Who would she have as her 'friends?' She would probably have a total of five: her mum, sister, and her three ghost-mothers. And that was more than a little sad. But Deborah managed to collate a whole three hundred friends – from where, Yasmin didn't like to think – but it made her sit taller. Even if they were paid friends, they made her feel popular.

Audrey created a few fake awards using Photoshop – first in her year in English; winner of a state debating competition; highly commended in an accelerated mathematics course.

And, for the grand finale – Audrey photoshopped Yasmin's face onto a picture of a woman stepping on stage to accept the award for the 'Walkley Young Australian Journalist of the Year.'

They printed everything out and placed the documents, awards and her social-media logins inside a manila folder.

"Wow. I didn't expect all this," Yasmin said, flicking through the flawless creations. She paused on the journalism award, placing her finger on 'her' formal gown, the trace of satin, the sheen of her smile. Yasmin felt proud as if she'd really earned that award.

"It takes a lot to fake an identity in today's connected world," Deborah said, handing her two sheets of marbled paper. "Final stop, the campus library."

Before the hour was out, Yasmin was lurking in some nook of the campus library, right beside the Subterranean Engineering section. It proved to be the least-visited section of the library.

Yasmin leaned against the wall, feeling the cool of the air

conditioning vent blast her humidity-frizzed flyaways. Tinny music emanated from a nearby student who couldn't afford noise-cancelling headphones.

Yasmin's mind wandered and, for some reason, she conjured a clear picture of her younger self: a precocious and uncoordinated ten-year-old, sitting alone on the steel benches at recess, grandmother-less, friendless, and without a father. She shook off the feeling. She would soon be a fabulously successful journalist at *The Woman's Standard*. She'd make it.

Yasmin fed the elements of her magically new-and-improved grades into the photocopying machine. She positioned her record, covering the grades with the faked print-out. She bent over the photocopier with precise concentration, carefully easing the papers with a slight nudge of her finger. The sheets of paper scratched as they slid over each other.

She lowered the photocopier lid as if she were re-boxing dynamite. The light skimmed underneath the closed lid, and then the paper mechanically regurgitated.

Yasmin watched as a perfectly passable, highly illegal, and potentially damning academic transcript rolled out of the photocopier. The marbled paper was green and official-looking.

It would be her undoing, but without it, she wouldn't have a chance of making it to the interview. Surely it would be worth it?

And, for the first time since she'd started uni, five years ago, Yasmin headed home to study.

3

*B*ack in her bedroom, Yasmin busily taped another photo, cut from the latest *Standard,* to the vast photographic collage on her ceiling. She stood back and admired her handiwork.

Audrey reached into the photo of her French Resistance farmhouse and plucked an apple from the tree. She picked another and gave it to Yasmin, who pointed to the collage.

"Do you like my vision board?" she asked.

"I don't know what a 'vision board' is, but this apple is delicious," Audrey replied.

Yasmin crunched on the fruit as she opened her laptop and googled articles on how to land your dream job. She studied what to say in the interview and how to make a good impression. She scoured articles on the magazine-publishing industry. She watched *The Devil Wears Prada,* making notes as if it were a textbook.

Every mention of *The Standard* sent a thrill through her.

She devoured every copy from her collection, from 1933 to now. She knew the royal family more intimately than Diana's biographer. And she had memorised every dinner-party recipe, conversation starter and cleaning trick.

She lay on her quilted bed, playing with the penny on its chain while her besties quizzed her. Nicole marked the score on her ever-present clipboard.

"Who was the editor from 1976 to 1983?"

"Who won the inaugural 'Woman of the Year' award?"

"Who was the first woman to scale Mount Everest, and which issue did she feature in?"

Yasmin fired out her answers, round after round, until she grew dizzy with facts and bored of her bedroom. But her ghost-mothers cracked on, as if they were readying an Olympic contender for a gruelling decathlon.

After a week of intensive training and study, Nicole declared Yasmin ready to make the call and her chest puffed like a proud mother tigress as she handed Yasmin the phone.

Yasmin dialled.

She cleared her throat. Her stomach hardened like her beloved aspic jelly.

She glanced at her besties. Audrey gazed back, like a movie siren; Deborah swayed to unheard folk music; and Nicole gave an overenthusiastic thumbs up.

"Yes?" a smooth female voice answered.

"My name is Yasmin Taylor-Lee, and Felicia Pine asked me to call for a position as a journalist at *The Woman's Standard*."

Her besties squealed with excitement, and Yasmin hushed them with a wave of the hand.

"Sorry about that," Yasmin said. "My friends are watching *The Bachelor*. Yes, so about that job?"

Weeks went by, then a whole month. Gargantuan Consulting had Yasmin's resume the entire time, and she hadn't heard a thing.

The first day was the hardest. She jumped at every call. She even ran to answer the door, with some weird notion that the recruitment agency would track her down and personally escort her, in Felicia's limo, to the interview.

After the second day, she only got up for phone calls, but they were mostly for her younger sister, Catina, and one from her mum's work.

After the week played out, Yasmin had assumed a prone position on the couch, the will to live slowly seeping out of her pores as she binge-watched *Mad Men* on Netflix.

She lay head-to-foot with Catina, fighting for legroom on the couch. Catina had purple tips in her black hair, a petulant smirk, and spent all of her free time hanging with her drama buddies.

Yasmin took note of the ladies' fashion on the show, wishing that she had been born in the sixties. She fancied she could have rocked a beehive. She was halfway into the fourth season when her mobile buzzed. She checked the screen – unknown number. She almost didn't pick up, but then Catina pushed her off the couch; she answered, just to let Catina know that she was still in control.

"Hello, Yasmin?" a lady asked.

"Yes."

"It's Jane, at Gargantuan Consulting."

Oh, my! Yasmin put on her most casual voice and replied, "Hello, Jane. Good to hear from you."

She slipped into the privacy of the hallway.

"Yes, well. I've got to say, your resume is top shelf – exactly what we're after."

"Um, thanks." Yasmin's voice came out in a squeak. She started a happy dance up the hall.

"Felicia wants you to come in tomorrow morning, first thing. I must say, on paper, you're our most promising candidate."

"I am? I mean, I'd be delighted."

"Can you be there at nine a.m.?"

"Yes! Sure, absolutely." She tried not to let the phone waggle too far from her ear, as her dancing became more erratic.

"Great. The job isn't for a journalist, I have to warn you. You'll start as an editorial assistant. And it's a tough role. Not many people make it."

"Yes, great. So I'll see Felicia tomorrow morning at nine a.m." She hung up the phone and let out a resounding "Whoooooop!"

Yasmin bounded up the stairs two at a time, bursting into her bedroom. In a few steps, she was at her mahogany wardrobe, riffling through the dresses, skirts and blouses. She shoved an unusually puffy petticoat out of the way, and tossed dress after dress onto her bed for consideration.

"Oh my God, oh my God, oh my God!" she said to her ghostly friends, watching their beaming faces appear. "I did it! I got the interview!"

Her ghost-mothers shrieked and moved in for an awkward, cold air-hug. Yasmin shivered as their forms touched her skin.

"What a gas!" Audrey said.

"Far out," Deborah said.

"Way to go, Yasmin!" Nicole said.

They danced and squealed so loudly that her mother, Susan, yelled for Yasmin to cool it. Yasmin put a finger to her lips.

"You guys are going to give yourselves away!"

It was the most exciting day of her friends' lives, too, the highest validation Yasmin could ever give them. She put her hand over her heart, as theatrical as Catina, and smiled humbly.

Audrey pulled a champagne bottle and glasses from a photo on the ceiling, and popped the cork with a *bang*. Yasmin felt the splash of champagne as it exploded out the top. Glasses were re-filled. Raised. Downed in celebration.

Yasmin, a little drunk, spun on the spot, her eyes closed, feeling her skirt billow. After a minute of spinning, she fell onto the bed, ecstatically giddy.

"Dreams do come true," she said.

Her friends joined in a chorus of 'For She's a Jolly Good Fellow.' Nicole and Audrey's flighty sopranos and Deborah's hearty contralto mixed together, in the swelling culmination of her dreams.

It felt as if all her birthdays had come at once.

A knock at her door hushed them. A fresh champagne cork ricocheted off the door in the awkward silence.

"Yasmin? Could you turn the volume down, please? My head," Susan said.

"Sorry, Mum." Yasmin stifled giggles with the back of her hand. She peeked out of the bedroom door. "I got the interview at *The Standard*."

"You did? I'm so pleased for you." Susan hugged her daughter. "Now you can finally pay me back and move out, you know – into the adult world."

Fleeting annoyance crossed Yasmin's face. Why did her mother have to go and ruin the happiest moment of her life? But she returned the hug.

"I'll pay you back with my first paycheque," Yasmin said.

"You owe me a lot of money; it will take quite a few paycheques," Susan said. She patted Yasmin on the head as if she were a two-year-old who had successfully peed in her potty. "I'm just going to rest, so hush up the celebrations. Who have you got in there, anyhow?"

Susan popped her head into the bedroom, peering straight through Yasmin's fairy ghost-mothers. Audrey gave a petulant wave, and Deborah stifled giggles.

"Nobody. Just me," Yasmin said.

Susan shivered, frowning at the closed window. "Your room is always so draughty."

Yasmin's ghosts moved away from the bedroom door to the farthest corner of the room. Susan stopped shivering.

"Bye, Mum." Yasmin closed the door and turned to the subdued gathering. Deborah blew a party whistle; the paper curled out and then back again, ending on a flagging note, just like their deflating happiness.

Yasmin did owe her mum a lot of money. She'd borrowed funds for her living expenses for years – on top of the uni fees. She was twenty-four and broke, and she'd just been told, in no uncertain terms, that there was an expiry date on her meal ticket in the family home.

Stuff it – she had the interview, and her life was about to turn a very sharp corner.

She stepped back to her bed and perused the dresses she'd thrown there for consideration.

All she had to do was impress the great Felicia Pine.

Yasmin lay awake for most of the night, turning from one side to the other. When sleep finally came, in the quietest part of the night, she fell into fitful dreams.

~

Yasmin is pressed up against Audrey behind a French farmhouse. She can feel the scratch of the uniform jacket on her cheek. A rock bites into her bare knee as they crouch in the dirt.

Ragged chickens peck around them, too stupid to be terrified. They're used to the sound of gunshots and shells. All Yasmin can hear now is her breath, coming in pants, rattling out of her throat.

One of the chickens makes a beeline for them, its flaccid comb flopped to one side. She must have fed it before, and it's slim pickings on the packed dirt. She shoos it away, ducking her head further beneath the woodpile, feeling the splinters poking her neck, smelling gunpowder and pig manure.

"Now!" Audrey yells and grabs Yasmin's arm. They sprint over to the open door of the farmhouse and dive inside.

Audrey's already on her feet; Yasmin rolls onto hers. Audrey pokes her STEN submachine gun through the curtains, and ducks as a rapid-fire round of bullets digs into the side of the house. Yasmin's mouth tastes acrid, and adrenalin courses through her body.

Audrey nods to her and pops up, firing a round into the bushes outside. Yasmin careens into the kitchen. Opens the cupboard under the sink. Retrieves the package wrapped in brown paper and packing string.

"Got it!" she says.

Audrey flicks her head at the back door.

Yasmin sprints, propelled faster by fear, cradling the package underneath her arm. She glances back and sees Audrey sneak out and grab a rusting bicycle, which was leaning against the rear of the house. Yasmin finds another paint-flaked bicycle beside the pig pen, and they're off along the dirt road. Audrey slings her gun over her shoulder, the metal barrel clicking against the buttons on her uniform. Yasmin's bike spokes seem flimsy as the wheels turn, and she can't pedal fast enough. She guesses she'll never be able to pedal fast enough.

Men shout behind them in German.

They put everything they have into pedalling, but the wheels slow down, rather than speed up. The Germans are on their tail, their shouts closer. The more they pedal, the slower they seem to go, the bikes clattering under them, breaking apart into dust. The Germans are on them, grabbing with rough hands, knocking them off their feet...

Yasmin sat bolt upright in bed, her nightdress twisted, her hair escaping the rag curlers. What was that noise?

Her alarm jittered on the bedside table, shaking the wood beneath. It was an old-style clock with a real face and hands – like clocks used to be, before phones and computers told time electronically.

And it made an unholy racket.

She flicked off the alarm, and the clock sprung back into healthy, friendly ticking, as if nothing had been amiss, as if the world was okay again. As if the Germans never existed.

"Did you have a nightmare?" Audrey asked, materialising from her picture, hovering translucently by the bed as she straightened her blue air-force tie.

She pulled a compact from her handbag and applied rouge, angling the mirror to catch Yasmin's reflection.

Nicole and Deborah appeared too.

"No, I was dreaming about Grandma," she lied, shaking sleep from her head. She didn't want Audrey to worry.

Yasmin sniffed, stretched, and felt the state of her hair with her hands – it was a mess of tangled curling rags and matted hair.

"So, big day today," said Audrey.

"Big day?" Yasmin was still chasing the adrenalin-charged feeling of being pursued by men in uniform who wished her harm. She took a deep breath and slowed her breathing, feeling her heart knocking inside her like a caged animal shaking its bars.

"Come on, lazybones," Nicole said, perky as always, easing

into her lab coat. She pushed her reading glasses up her nose and tapped her forehead with a ballpoint pen.

Yasmin peered out of the lace curtains at the burgeoning summer's day. The harsh sunlight already heated the air. The temperature would probably push forty again.

"You're going to be late!" Deborah barked in a tone that could rouse a whole commune. She adjusted her flower headband and splayed her bare feet in a power stance. "You wouldn't be going for the interview at all if I hadn't had my way with the patriarchy all those years ago."

Wait – the interview!

"Oh, darn," Yasmin said, leaping from her bed, the sheets tangled around her legs. She face-planted into the bedside table, upsetting a stack of *Standards*.

"I wish we could come with you," Deborah said, charging the door with her shoulder. But she was flung back into the bedroom by some unseen force. Deborah shrugged. "I always think that will work."

"I wish you could come too," Yasmin said.

"But we can't leave your bedroom," Nicole said sadly.

Yasmin hurriedly showered and grabbed her resume on the way out, sprinting the last hundred metres to catch the 426 into town.

She settled into a seat and took a calming breath. She'd make it.

In the back of her mind, Yasmin wondered why the role had come up. What had happened to the last editorial assistant? Working at *The Standard* was a dream for many people. The Warner Williams Corporation was the original media dynasty, printing the first magazines in Australia; whoever ran *The Standard* would have the ear of the country's most powerful families. They wouldn't be shy about voicing opinions or having someone fired – someone like Yasmin, if they found out she had never worked in a magazine company before, or anywhere else for that matter. Her skill set was built on the strength of the tall tales she told herself.

But everyone told little white lies to get jobs, every day. It's how the recruitment industry worked, right?

She exited the bus on Elizabeth Street and headed to the familiar WWC building. As she reached the foyer, she caught a glance of her shapely green fifties' frock, too-bright lipstick and white cardigan (which, she realised now, of all times, was too tight), and elbow-length gloves. Gloves! Whose idea was that? She quickly stuffed them into her handbag.

She strode right up to the front desk. The faultlessly presented young thing behind the counter lay her disdainful eyes over Yasmin's outfit.

"I'm Yasmin Taylor-Lee, here to see Felicia Pine," Yasmin said.

Buckley, the all-too-familiar security guard, hovered behind the receptionist.

"I thought I told you not to come back?" he said, resting his hand on his walkie-talkie.

4

*B*uckley had a hold of her arm and waited until she stopped struggling.

"Will you take your hands off me," Yasmin demanded.

Buckley thought about it for a minute, then grabbed her harder.

"I'm here to see Ms Pine," she continued.

"You've tried that one already."

"Jane at Gargantuan specifically said I was to present myself here at nine a.m. If you don't believe me, check the visitor schedule."

Buckley turned to the receptionist, giving a 'can you believe it?' toss of the head.

"Yasmin?" a voice called from the other side of the foyer. "Ms Yasmin Taylor-Lee?"

"Me!" Yasmin exclaimed, shooting her free arm in the air. She turned to Buckley. "That's me."

He released her and said, "Seriously?"

"Thank you," Yasmin said, huffing and making a show of pulling at her cardigan, which had ridden up over her hips.

She almost ran over to the petite, edgily dressed woman, whose short hair was shaved on one side. She didn't seem much older than Yasmin – maybe around twenty-five – but there was something about the set of her posture that said she absolutely belonged in the building.

"I'm Tasha Towns, Felicia's junior sub-editor."

They shook hands. Yasmin's were clammy. Tasha pointed towards the lifts.

As they approached the security gates, Tasha nodded at the receptionist, who was now painting the perfect picture of hospitality.

"How was Friday?" the receptionist whispered as they passed.

Tasha rolled her eyes. "Oh my God. I was so trashed."

"Me too!" The receptionist buzzed them through.

Yasmin, however, concentrated on the gate as it swung open before her, the lifts just a few steps beyond. She felt a jolt of new excitement shoot through her tummy.

I've done it – even if I don't get the job, I've infiltrated WWC and all the family dynasty secrets within.

Yasmin stroked the visitor badge pinned to her white cardigan until she noticed Tasha staring. Yasmin stopped.

"Did you find the office okay?" Tasha asked as they waited for the lifts.

"Oh, I come here every day."

Tasha clearly hasn't heard that answer before.

"Ah…actually…" She wondered whether she should just say it. She did. "I've wanted to work here since I was ten years old."

"At *The Woman's Standard*?"

"Yes."

"As in, before you were even a woman?"

"Yes."

She looked at Yasmin as if she had grown a second ear.

"Strange thing for a ten-year-old to even think about."

"I guess."

Where's that bloody lift before I dig myself in deeper?

"Well, I was an exceptional ten-year-old, it has to be said. Some say, gifted…"

The lift *dinged* and Tasha waved Yasmin ahead.

They arrived at the atrium. Several frosted glass doors led into the main office. Yasmin was disappointed not to see a fancy, branded foyer, like the publishing houses in the movies: something with a wood-panel-finish and glinting gold lettering.

"We've got you in the Eleanor Gilbert Room," Tasha said.

"As in, Eleanor Gilbert, the editor from 1956 to 1962?"

Tasha gave her that look again.

"I mean…" she back-pedalled. "Great. Fabulous."

Tasha buzzed them through to a corridor, which was flanked on one side with glass-walled meeting rooms. They arrived at the largest room.

The long boardroom was filled with high-backed, black chairs, which framed a white, expansive table. Tasha indicated a seat, suggesting Yasmin make herself comfortable. The room seated about twenty people, an imposing show of power. Yasmin wondered what else, besides job interviews, took place in this room. She bet they brought people in here to fire them. Maybe the odd decapitation?

At the thought, Yasmin felt her heart nudging her chest, just letting her know it was there, ready to implode as soon as she opened her mouth. She sat on the chair closest to the hallway and crossed her legs.

"Felicia will be here soon," Tasha said, then added as an afterthought, "good luck."

"Thanks." Yasmin watched Tasha close the door behind her.

Yasmin stretched out her fingers, trying to work out the tension. She straightened her cardigan, its buttons straining against their holes. She hoped one didn't pop off mid-interview and blind Felicia.

And, with a flurry of earth-coloured scarves and the click of an efficient heel, she was there, right in front of Yasmin, holding out her hand.

"Hello. I'm Felicia Pine."

Felicia held her shoulders in a way that screamed high society. She reminded Yasmin of an older Cate Blanchett: the effortless class, the way she made you feel like a bogan for not wearing couture. Felicia studied Yasmin, raising her eyebrows slightly – as far as was possible on her botoxed face.

"We've met," Yasmin said. "In your basement car park."

Felicia drew a blank, then, leaning back, remembered.

"I thought I told you I'd call the police if you kept stalking me."

"I'm not…no…Jane from Gargantuan sent me. Said my resume was 'top shelf.'"

Felicia seemed unconvinced, so Yasmin stood up and held out her hand. Felicia reluctantly shook it. Her palms were even clammier than before. Felicia snatched a tissue from the box on the table and discreetly wiped her hands.

"I'm sorry," Yasmin said. "I'm just incredibly in awe of seeing you again."

"Most people are."

Tasha entered the room and passed a manila folder to Felicia, then exited, shutting the door behind her.

Yasmin was trapped in a room with the most powerful woman in publishing, and they were off to a bad start.

"Well, you're here now," Felicia said. "Let's take a look at you."

Felicia opened the folder and perused the two-page resume within. That ghastly headshot, Yasmin now realised, was insufficient. She should have had someone take it who knew their way around a camera. She most certainly should have photoshopped herself to the nth degree. Whitened her teeth. Straightened that crooked incisor.

"So…" Felicia flicked between the pages with an expert, editing eye. "Yasmin. That's a pretty name."

"Oh, I'm Australian. I'm a citizen with a right to work here and everything."

"I didn't think otherwise."

"Oh. Sorry."

"We are not sorry in this office."

"Right. Um, well, I think it's Persian or something."

"It's lovely."

"Thank you."

Yasmin shifted in her seat. They hadn't even reached the proper questions yet.

"So, I see that you graduated from Sydney University, with a degree in—"

"Journalism," Yasmin said, pleased with herself for remembering.

"I don't need you to put words in my mouth."

"Sorry."

Felicia peered up at Yasmin, hands poised on the resume. Yasmin shook her head by way of – yet another – apology. Felicia waited for a second, then continued reading.

"So how did you find Sydney University?"

"Oh, I loved it," Yasmin said without conviction.

"And you have a little experience with the university paper. You were…" Felicia peered closer. "Chief editor?"

Yasmin screwed up her face, her eyes flitting to the ceiling for the answer. "Yes, for my last semester. Before that I wrote features."

"I see."

Felicia read the rest of the page. The *sffft* of the paper scraping against itself seemed amplified. Was she buying this?

"Worked in Gleebooks, blah blah," Felicia said almost to herself. She straightened, glaring at Yasmin, who withered, and not just a little. "So why are you applying for this exact role, in this exact company?"

"I've wanted to work here all my life. At *The Standard*."

"All of your life?"

"As much of it as I can remember."

"So as a, say, primary-schooler, when someone asked you what you wanted to be when you grew up, you said you wanted to work for *The Woman's Standard*?"

"It used to freak people out. Or amuse them."

"Well, I am neither freaked out, nor amused."

"It does sound a little ridiculous, but it's true. I've read every issue, dating back to 1933."

"And how, exactly, does being *The Standard*'s biggest fan help my editorial team?"

Yasmin thought for a second. From the angle of Felicia's raised eyebrow, it was a second too long.

"I guess I bring a certain kind of passion that nobody else does."

It seemed lame even as she said it.

"Many people want to work here. Many people can be passionate."

"I understand that, but I feel like I was born to this. Like I have no other purpose in life."

"So you'd be prepared to work hard."

"Of course."

"Harder than anyone else on the team?"

"Absolutely."

"Then you're a super-fan. Nothing more." Felicia stood, and Yasmin did, too. Was she being dismissed?

"I don't think you understand, I've been working towards this moment all my life, and I am absolutely the person for the job."

"Then I will absolutely make sure that my assistant gets back to you." Felicia rose from the desk.

"Wait," Yasmin said, jabbing at the zip of her resume folder. "I have something to show you."

She pulled out a sketch pad, filled with a magazine collage.

"Here. It's the latest piece I'm working on."

Felicia wavered, clearly thinking of the next young hopeful waiting to be interviewed, but instead, stepped towards Yasmin. She leaned – with reluctance in all her movements – towards the collage.

Yasmin had laid it out like a magazine centrefold, covered with the portraits of famous Australian women throughout history.

"There's the first lady to circumnavigate the globe in a single-person aeroplane. There's the first female Governor-General. And finally, our home-grown Darling of Hollywood, our first to crack the golden screen."

"When did you write this?" Felicia pointed to the article within the collage.

"Oh, that? A few months ago."

Yasmin saw an almost imperceptible twitch in Felicia's eye. She took the folder, holding it closer, skimming the first couple of paragraphs. She even sat back down again.

When she finished, she made a dismissive sound, something between a *hmph* and a *hmm*. She pushed the folder back into Yasmin's hands.

Felicia read the resume more closely.

"When did you leave *The Guardian*?" she asked.

"Sorry?"

"Your previous job?"

"Oh yes, of course. My previous job at *The Guardian*."

"Yes, that's what I just said. Are you going to keep telling me things I've just told you?"

"So – I mean, well, yes – not long after I wrote that article, you know, under my maiden name."

She'd printed the article from the website, the byline reading Yasmin Whittaker. But of course, that was a different Yasmin. A little white lie to get her over the line…

Felicia read the first section of the article.

"An extraordinary piece of journalism…"

"Thank you," Yasmin said, trying not to overdo it, remaining humble. But – she had her! "It's just something I pumped out on spec…"

"This article opened the Graham Inquiry," Felicia said. "It was unflinching, ground breaking."

Yasmin smiled demurely at Felicia, who composed herself. For a moment, Yasmin saw real esteem there, even if it was for something she hadn't done. Felicia respected the journalism. Her features slid back into disinterest.

"Well, it's not the sort of thing we write here."

Felicia stood up.

"But it could be…" Yasmin said.

Felicia remained standing, making it clear the interview had concluded.

Yasmin wasn't sure if it was enough. She wasn't sure of anything about Felicia Pine, who had already turned for the hallway.

"So thank you for seeing me." Yasmin held out her hand, and Felicia shook it as if it were a limp beef steak and she was trying not to get bloodied.

"Tasha will show you out of the building."

And with that, Felicia vanished.

5

*Y*asmin pushed open her front door, heels in hand. She'd had plenty of time to replay the interview over in her mind on the bus home. And the more she thought about it, the more she remembered that one moment – when she had Felicia – and then Felicia's features had turned back to stiffened disinterest.

She froze that memory and replayed it over and over again: Felicia's rapture, disinterest. Rapture, disinterest. Rapture…

Felicia saw Yasmin's brilliance – even if it was borrowed. But that hadn't been enough, had it?

Her friends were waiting in her bedroom. Nicole, the most diligent of the lot, accosted her first.

"So when do you start?" She dabbed at proud tears with a tissue.

"What was it like to infiltrate publishing royalty?" Audrey asked, resting the radio signalling component that she was repairing on her lap.

"Are they paying you enough?" Deborah said, stuffing an envelope with protest leaflets.

"I don't know, guys," Yasmin said, slumping on the bed. She hoisted her resume folder, as if it were a weight from a training pack, onto the desk. Her limbs felt heavy. She lay back on the bed, staring up at the ladies. "I think I tanked."

Nicole let out a little 'Oh!'. Audrey started punching her fist into her other hand. Deborah merely smiled.

"See?" she said. "'The man' will take everything that's good in this world and *smash its little face in.*"

"I'm pretty tired, actually," Yasmin said. "Let's talk about it later."

Nicole looked positively scared, as if Yasmin would leap out of the first-floor window and break both ankles. Audrey shook her head as if Yasmin had just conceded the war to the Germans. But Deborah? She grinned as if she had seen it coming.

"There's only one thing to do in situations like this," she said.

"What's that?" Yasmin said.

"Jimi. Hendrix."

Deborah set the needle on the record and the iconic jangling guitars and piercing electric solos filled the air.

"I'm not in the mood for Jimi," Yasmin said.

Deborah recoiled as if she'd been slapped. "Not in the mood for...What a square."

Yeah. That's me – the square.

Yasmin sat up, remembering the marble foyer, its other-worldly inhabitants, the glitz and pizazz. She smiled coyly.

"But, Felicia Pine – you should have seen her!"

Her besties crowded in to relish the details.

A few days later, Yasmin sat at the dining-room table, dressed in slacks and a blouse, barefoot, with a towel wrapped around her wet hair. Catina slouched beside her, hiding behind her too-long, too-black fringe.

Catina twirled her nose ring around.

"Would you mind not picking your nose at the dinner table?" Yasmin asked.

"I'm not picking, idiot. You have to keep moving piercings around. So they don't grow over."

"Oh, yes. Piercing-care is an exceedingly useful life skill."

"Loser."

"Hey, you two!" Their mother butted in. "Family dinner time."

Family dinner time was true to form then.

"So I thought we could come up with a brainstorming session, you know, help Yasmin get a job," Susan said, checking the watch pinned to the pocket of her nurse's uniform.

"If it means her moving out, I am so in," Catina said.

"That's another topic up for conversation," Susan eyed Yasmin carefully.

"What, the 'get a job and kick me out of home' conversation?" Yasmin said.

"Honey, that's not what this is. Consider it more of a career-counselling session. Or like those life coaches. You'd pay a lot of money to see a life coach."

The house phone rang.

Catina shoved her chair back, and Yasmin had no chance of beating her. Yasmin knew it would be for her sister anyway.

"Yes, Yasmin lives here," she heard Catina say. "No, I don't think she's home—"

"Hey!" Yasmin shot across the room and wrenched the phone from her sister. "Hello? Yasmin speaking."

"It's Jane. From Gargantuan Consulting?" a smooth voice said on the other end of the line.

"Oh, yes. Hello, Jane." Yasmin felt a spiral of panic traverse her stomach, writhing like a newly birthed, tiny demon.

"I'm sorry to call so late, but I've been trying to reach you on your mobile phone, and it's going straight to voicemail. I just wanted to make sure you got my message."

Yasmin hadn't checked her phone today.

"My phone's been stolen. We had a break-in."

Her mother shot Yasmin a greasy stare. She hated it when Yasmin lied.

"So I guess this is the big news you've been waiting for." Jane took a deep breath. "Felicia Pine wanted me to inform you that you're the new editorial assistant, if you are still available."

"Yes!" Yasmin wound back her enthusiasm. "I'm definitely available."

Susan shot Yasmin two thumbs up from the dining-room table. Catina smirked. Yasmin turned around for some privacy.

"Good, that's fantastic," Jane said. "So the package is the same figure I mentioned before."

"Yes, that's fine."

Jane paused. Yasmin wondered if she had said anything wrong. Should she have accepted so enthusiastically?

"So you accept the job," Jane said, "without negotiating the pay?"

"Is that normal?"

"And even though Felicia will steal all your ideas and is constantly looking for an excuse to fire you?"

"Pardon?"

"Oh, and the rumours you've heard about Felicia? Multiply them by about one hundred."

"Why are you telling me this?"

"Because we've been the recruiting agency for Felicia's team for the last five years, and I finally want some commission out of the account. We don't get paid if you don't stay in the job for more than a year."

"I plan on being there long-term."

"I want to believe you. You probably believe it yourself. We have others on the books who could step in now, but if I take a chance on you and it doesn't work out, it's another round of recruiting and advertising. I'm on annual leave in a week, and nobody else will touch the account. So I want you to be sure. Why don't you think about it?"

"No, I'm ready now. When can I start?"

"I'll call you in a couple of days, and you can give your final decision to me then."

"No, wait—"

The line went dead on the other end.

Catina sidled over to the phone. "So did you get it or didn't you?"

"I'm going to think about it."

Her mother jumped up from the table, upsetting her cutlery. She enveloped Yasmin in a bear-hug, rocking from foot to foot.

"Yes!" She kissed Yasmin's cheek. "This is what you've been working towards for such a long time. How do you feel?"

Yasmin thought about it for a second.

"Confused," she said.

Yasmin sits in the Eleanor Gilbert Room, swivelling on a black, high-backed chair. Around and around, until she's giddy. She is ecstatic, for reasons unknown, but somehow it makes total sense.

"Stop swivelling!" Tasha hisses. "She's coming!"

But Yasmin doesn't stop swivelling; she spins faster, as if she's on a child's merry-go-round. It's fun, and she feels dizzy.

As vertigo sets in, she lowers her head and pulls in her knees to keep the centre of gravity closer to her body. That's when she realises she is naked – and it has been a long time between waxes.

She covers herself with her hands, mortified. Felicia is on her way!

And just like that – ta-Ding! – Felicia is sitting on the other side of the table, eyeing Yasmin's resume, as if it were perfectly natural that Yasmin should sit across from her, in the buff.

"So," Felicia begins, "why do you want to work at The Woman's Standard?"

Before Yasmin can speak, someone on her left side pipes up – a young, ambitious lady wearing a power suit.

"I've wanted to work here all my life," the girl says, confidence oozing from her like sticky sap from a tree.

"All of your life?" Felicia asks.

"As much of it as I can remember."

"Hey – that's my line!" Yasmin says, just as a second person materialises, this time on her right.

"I've wanted to work here all my life, too," the second girl says. She

37

wears a flowing tie-dyed maxi dress and a woven hair band, and she glares at Yasmin.

"Me too." A third girl appears right beside Felicia, smiling angelically, dusting her army fatigues. Seriously? This third woman pushes a three-dimensional holographic resume towards Felicia. Her face glows in the blue light.

"Impressive," Felicia says.

"Hang on a minute." Yasmin is indignant. "I said that first. I've always wanted to work at The Woman's Standard; *none of the rest of you deserves to!"*

The three girls ignore Yasmin. They say in unison: "I've wanted to work here all my life. All my life. All my —"

Tasha joins them in the meeting room. She holds a phone out to Felicia.

"Yasmin's reference is on the phone. He doesn't work at The Guardian. *He works at the local fish and chip shop – wrapping the news, not writing it!"*

"No!" Yasmin says. "I wrote it…I'm a real journalist…Please don't fire me!"

Yasmin flinched as she woke to her darkened room, well before sunrise had teased life into the sky. A fruit bat moved from branch to branch in the tree outside the window, shifting the weight of the leaves, cackling every now and again.

What if Felicia finds out I haven't written a single article for my university newspaper, or anyone else for that matter?

Yasmin tried to shove the image down, *way* down, but it only played out more overtly in her mind, like a song stuck on repeat. She fell back into erratic sleep.

When her alarm buzzed her awake into a harsh new morning, her besties were already waiting. Audrey had made a victory breakfast, plucked from an Aga in the kitchen on the ceiling.

"Hello, sleepyhead. Have some hen fruit!" she crooned. She held out a frying pan, filled with spitting bacon and oily eggs.

"No thanks," Yasmin said, her dream still fresh in her mind.

The morning had an odd feeling, as if she wasn't quite herself. She didn't feel optimistic about the phone call she'd soon have to make.

"You need protein to build muscle," Nicole said, nabbing a slice from the frying pan with her fingertips.

"Pretty sure I don't want to build any muscle, but thanks," Yasmin said.

"Bacon is for murderers, anyway," Deborah said, eating an orange. "Pigs are the Proletariat, too."

Yasmin felt panic start to take hold. She had to get out of her room. She headed to the door.

"Where are you going?" Deborah spat an orange seed onto the floor at Yasmin's feet.

"I'm not taking the job. I have to call Jane."

"What?" Deborah dropped her orange and the juice stained the carpet.

"No, no, no." Nicole moved to the part of the ceiling closest to the door.

"Oh, Yasmin," Audrey said, her shoulders slumped in disappointment.

Yasmin sighed, long and low, and ended in a frustrated, "Aaaaaagghhhh!"

They would find out eventually when she failed to turn up for work each day. There were no secrets in this bedroom.

"Jane made it sound awful," she said, "and anyway, I don't think I can handle Felicia. She's so…well…famous. And I don't have any experience. I think I should start somewhere else, somewhere a bit friendlier, and maybe think about working on *The Standard* once I have, you know, actually worked as a journalist."

Her ghost-mothers stared, not quite believing it.

"Maybe you shouldn't take the job," Audrey said, sitting huffily on the bed. "You should concentrate on going to dances and meeting a nice boy to marry."

"Yeah," Nicole piped up, missing Audrey's sarcasm. "Wait for a better-paid job. Don't let them demean you like that. And anyway, isn't *The Standard* an old ladies' magazine?"

"Horse doo-doo," Deborah said, lighting a joint and blowing smoke out the window. "If you don't take the job, you'll set back the whole of the feminist movement. That job is your power, a chance to have a voice."

Yasmin felt her energy seep into the mattress.

"I'm not smart enough. Even Mum and Catina can see through me now – how long will it take for Felicia to twig? And what if I tank at the job? My only dream, shattered, and then what will I have to live for? I don't have the courage for that kind of disappointment. And I'm not good at making friends – you're my only friends – and you're not even real! You need allies in an office to have your back. I don't know the first thing about getting people to like me. Usually they hate me."

She wiped her nose on Grandma's monogrammed hanky. No point in putting it off.

"I'm going to ring Jane now."

"Wait," Nicole said. "I have intelligence enough for the both of us."

Audrey smiled. "And I'm the most death-defyingly courageous person here."

Deborah rested an arm on Yasmin's shoulder. "And if you need to know how to make friends and influence minds, I'm your gal."

Yasmin hiccupped. "How does that help me?"

"We can come with you. For moral support," Nicole said.

"What are you talking about?"

"Yeah, we can totally help you out. Put our heads together, have your back. Kick Felicia in the rear when she's out of line…" Audrey said, a grin forming on her face.

"Stuff this room. Time for freedom. I'm in," Deborah said, throwing her smouldering joint on the floor.

"How would that even work?" Yasmin said, picking it up and tossing it out of the window. "You've never been out of this room."

"We're your fairy ghost-mothers," Nicole said, "and that means you can make up the rules."

6

*C*ould Yasmin make Audrey, Deborah and Nicole into real people, in the physical world? She felt the three of them staring at her like hopeful puppies on a farm, begging for adoption to a respectable home.

"I don't think it's a good idea. There's just so much that could go wrong," Yasmin said. Did she sound whiny?

"You're in charge. You brought us to life," Audrey said. "So if you don't want anything to go wrong, it won't."

"Just think of what you could achieve with us at your back!" Nicole said.

"Don't be a pussy," Deborah smirked.

"Do not move," Yasmin said as they crowded around, their cool presence making her shiver. "Stay right where you are."

Audrey put on her army cap – something she'd never worn since materialising – and slipped her handbag over her elbow.

Nicole wedged herself into a pair of comfy dress shoes and her lab coat.

Deborah slung a beaded cotton shoulder bag over her head, donning a pair of sandals and round, blue-tinged sunglasses reminiscent of John Lennon.

"Guys, wait!" Yasmin said. "I have to think."

"I thought I smelt something burning!" Deborah high-fived Nicole.

Yasmin shook her head, trying to dislodge the fear that took hold of her gut.

This had major potential to go belly up.

Until now, she'd hidden the existence of her ghostly friends from her sister, her mother and the world at large. They were Yasmin's pets, and they were hard enough to control from within the confines of her bedroom. She wasn't sure it was a good idea to unleash them into the real world where they could do catastrophic damage. And would that mean that other people could see them too?

Plus, they could up sticks and leave once they were free of her bedroom. She may never see them again! That would be horrible, even though she was twenty-four years old and well overdue for parting with her childhood imaginary friends. As much as they were pains in the rear, and as much as they bickered and bullied, Yasmin needed them. She couldn't remember a time without them.

She didn't feel like an adult yet. Yasmin decided that they were right. She couldn't do it alone. What if having them at her back gave her the confidence to take the job? To live the dream she had dreamt since childhood?

Would it be worth the risk?

"So," Deborah began. "You're busy talking yourself out of this, I can tell. Let me tell you why you have to go ahead."

She flipped on a record: 'With a Little Help from My Friends.'

Yasmin shook her head. "I'm still thinking."

"And that's your problem," Deborah said. "You've got to let go; you're holding on too tight. You exist in such a tiny world. You're not out there living. The world is this huge, cosmic thing, you need to expand your mind, you know?"

"It will be okay, love," Audrey said.

"You talk big. Now it's time to live big." Nicole reached out and gently rubbed her back, her cold touch strangely reassuring.

"What the heck," Yasmin said. Her besties' faces lit up as if they'd just tasted salted caramel ice cream for the first time. They'd had enough of being cooped up in there too. "But you've all got to behave."

Audrey and Nicole nodded.

Yasmin glanced at Deborah. "You too," she said.

"Sure, sweet cakes. I can behave."

"Let's do it," Nicole said.

"Everyone, gather around me in a circle."

She pulled out her penny on its chain, hidden beneath her pyjama top. She held it out for her besties to see. They crowded around.

The penny was a dull, tarnished bronze, but the three women's profiles were still visible.

Yasmin hadn't studied the coin for some time.

"It's Grandma's magic coin," Yasmin said, "and it first brought the three of you into existence."

She admired the three women on the coin: Audrey, Deborah and Nicole. She turned it over and peered at the inscription and three interlocking ovals.

"I already tried wishing to win the lottery, and for Catina to be adopted out to a family in Denmark, and for Matthew Crispin to get the bubonic plague. But none of those things happened," Yasmin said, turning the coin in her fingers.

"You might be out of wishes," Audrey said.

"What does the inscription say?" Nicole donned half-glasses and peered closer.

Yasmin held it up to the light. "*Reserare se serum tuae.*"

"What is that?"

"Italian?" Audrey asked.

"No," Nicole said, taking off her glasses. "It's Latin."

"What does it mean?" Yasmin rubbed at the inscription with her thumb.

"I believe you have access to something called Google these days?" Deborah said.

"Oh, right." Yasmin fired up her laptop and loaded Google Translate.

"It means, 'unlock your true self,'" she said. "I'm not sure that I like my true self."

"Would you prefer to lose your dream and entire reason for being?" Deborah asked.

Yasmin contemplated the rest of her joyless life if she couldn't work at *The Standard*. She felt the profound loss as a physical thing, a lurking weight across the backs of her shoulders.

Just then, the coin vibrated in Yasmin's hand. It began to pulse between her fingers, minutely at first, and then revving up, the colours of the sharp-edged circles iridescent in silver, red and gold.

"It's working!" Yasmin said, almost dropping the coin as it radiated its gentle heat.

"Turn it over!" Nicole said.

The three women were lit up in their respective colours: Audrey in silver, Deborah in red and Nicole in gold.

"This happened last time!" Yasmin yelped, her face transfixed.

She motioned for her besties to hover closer. She had to try. She couldn't face Felicia Pine and her chic, designer-wearing editorial team without backup.

To pull it off, she needed Nicole's brains, and Audrey's courage, and Deborah's way with people.

They stood there, expectantly – as if a thunderbolt were about to charge through her roof and tear her collaged ceiling to pieces. Yasmin appealed to each of her ghost-mothers.

Audrey's hand went to her hip where her holster sat, exhilaration painted on her features. Nicole seemed warier, as if waiting for the results of a dodgy scientific experiment to take shape. And Deborah closed her eyes, her face tilted towards the roof, her arms spread wide.

Existentially long seconds passed. Deborah opened one eye, the other still squinted shut. Yasmin felt Deborah's gaze land on her.

"Ah, I don't know how this works," Yasmin eventually said.

Audrey threw her hands up in frustration. Nicole sat back on the bed. Deborah pushed her blue-tinted glasses up her forehead.

"It's a good idea," Yasmin said. "But none of you are real. What the hell was I thinking?"

She could tell she'd hurt thier feelings with the accusation that they were merely a part of her imagination, but to their credit, her besties let that one slide.

Audrey stepped forward.

"Do you remember the first time you saw me?" she asked.

"Yeah, of course," Yasmin said. "You scared the heck out of me."

"Tell me what you saw."

Yasmin took a few deep, meditation-worthy calming breaths, closing her eyes. She waited until the light stopped shooting around the backs of her eyelids, easing into a swirling ribbon of blue, a serpent-like wave, gentle and undulating. She felt the warmth of the coin in her palm.

Yasmin concentrated for a moment.

Then she told them.

Ten-year-old Yasmin watched Grandma, propped up in a hospital bed, smaller and skinnier than ever. She was like a skeletal bird, bent timidly over the tray of hospital food, so far removed from her delicious roasts.

Yasmin felt overwhelmed by the pings *of the strange machines, attached by wires to Grandma's chest, and the tubes of oxygen fitted to her nose.*

"Come closer, it's okay," Grandma said. "I have something for you."

Grandma reached over to her ornate handbag, pulling out an aged penny on a tarnished gold chain. Both sides were smooth and blank. She held it out to Yasmin.

Yasmin stepped closer to the bed, peering at the coin.

As she touched it, the outlines of three women magically etched themselves onto the coin. The coin grew hot to the touch. Yasmin gasped and stepped back, dropping the penny onto the hospital bed. Grandma's eyes twinkled.

Yasmin tentatively closed her fingers over the penny.

"Have you ever heard of 'fairy ghost-mothers?'" Grandma said.

Yasmin shook her head, her eyes wide.

"They're helpers. They can help you feel less sad – you know, after I'm gone," Grandma said.

"But where are you going?" Yasmin asked, her voice soft.

Grandma erupted into a coughing fit and lay back. Yasmin felt scared. Scared of the hospital and the strange bleeping machines. But mostly for Grandma, who seemed frail enough to disappear right into the bend of the bed. Yasmin stepped back.

"It's okay," her mother said, returning from the canteen and placing a steaming cup of tea on the set of drawers. "Grandma's just resting."

But Yasmin saw the bruised-blue lids and Grandma's pale face without her usual makeup, her hair a mess against the pillow. Yasmin became transfixed by a lavender vein snaking up Grandma's neck, pulsating erratically.

"We'll come back tomorrow. You rest now," Mum said to Grandma. Then to Yasmin, "Say goodbye to Grandma."

And Yasmin whispered it.

To this day, she's not sure if Grandma heard.

At the wake, Yasmin left the adults in Grandma's house with their cut sandwiches and solemn faces.

She let down the steps of the caravan in the shed. She wedged herself into the seat at the dining nook and felt the give of the cushion beneath her rear. Grandma's talc wafted up from the foam.

Her feet kicked against something underneath the table. She bent her head and found a cardboard box, its lid taped shut, its sides softly dented with age.

Intrigued, she pulled out the box, tore off the tape and peeked inside. The smell of old printer's ink and yellowing paper hit her first. The box was filled with back issues of The Woman's Standard.

On the first cover was a woman in uniform, gazing out. And, underneath the image of the woman, were the words: "Lest we Forget – Audrey Elizabeth Stewart, 1920 – 1950."

Yasmin read Audrey's obituary, and things seemed somehow better, as if all Yasmin needed was to buy the oil for Audrey's 'damp set' curl, *put on a stiff upper lip and knit jumpers for the war effort. She thought Grandma might have been like Audrey in her younger years.*

Back in her bedroom, Yasmin wished Grandma was still with them so that she could ask her about the coin. She felt the sadness of her loss.

As the loss began to fill her, until she couldn't bear the tightness in her chest, one of the profiles on her coin glowed silver!

Yasmin turned the penny over, then back again. Where she'd seen the same bronze of the penny only moments before, one of the women was now silver.

"What magic is this?"

Yasmin put the chain around her neck and held the coin, the glow showing through the tips of her fingers.

"If I get three wishes, I know what my first wish will be," Yasmin said. "I wish Grandma wasn't dead."

Yasmin opened her eyes.

"And then you appeared for the first time," Yasmin said to Audrey.

"So make another wish," Audrey said.

Yasmin squeezed her eyes shut and wished with everything she had. She wished that Audrey was a real person that she could share adventures with. She wanted to take Audrey out into the real world, spend time with her wandering the cobbled streets of The Rocks historical area, take her to an old picture theatre, and motor up Parramatta River on a replica steamboat.

She wished to set Audrey free.

Yasmin opened her eyes – and there she was; Audrey was luminescent! She glowed with a silver halo around her body. She radiated a hot light and began to fill out, her limbs covered in a film, like a silver spider web. Her limbs then lost their glow, dulling to a sepia-toned sheen. Her form became three-dimensional. Yasmin could no longer see through Audrey, her skin was golden and brown, as it appeared in her photograph, and her feet touched the floor and everything. She was a fully formed, wonderful, real woman!

Audrey's face had an expression of pure wonder. Yasmin poked her, and she was solid. Her hand no longer went through Audrey, who no longer felt cold to the touch.

"You're not a ghost; you're a real woman!" Yasmin said.

Audrey wavered slightly, getting used to feeling the pull of gravity. Then she found her balance, and she stood there, in front of Yasmin, a head or two shorter.

Audrey took in her new form. She stood there, right next to Yasmin.

"What a gas!" she said. "Girls, you have to try this!"

Yasmin hugged her with a strength that almost knocked them both for six. Audrey felt real enough – round and buxom – and Yasmin smelt the scent of her damp-set hair oil.

"Me! Do me!" Deborah said, hovering above the carpet, cross-legged and attentive.

"I'm on it," Yasmin said. "Let me concentrate first."

She breathed in the sweet scent of Deborah's smoke and closed her eyes.

Yasmin couldn't wait to see Clementine, her best friend, and tell her about Audrey. Maybe adults couldn't see Audrey, but other kids could. But as she approached Clementine, she saw Matthew and some of his friends were gathered around for the kiddie-kill, pushing Clementine roughly against the wall of the primary-school classroom.

"You're always reading books, cause you've got no friends," Matthew said, grabbing a fistful of Yasmin's hair.

"Stop it, please," Yasmin said, fighting back tears, "or my Dad will arrest you. He's a police detective, specialising in cruelty to children. He can have you sent to Guantanamo Bay."

Matthew pushed Clementine so hard she fell to the ground and grazed her knee. She drew a pained breath as the blood bloomed in little droplets.

Matthew's voice rose in a cruel, pre-pubescent giggle. "If I ever see you hanging out with bookworm-hole again, I'm going to jump you on the way home from school." He spat next to her knee. The air bubbles of his saliva popped into the asphalt. He laughed, and his friends joined in.

"And you," he said to Yasmin. "Stay away from me, liar. Your Dad's not a cop."

He shoulder-charged her on his way past, and it hurt like the blazes.

Stunned, Yasmin reached a hand to Clementine, who stood up, wincing at her grazed knee. She held the skin together to stem the blood that began to drip down her leg, as if it were paint on modern artwork.

"I'm sorry. I can't keep doing this. We can't hang out anymore," Clementine said. She couldn't look at Yasmin. She limped into the playground, weaving between the handball courts.

Yasmin couldn't believe it. Did she mean it? How could she drop her like that? Her best friend.

"Oh, you can't hang out with me?" Yasmin yelled after her, feeling the strength of her anger rise, creating a righteous feeling – as if she could say anything without consequence. "It doesn't matter, I have plenty of other friends. I decided to hang out with you. You were lucky I chose you!"

Yasmin looked to the empty wall, and to the void of space around her in the playground – a solid force field keeping the other kids away.

After school, Yasmin rifled through the boxes of her grandma's magazines, and matched the hippie from the coin to one of the covers. Deborah was seated, in peaceful protest, in a ring of defiant women. The cover read: "The women's movement's first martyr. In loving memory of Deborah Anne Reece, aged thirty."

Yasmin rubbed her fingers over the magic penny. If Deborah had all those friends, maybe she could help Yasmin find some more herself? Yasmin would be okay if she could find a friend to replace Clementine. A better friend – someone who was a year older, with a swimming pool and a miniature poodle!

She grasped the penny, closed her eyes and calmed her mind.

She opened her eyes and – sure enough – Deborah's profile glowed red.

This was it! She held the penny, closed her eyes again, and waited for the wind.

"I wish I had a friend," Yasmin said.

• • •

Back in the present day, Yasmin wished for Deborah to be real too, so they could march together on International Women's Day. She wanted Deborah to show her the spot where she was first arrested in Hyde Park. She wanted to see the squat Deborah had lived in, which would now be exclusive inner-city real estate. Yasmin wanted to show Deborah their first female Prime Minister's photo in the halls of Parliament House in Canberra.

Yasmin opened her eyes, and Deborah shone too, her light a pulsating red. She filled out, becoming solid, her feet lowering to the ground. She swayed as she morphed into a substantial, real being. She also retained her faded magazine colours, like well-washed blue jeans. But she was solid and gave Yasmin their first real hug. For the first time, Yasmin felt warmth radiate from Deborah's arms.

Deborah stood back, nodding in her cool way, with pink in her cheeks and a brightness to her eyes that matched the seventies' era photography on her magazine cover. She danced, kicked off her shoes and dug her toes into the carpet.

She gave Yasmin a peace sign. "My little anarchist," she said proudly. She gave a considered wink. Yasmin sighed with relief; she had finally made it into her club.

"My turn," Nicole said.

Yasmin found she couldn't speak. She heaved in a breath, her face lowered.

"I found you after Dad—"

Audrey and Deborah moved in closer, hugging her. Yasmin felt the true strength of their arms, their breath on the back of her neck, the heat radiating off their bodies. At that moment, some of their light shot across her back, her shoulders, her neck. She felt strong, plugged in and charging. She didn't want to pull away, but she couldn't forget Nicole.

Yasmin pulled free and closed her eyes.

• • •

Two weeks after Grandma's funeral, Dad, Mum, Catina and Yasmin sat amidst packing boxes on cushions on the floor, around the upended cardboard box they used as a table. All their furniture had been taken away by the moving van to a storage shed not far away. A family-sized supreme pizza sat in its box on their makeshift table. Yasmin picked off the capsicum, lifted the slice to her mouth, and tasted the sweet crunch of pineapple as the juice dripped down her chin.

Dad marked notes on his linguistics paper, and Mum rolled her eyes.

"You haven't helped in any way with the packing!" Mum turned on Dad, trying to rouse him.

"My article is due, and I can't be sloppy with my work right now," Dad said. "They can still cancel my secondment."

"Our house is in chaos," she said, "and our family even more so."

"You and your overly dramatic signifiers."

"How's this for a signifier?" Mum said and thrust a middle finger at him.

Catina started bawling, so Yasmin picked her up and trudged upstairs. She knew the best time to bail out. She plonked Catina in her cot. She threw a teddy bear her way but Catina grew redder in the face. She then turned from red to bloodlessly white, her face screwed into complete tantrum mode.

"Shut up, will you?" Yasmin yelled, but now Catina's eyes were closed, and she was beyond listening to reason. She morphed into crying-so-hard-she-was-holding-her-breath. Yasmin picked her up and waited for the hysteria to pass.

"It's all your fault," Yasmin said, feeling taller with anger, jigging her sister up and down. Catina's cries matched each jerk on Yasmin's hip bone. "You're the reason that Mum and Dad are fighting all the time."

Even at ten years old, Yasmin knew the real reason Mum and Dad fought all the time. They didn't love each other, not in the same way they had when they were first married. Mum had told her this many times, in calmer moments.

But this was the first time Mum had told Dad, and he took it badly.

Dad left for New York the next morning. Mum had the movers bring their stuff back from storage. She acted as if they weren't going to move in the first place.

Yasmin would always remember the door closing, softly, as he left the house. How gently it hitched into place. Totally normal. The cockatoos screeched outside, and it seemed like an everyday morning, like all the others before it, except that her dad would never come back. And somehow, Yasmin knew it.

How many more people could she lose? First her grandma, then Clementine, and now her father?

And out of all of them, why did this one sting the most?

She felt herself go numb, an empty vessel. Her face became expressionless. She held her hand over her chest, feeling the kick of her heart underneath.

She turned from the landing and closed her bedroom door behind her, the house now eerily still.

She pulled the coin out from around her neck, comparing the third relief to the real woman's profile in the magazine. It was Nicole; she'd already found her, halfway through a pile on the floor next to her bed. Nicole, smart in a lab coat, peeked over the top of her glasses, fresh from her research study. She was the joint recipient of the Nobel Peace Prize for her contribution to our understanding of climate change, and how to reverse its disastrous effects. Her obituary from the year 2000 lamented the loss of one of science's greatest thinkers, and tragically young too — only thirty years old at the time of her death.

She might well have had an office at the university next to her father, eaten at the same teacher's cafe, crossed paths in the campus library.

Yasmin rubbed the coin and closed her eyes. She felt this one keenly. It seemed the most important wish she could make.

"I wish Daddy didn't leave," she said.

Yasmin wished for Nicole to be real so that they could wander the boulevards of Nicole's campus, pointing out the rooms where she made her research breakthroughs. Yasmin would show Nicole the wind farms that generated green electricity and read articles in *The Guardian* about the Scandinavian countries becoming carbon-neutral. They would watch documentaries together at the Dendy and debate possibilities for the future over hot chocolate at a late-night café.

Yasmin watched Nicole, whose light strobed gold. She filled out and touched down onto the carpet, her skin electric, like criss-crossed neurones.

She was glossy, with overly bright colours, just like her magazine from the year 2000. Her conservative blouse crinkled in a real way. She was a solid, odd-looking person too.

"I feel amazing," she said.

Nicole gave Yasmin a heartfelt, warming hug, taking a moment to relax. Yasmin felt elated.

The four of them broke into laughter, the three ghost-mothers poking each other to check that they were real.

Yasmin's friends were in physical bodies for the first time since their deaths. They were pretty clumsy, it had to be said. Deborah stood on Yasmin's foot more than once. Yasmin began to wonder if it was on purpose.

They flopped onto the bed, catching their breath, and lay there for a while. Yasmin wondered if this is what slumber parties with your best friends felt like. But then the excitement dissipated, like fizz from the surface of lemonade.

"Now what?" Yasmin asked.

Nicole handed Yasmin the phone. "I believe you owe a phone call to Gargantuan Consulting."

Yasmin rang Jane, who asked her to start the next day. Yasmin had landed her dream job!

Audrey, Deborah and Nicole, however, were keen to explore the house. Yasmin agreed that they should test out their new, solid state to see how it all worked.

Audrey was the first to test Yasmin's bedroom door. Before their latest transformation, it had slammed in their faces whenever they tried to leave the bedroom, trapping them inside. Would the same thing happen now?

Audrey approached the door. She stood by it, reaching out a tentative hand.

She gripped the handle.

She turned it and flung the door open!

Audrey glanced back at the girls, who wore the grins of escapees scaling prison walls.

"Freedom!" Deborah whooped, and the three ghost-mothers fell – literally – over each other in a rush to the landing, ending up in a pile of uncoordinated limbs and muffed hair.

They pulled themselves up onto the banisters, marvelling at the hallway and peeking into every door on the top landing.

"Can you stop that for a moment?" Yasmin hissed.

"Your house is enormous," Audrey said, wonder lighting up her face.

Yasmin led them along the hallway. They were like kittens first encountering stairs, wrong-footed and bumping into the walls as they went. They still had to get used to their bodies.

"This whole walking thing is overrated," Audrey said, stubbing her toe on the railing.

"Yeah, floating is way easier," Deborah said.

"And this is our living room," Yasmin announced, sweeping her arm in the direction of the television, couches and coffee table.

Yasmin stepped back proudly, watching them poke at the bookshelf and turn the television on and off.

"Hey, loser," Catina popped her head up from where she lay on the couch. She mashed sleep from her eyes.

"What are you doing here?" Yasmin asked, peering discreetly from friend to friend. They all froze, then wilted into nothingness. One minute they were there, then the next, they morphed into invisible beings. Nicole's book hovered in mid-air, her body gone. Yasmin could see a faint outline of the ghosts, a slight shimmering at their edges. Could Catina see too?

"Did you just say 'this is our living room?'" Catina asked.

"Ah, no," Yasmin squeaked.

"Pretty sure you did. Who were you talking to?"

Yasmin scanned from bestie to bestie. Or the places where their shadowy outlines stood.

Catina followed Yasmin's gaze, staring straight through their outlines, then shook her head.

"Play fantasy real-estate agent somewhere else. I'm trying to nap." She rested her head on her arm and closed her eyes.

Yasmin smiled at her friends and watched the book hover across the room to the kitchen. The book opened, seemingly magically, and the pages turned as the invisible Nicole speed-read the first chapter of *Harry Potter and the Philosopher's Stone*.

Yasmin jerked a thumb to the dining room, watching the chairs scrape back as if mechanically driven by their shadowy outlines. One of her friends missed the chair and landed on the floor with a thump.

"Oof..." the invisible Deborah said, righting herself.

The chairs scuffed back as Yasmin's besties sat.

Her mother entered the dining room, placing her MacBook Air on the table. She frowned at the skewiff chairs and pushed them back into the table, squishing Yasmin's imaginary friends in tight. Nicole squealed as the air pushed out of her lungs.

"What's wrong?" Susan asked.

"Sorry, I've got wind." Yasmin scanned her outlined besties. So Susan couldn't see them either!

"I saw a cute share house on Flatmate Finders." Susan slid the MacBook across the table.

Yasmin watched the outline of the invisible Deborah push her chair back. Susan frowned at the chair magically displacing itself. Yasmin leapt over, pretending to kick the chair with her foot.

"These chairs are so light. Have you ever noticed that before?" Yasmin said with a chuckle, as if to say, "Chairs, huh?"

"Not really," Susan said, shrugging. And she wandered off, humming to herself.

Her besties hardly waited until Susan was out of earshot before reappearing.

"They couldn't see you!" Yasmin said.

"So," Audrey said, rendering herself visible again, "looks like we have the camouflage part down."

She encased Yasmin in a bear-hug.

Nicole and Deborah leapt up too, and they all embraced, jumping around in a circle like maniacs. Catina approached the kitchen, reading a text on her phone.

"Invisible!" Yasmin shouted. Her ghost-mothers disappeared.

Catina watched as Yasmin landed, her face sheened in sweat from the exertion. Yasmin tucked her hair behind her ear and curtsied.

"Oh my God!" Catina said, rolling her eyes.

Yasmin gave her sister two thumbs up and rushed her besties outside. They practised turning invisible, then visible at will. It took immense concentration. Deborah was the least apt, having the shortest attention span, and Nicole, of course, excelled. Audrey was fine until she needed to move while she was invisible. She found the need to check for potential threats around each corner of the house, which added an extra layer of effort on her part.

They became visible again just as their neighbour poked her head above the fence.

"Who are your friends, Yasmin?" she asked, recoiling as the ghost-mothers faced her, their weird colouring giving away their other-worldly existence.

"Oh, they're friends of Catina's. You know, for the musical."

Yasmin turned to where her ghost-mothers stood, but they had disappeared entirely in the eyes of her neighbour.

Her neighbour shrieked and dropped her washing basket, running into the house.

"Ah, don't ever do that again," Yasmin told them once they reappeared.

Deborah grinned as if she'd just fished a winning lotto ticket from her pocket.

"Okay ladies," she said. "Let's prepare our battle strategy."

They had a big day tomorrow.

7

*Y*asmin and her invisible ghost-mothers began a protracted walk to the bus stop, taking twice as long as they should have. Her friends detoured into laneways and other people's gardens. They were curious about everything in 'the future.' Yasmin guessed she might have been as well if she had jumped twenty-odd years, or nearly fifty, or almost seventy, in Audrey's case. When Yasmin tried to think of the world through her besties' eyes, she could understand their wonder.

Yasmin felt as if the world was brand-new too as she explained the electronic bus tickets and automatic revolving doors. She had to tell Nicole several times that, unfortunately, cars could not yet fly.

They let a couple of over-crowded buses pass before flagging down one with spare room to huddle along the back seat.

"The first perk of being invisible to everyone except Yasmin," Deborah said, "is that we don't have to pay bus fare."

When they disembarked at Elizabeth Street, her besties' concentration wavered, and they dipped in and out of being visible. But, in true commuter form, nobody looked at them too closely or batted an eyelid at their unusual appearance. Yasmin supposed they could have been taken for a promotional troupe handing out free protein balls or the like.

Yasmin's wristwatch ticked over to 8:30 a.m. as they arrived at the foyer of Warner Williams Corporation.

"Quick you guys, you can't be seen," Yasmin whispered. Her ghost-mothers vanished just as Buckley turned around. He spied Yasmin and spoke into his walkie-talkie. Yasmin threw a smirk his way and announced herself to the receptionist. She sat and waited for a few minutes on the plush white couches in the foyer.

"Yasmin?" Tasha called from the other side of the security gates. She wore a flowing printed dress and Saturday-night-ready heels, her eyes crinkling with a smile. Friendly enough. "Come on up."

Tasha tapped her security pass against a sensor on the wall and the gates swung open.

Yasmin sidled through, beaming at the space where the shimmery outlines of her crew stood. But they were too slow, as a worker was knocked over by an invisible bestie.

The worker found her feet, confusion and anger spreading on her features. "Do you mind?" she yelled, dusting off her designer jacket.

"I'm sorry!" Deborah said, much to the worker's surprise.

Tasha seemed distracted but quickly reverted to professionalism. She pressed the lift call button. "Did you have a good trip in?"

DING!

Their lift arrived.

All three ghost-mothers struggled to stay invisible as they concentrated on negotiating the security gates.

Deborah was wedged halfway through the turnstiles, Audrey failed an attempt to hurdle the accessibility gate, and Nicole apologised to people who recoiled at her weird colour. Her sheen looked as if she'd bathed in a tub of olive oil.

"It will be a nice ride to the fourth floor!" Yasmin said dramatically, for her besties' benefit.

"Well, I suppose," Tasha said carefully.

"I like lifts," Yasmin said, by explanation.

As the lift doors closed, Yasmin watched Buckley escort her three now-visible ghost-mothers out into the street.

Yasmin and Tasha hurtled upwards. Yasmin's heart fluttered irregularly. Dammit. How would she make it through her first day without her besties? That was the whole point of making them real. The most significant moment of her life to date was about to present itself. And now she had to navigate the day alone.

The lift doors swept open to show the fourth floor vestibule. Tasha swiped her pass and led them through a second frosted entrance into the belly of the office.

The office of *The Woman's Standard*.

Yasmin saw the office for the first time – row upon row of open-plan, industrious, sleek, white desks strewn with the detritus of the busy office: Post-it notes, pages of copy and mocks, half-drunk takeaway coffee and photos from shoots. Workers hovered over keyboards. The sound of phones and chatter filled the air. Yasmin savoured the smell – printer's ink, photocopy toner and eau de parfum.

The industrious atmosphere suggested the whole floor had been there long enough to settle into their day, with every desk occupied. High-end-fashion-clad workers tapped at keys or answered phones in the open-plan layout. All had a stressed set to their shoulders as if they were awaiting a small bomb to detonate. It seemed a joyless place. Even to Yasmin, who was filled with enthusiasm and ecstatic with the newness of the experience.

She glimpsed flashes of the latest cover on someone's over-sized Mac screen – she would now be privy to covers before the general public! Her heart raced as she recognised Harry's cheeky mug featured on a half-finished design with the headline, 'The Princess and her untameable Prince.'

Yasmin's knees threatened to buckle as she followed Tasha down the line of desks. Oversized posters of magazine covers hung in metallic frames on the farthest wall. Gracing the covers were: a woman wearing a doctor's coat and stethoscope; a woman in a purple pantsuit; Lady Di; and Nicole Kidman. All four women beamed and, on those covers at least, had found the answer to life. They were the epitome of cool, calm and fabulous.

Yasmin noticed a heavy wooden door next to the posters, leading into a private glass office. The door was closed, with the blinds drawn, but she could see daylight filtering through the cracks.

There were at least thirty people in this section of office alone – a hive of creativity and concentration. Only a few people talked to each other – everyone else had their jobs and worked in a focused way. There were enough designer clothes on these people to stock all of the high-street shops in town.

"I'll introduce you later," Tasha said, leading her to a clear desk with a computer, two large monitors and a multi-buttoned desk phone. "This is you."

Yasmin tried to take in the moment – being presented with her desk at *The Woman's Standard* – and she couldn't help the flits of excitement in her stomach. Tasha motioned for her to sit, so she did.

"Thank you," Yasmin said.

"You're welcome." She handed a manual to Yasmin. "Read this through if you like."

Tasha headed to the desk opposite; a low, frosted partition separating them. When she sat, Yasmin could easily see the top of Tasha's head over her monitor and, if Yasmin reached her chin up, the upper half of her eyes.

Yasmin pretended to read the manual, but preferred to sneak glances about the office, trying not to pry or linger on any one person for too long, or give away too much of her exhilaration. It didn't seem the cool thing to do, and who knew who these people were? She didn't want to spend her first day ogling someone who turned out to be her superior.

Then she realised that absolutely everyone in this office *was* her superior. She could be certain that even the roving mail clerk outranked her.

She listened to the various office phone tones and the chatter of a distant worker making a sales call after hamming it up about her weekend on the harbour. Tasha seemed busy, so Yasmin concentrated on her workstation. She found the on switch for her computer, pleased with herself as she waited for the boot-up sound, and a blue login screen materialised. She had no idea what her password could be.

She lifted her chin so that she could see Tasha's half-eyes over the partition. But Tasha's brow was furrowed in a deep and well-rehearsed frown. Yasmin would bother her later.

She picked up the receiver of her large, flat phone, pressing it to her ear. She was pleased to hear a dial tone. She didn't know what else she had expected and had nobody to call, in any case.

She rummaged around in her desk drawers, which contained a soggy packet of gum and an empty bottle of vodka. Not the best sign.

For want of something better to do, she pulled some photos from her handbag. They were of Audrey, Deborah and Nicole, unpicked carefully from her bedroom ceiling. She found some Blu Tack and stuck them to the wall of her partition, her hands shaking slightly with the weight of the situation.

She wished her besties had made it inside.

Tasha popped her head up over the partition.

"IT will be with you shortly," she said. "Until then, here's some back issues to flip through."

She handed over a stack of *Standards*.

"Oh, I've read them all," Yasmin said, sifting through each cover.

"Well, reread them," Tasha said, a little tersely.

"Right, sure, sorry."

Tasha disappeared behind her partition.

Yasmin was off to a great start already. She flipped through the magazines, but couldn't concentrate on the page. She checked out her fellow workers surreptitiously, like a commuter on the bus peering over the top of a broadsheet newspaper. She felt just as pervy.

A harassed blonde bent over the lightbox, a loupe to her eye, scrutinising photo negatives. Several people typed as if they were completing a test on the Amazing Race. A couple of journalists conducted phone interviews, and a photographer dumped her kit on a table littered with SLRs and lenses in ever-increasing size. A few sales reps huddled in the corner, chewing pens as they made their sales calls. Everyone else pounded on keyboards, pressed deep into office chairs. Yasmin hadn't seen a single man since she'd arrived.

The girl at the desk beside Yasmin caught her eye – a sleek brunette with the most gorgeous, sheer blue blouse, with her white bra showing through. She was assembling the Prince Harry feature and fussing over the cover image, placing it 'just so' with a stylus on a touchpad. Her eyes grew wide in concentration as she moved the image across a few pixels. Crooked her head. Moved it back again.

She felt Yasmin staring and looked up.

"I love your outfit," Yasmin mouthed.

The designer grunted and turned back to her work. Okay, not the friendliest of offices, but Yasmin guessed everyone was busy. Covers were important work. You certainly judged a magazine by its cover.

IT arrived fifteen minutes later, by which time Yasmin was swivelling on her chair, pretending – in her head of course – to have phone conversations with her ghost-mothers. Yasmin mentally told them about her day so far, how the work was hard, but she thought she was up for the challenge. She was just about to give the scoop on her latest feature article when a small Indian lady with a severe fringe and a sedate smile approached.

She introduced herself as Rachna and was affable enough. She presented Yasmin with her swipe card and login and explained how to use the phone. Yasmin smiled, only understanding about half of Rachna's instructions.

"Welcome and I'll leave you to it," Rachna said, with a hint of an accent.

She hurried towards the door.

"Rachna's good," Tasha said. "Really knows her stuff. Be sure to make friends with her."

Yasmin laughed nervously. She watched as the designer flagged Rachna down.

"Ah, I have a problem with my stylus," she said.

Tasha raised her eyebrows. "It's not her stylus that's the problem," she mumbled under her breath.

Rachna clearly just wanted to leave. Tasha cleared her throat and took another sip of coffee.

"So, you do realise," Tasha addressed Yasmin, standing up and stretching, "that I was the last person to make it through probation."

"Oh," Yasmin said, grateful for the conversation. "And how long have you been with the company?"

"Five years."

She sipped her coffee and let this sink in.

"So nobody's made it through probation since you?"

"Exactly." She leaned over the partition, and whispered, "Doesn't matter anyway, the magazine's going to fold after the next issue."

"Wait – what? Fold, as in, cancelled?"

"Yep. Unless we hit 100,000 circulation for the 85th anniversary issue."

"That's – when?"

"We go to print in a month. Don't get comfy, is all I'm saying. If *The Standard* folds, the whole company goes under. It's our flagship title."

"It can't…What will I…but it's been published since 1933."

"Yeah, she's had a good run." Tasha's face crumpled, and she sat down. A few seconds passed. The top of Tasha's head shook as she stifled sobs. She blew her nose.

This couldn't happen. How could Yasmin's precious magazine be in danger of folding? She had just landed her dream job, and it was only temporary? What would she do if she didn't work at *The Standard*? How could she fulfil her life's purpose, and what mail could she look forward to receiving? How would she find out about each breaking royal scandal? And what about her fairy ghost-mothers? Would they still be able to visit?

Yasmin stared glumly at Rachna, who wrestled to shut the door behind her. What was wrong with that door? She was small in stature, but put her weight into it, pulling it a few centimetres, before it wrenched backwards. Jerking back, forward, back. What was going on?

Yasmin swore she heard a muffled, "Put your shoulders into it!"

It sounded like Deborah.

Yasmin's ghost-mothers, who were shimmery only to Yasmin, and invisible to Rachna, were trying to chock the door open! They had somehow made it through the security gates and up the lift to the fourth floor.

Rachna strained.

"This...door...won't budge!" Rachna said through clenched teeth.

Deborah became partially visible as she performed an impressive backbend and slipped through. Yasmin watched a slight wavering in the air as Audrey commando-rolled past, popping upright straight away. Nicole's almost visible arms let go of the door, and Rachna catapulted back into the room, the door slamming before her. A few desk-bound workers glanced up and, just as quickly, returned to their work. Rachna seemed perplexed and a little embarrassed.

"I'll get maintenance to see to that," she said, although nobody paid her mind. She carefully opened the door, as if handling a Jenga tower, and left, watching the door click to. Her shadow wavered through the frosted glass, slinking to the lifts.

Yasmin's ghost-mothers were in the office!

She checked to see if anyone had noticed. Tasha blew her nose on a fresh tissue. Everybody else stared straight through the three shadowy outlines lurking at the door.

Yasmin casually got up from her desk, stretching and cracking fingers.

"I'm just going…over there," she said, lamely, "you know, in case you need me."

"I definitely don't need you," Tasha said, occupying herself with a database of some sort.

"Great!"

Yasmin traversed the room. She grabbed the arms of her besties and dragged them to the least-populated corner, next to a fake tree in a pot and the wooden door to the glass office.

"Stay invisible, please!" Yasmin whispered, lips as still as a ventriloquist's.

Deborah waved her arm in front of a passing worker to make her point. The worker frowned at the displaced air but kept moving.

"It's pretty tiring being invisible," Deborah said. "It requires concentration."

"For you maybe," Nicole retorted.

"Okay, but it looks like I'm talking to myself," Yasmin whispered. "Just keep a low profile, okay?"

Nicole magically straightened one of the posters on the wall. The leaves of the fake tree bobbed as Deborah stroked them. Audrey dangled a nearby mouse mid-air by its cord.

"Stop it!" Yasmin hissed. "Stop touching things!"

The stressed blonde at the lightbox watched the levitating mouse from across the room. Audrey placed the mouse back on the desk, sensor-side-up. Yasmin smiled sweetly and the blonde picked up her glasses from the table and put them on. She squinted across the room. Yasmin waved as the woman bent back to her loupe.

Yasmin gathered her besties into a manageable bunch.

"Do you not remember me asking you to behave?" she asked.

Just at that moment, Felicia Pine stepped from behind the wooden door, right into their enclave.

Then ricocheted back.

The ghost-mothers lurched out of the way, and Yasmin feigned being closer, to account for the collision.

"I'm so sorry, Ms Pine," she said.

"Why the blazes are you spying outside my office?" Felicia straightened. "And who are you?"

"I'm Yasmin Taylor-Lee." She held out her hand. Felicia declined to shake it. "The new girl."

"Well, get away from here and don't ever snoop on me again!"

"Yes, Ms Pine."

Felicia huffed and straightened the large cardboard mocks of the covers that she carried in one arm. Yasmin retreated to her desk; her friends followed.

"Is that—" Nicole whispered.

"Shhh!" Yasmin warned.

Yasmin studied the faint outline of her three ghost-mothers, the hazy border drawn around their shapes. Lightbox Girl stared straight through them as they passed, then went back to her negatives.

Yasmin and her friends huddled around her workstation.

Audrey rested her rear on Yasmin's desk. Nicole observed the monitors, marvelling at the multi-flat-screen set-up. And Deborah sat on an empty chair and spun.

Tasha popped up, frowning at the chair spinning of its own accord.

Yasmin put a hand on the back of the chair and gave it a push, as if she'd been in control of its momentum all along.

"Don't you just love chairs?" Yasmin asked.

Tasha smiled at that, her tears forgotten.

"Newsflash," she said. "You're most definitely not making it through probation."

Yasmin's stomach growled with an ever-increasing intensity as lunchtime came and passed, without any discernible interruption to the workers' day. She could murder a steak and three veg right about now. Her besties sat on her desk, legs swinging, sick of not talking. Yasmin felt much the same way; the novelty of her first day was starting to wane. Were they going to give her any actual work?

She opened her emails for, what felt like, the fiftieth time but didn't understand the jargon in the *pings* in the chat window. She read one:

Flag CMS error with SS.
DPS use PMS 185. B&W DL by COB.

It seemed to be in an alien language. None of the messages were addressed to her personally, so she hoped that meant they didn't expect a reply.

Her phone rang, and Yasmin felt a thrill in her stomach. Her first real call! She cleared her throat and composed her most serious face. But before she could answer, Tasha picked up the line from her desk.

This was getting ridiculous.

As she listened to Tasha's posh telephone-voice, Yasmin wished she'd had breakfast. She'd been too nervous before she left home. She wondered if people who worked on *The Standard* were allowed lunch breaks. What about bathroom breaks? She didn't remember anyone leaving through the frosted doors, and she started to worry.

"Ah, I'm sorry to bother you, Tasha," she said, standing up so she could see over the partition. "Would you be able to point me to the bathroom?"

Tasha covered the receiver. "Last door, to the left."

"Thanks."

Yasmin manhandled her friends down the hallway. They entered the tiny, two-stall bathroom. She moved to the mirror, springing her curls with her fingers.

"Oh my God, oh my God! You've got to hear this," she said, turning from the mirror. "*The Standard*'s folding!"

They didn't get it. They stared back as if she was a talking bear on a kid's commercial, and all they heard was growling. Yasmin reached for a paper towel and dabbed at a speck of mascara that had fallen onto her cheekbone.

Nicole cut the air at her neck.

"That's right. It means the magazine's cactus," Yasmin said. "Dead. No more."

Audrey waved as if directing a freshly landed B-52 around an A-bomb crater.

"Yeah, we're in trouble all right," Yasmin said.

The toilet flushed.

How had Yasmin not seen that closed stall door?

She was horrified. She'd been caught out – on her first day no less – talking to herself in the ladies' bathrooms. The flushee exited the stall, regarding her in an odd way – it was the designer from before.

"I wouldn't go around telling people that," she said, her blue see-through blouse gaping at the top as she vigorously washed her hands. She moved sportily as if expecting to intercept a passing netball at any time.

"No, of course not. There's nobody here, right?" Yasmin said.

"Right."

"Not unless they're invisible!" Yasmin said, then laughed. Then snorted. Then laughed at her snort. "Haha, there's no such thing as invisible people."

Deborah nodded in her cool way.

"Well, anyway, not that we know of, right?" Yasmin rambled. "I mean, my father, now *he* was a physicist, worked for the government – you never know what ASIO has in store for us. Well, I don't anyway, it's a matter of national security. He never could talk about his work…"

"I'm Erica," she said.

"Yasmin," she said, relieved at the change of topic.

They shook hands. Yasmin wondered if Erica thought she was a complete weirdo. Or maybe she was about to tell that huge security guard to collect her and throw her out on the street. At least she'd make Buckley's day.

"Well, keep those details on the down-low," Erica said. "If our competitors knew how much trouble we were in – the whole company was in – they'd start poaching all our advertisers. That's the last thing we need."

"Of course. Goes without saying," Yasmin said.

"Your job shouldn't have even gone through. There's a hiring freeze. Felicia did it to spite Oliver."

"I see."

"I'd make sure they pay you, is all I'm saying." Erica checked her out. "Nice outfit."

"Thanks."

She dropped her voice. "You know, I'm pretty sure they have a, 'last in, first out' policy when it comes to redundancies."

"Oh," Yasmin said. "What does that mean?"

"Just be sure you have a plan B."

"But I just landed plan A."

"I'm just being realistic, honey."

Erica sidled out of the bathroom. Yasmin watched the door click shut, listening to Erica's heels clacking down the corridor.

"Did you just hear that woman?" she said.

"Forget about her. What do you mean the magazine is folding?" Nicole said.

"Yes, dear. What does that mean?" Audrey asked.

"It's the man, isn't it? He can't take this away from us!" Deborah yelled.

"Shhh…It means Australia's longest-running women's magazine will be no more. And I'm out of a job."

"And if *The Standard* doesn't exist," Nicole reasoned, "we won't exist."

"What do you mean?" Yasmin asked.

"Think about it. We're only here because of our obituaries in the magazine, and we take everything from that. We're like our magazine selves. We're the same age we were in our obituaries. Our skin and clothes are the same colour as our respective pages."

"But we're dead," Deborah added. "The ghosts from magazines past."

"Ghosts need a place, or object, to haunt. And that place or object has to mean something to the living. If your magazine loses relevance, so do we," said Audrey.

"Can't you just hang out in my bedroom?" Yasmin asked, her voice small.

"It won't work. Nobody died in there," Audrey said.

"Pretty soon we'd be lost to those boxes of back issues again. Forgotten, just like your grandma forgot about those who went before us. Ghosts feed off human energy."

The three of them chattered away. Yasmin couldn't make out what they were saying. Her head started to spin with the noise and emotion. She put both hands on the basin, steadying herself. Her breath caught, short and painful – as if she were breathing after a dip in Arctic waters. Her body started to shake.

"What should I do?" she gasped.

Nicole stepped forward, cupping Yasmin's cheeks.

"You have to save it," Nicole said. "You have to save *The Standard*."

8

*Y*asmin knew that's what she had to do – stop *The Woman's Standard* from folding. She would have to find a way to prevent everyone in the room from being fired. The 'how' proved to be another matter though, considering she couldn't even work out her new phone.

She jabbed at all the red flashing buttons, but the English-accented automaton kept asking her to input a password she didn't have.

She began entering random numbers. 1-2-3-4 seemed obvious, but no go. Neither was 0-0-0-0 and 69-69. On the last attempt, the English automaton told her, in her posh voice, "That password is incorrect. Goodbye." Then she disconnected the line. Angry beeps followed.

"How rude," Yasmin said.

"Are you talking to me?" Tasha asked, her eyes wide.

"No, sorry, the answering machine."

"Oh yeah, she's annoying, right?"

"Right," Yasmin said. Phew. Forget saving *The Standard*. She just wanted to make it through her first day without getting fired.

Her friends busied themselves while perched around the desk, reading back issues and pointing out pictures and stories to each other. Their fidgeting would be distracting if Yasmin had any work to do. Her co-workers were too engrossed to notice three magazines floating mid-air, magically turning their pages.

Yasmin admired the pictures tacked proudly to her desk divider: one each of Audrey, Deborah and Nicole snipped from the front covers. They were the first images that had brought them to life, and they were Yasmin's most precious possessions, after her grandmother's magic coin. She rearranged the photos in a careful collage.

Tasha rounded on Yasmin's desk. Her friends tensed and Yasmin slapped the magazines onto the table. Nicole jerked her leg out of Tasha's way.

"Who are your friends?" Tasha asked.

Yasmin guiltily scanned the outlines of Audrey, Deborah and Nicole. Could Tasha see them now?

"Sorry?" Yasmin asked.

"Your friends." Tasha pointed to the partition.

"Oh, the pictures!" Yasmin said, relieved. "I thought I'd put up some inspiration."

Yasmin winked at her ghost-mothers. Tasha noticed. Yasmin blinked rapidly and pretended to pull dirt from her eye. Tasha examined the covers.

"You've got good taste," she said.

"Thanks. So do you." Yasmin blushed. Why did she say that? Was she referencing Tasha's pictures? She didn't have any, so that was a weird thing to say. "I mean, you've got good taste in clothes and all that. Of course, my brother is an insane stylist. He works with Vera Wang. He can get me any sample he wants before it hits the store. Not that I'm wearing that today, of course. I opted for a more conservative look..."

Tasha dumped a pile of lever-arch folders on the desk.

"I may wear Gaultier tomorrow," Yasmin continued, putting her palm to the stack to stop them from sliding to the floor.

"Well, at the moment you're *wearing* Target."

"Not true. I made this one myself. I'm quite the seamstress... My brother designed it, of course. So, you see, it's a prototype. Target must have copied the pattern..."

"So anyway, I'll start you off with something even you can't stuff up." Tasha pointed to the lever-arch files. "Here's some back issues of our magazine to get you acquainted with our editorial. You need to make a list of all the contributing writers and start a spreadsheet. You know how to make a spreadsheet, right?"

"Of course." Yasmin hadn't used a spreadsheet since high school, but how hard could it be?

"Once you've made your list, you need to go through our database and add their contact details. You get it?"

"Got it."

"And make sure to list which issues they featured in. That's important." Tasha glanced at the desk phone, which was lit like a crazed Christmas tree. "You'd better take down those messages. Could be important."

She wandered back to her desk.

Yasmin glanced at the red blinking lights. They seemed to speed up and flash erratically until she felt like she would have a seizure. She had no idea how to work that thing.

"I tried but the lady just said 'goodbye,' and then she hung up," Yasmin said.

But Tasha was already seated, donning an oversized pair of noise-cancelling headphones.

Yasmin mashed a few more buttons, but the phone made a loud *buh-bow* sound. Even Erica roused herself from her cover design and gave Yasmin the stank eye.

Finally, Tasha relented. "You'll have to get IT to reset your pin."

"Thanks," Yasmin said, moving onto her computer. "I'll just send her an email, shall I?"

Tasha didn't respond, so Yasmin enlisted her ghost-mothers' help. Nicole at least understood the concept of a computer, having used several in her work at the university. Audrey and Deborah both cooed like grandmothers inspecting their grandchild for the first time. They clapped their hands whenever the computer made a noise or opened a new 'whatsit.'

Yasmin assumed the email for IT was just it@thewomansstan-dard.com, but that just sent a bounce-back.

Erica took pity and ducked over from the next desk. Tasha pretended to be in deep concentration, in 'the zone,' while Erica pointed Yasmin to the icon for something called an 'in-tra-net.'

"It's like the internet, but just for our office," Erica explained, pointing helpfully at the little links on the page, "and you can find pretty much anything you need on here."

"Wow, thanks for the tip. How wonderfully useful!" Yasmin gushed. Tasha stewed on her side of the partition. Yasmin swore she felt the heat through the desk.

Erica smiled and returned to her seat.

Yasmin found a contact list, located the real IT email and shot off a request for help.

Dear Internet Thingy people,

I would be very much obliged to make your acquaintance again, as I seem to have a problem with my phone. The lady on the other end has prevented me from accessing the many messages that I have been sent. I am sure they are critical and needed by Ms Pine most urgently. In fact, she has personally asked me to retrieve the messages as a matter of prior-ity. I would appreciate your help so that I am not fired, and Ms Pine can continue her long and illustrious reign as Chief Editor of The Woman's Standard (magazine).

Yours utmost faithfully,

Yasmin Taylor-Lee.

While she waited for a reply, she noticed that Audrey was fascinated by everything Yasmin did. She opened a new webpage and googled 'what is a spreadsheet?' She kept the YouTube tuto-rial running for Audrey to follow along.

She opened up Excel from her desktop and entered the infor-mation almost by rote, she didn't have to check the magazine too often. She was just pointing to the Excel cell to show Audrey where she was up to – when Tasha checked on her.

"What are you doing?" she hissed. "You can't be that stupid?"

Yasmin paused the video, her face flushed. Now Tasha thought she was a complete idiot.

"At least use headphones, please," Tasha huffed. "The rest of the office is trying to concentrate on important work. You know – saving the company, yada yada."

"Sorry."

Yasmin shut down the YouTube page.

Nicole put her head close to Audrey's and whispered, "I've used Excel extensively for number-crunching large data pools. I'll show you how to use it."

At 5:30 p.m. on the dot, Yasmin had finished her spreadsheet. She was well on her way to becoming a data-entry whizz – although she still typed with her two index fingers.

She admired the little Excel icon on her desktop. Her first piece of work as an employee at *The Woman's Standard*. She was so pleased that she snapped an Instagram pic with her iPhone. She named the Instagram pic, 'Yasmin's first file.'

She felt pretty darn good about her first day.

Yasmin was just uploading her Instagram pic when Tasha caught her – again.

"Oh my God, you're way too excited about that," Tasha said. "Have you never worked in an office before?"

"Of...of course!" Yasmin back-pedalled. "Just not *this* office, right?"

Tasha's phone rang again and she left to answer it. Yasmin let out the breath she had been holding.

Audrey tucked her notes into her handbag, and Yasmin spent the next few minutes trying to figure out the database.

Nobody seemed even remotely close to finishing up for the day. So Yasmin checked her inbox, and Rachna from IT had responded! She had provided a temporary pin, which Yasmin plugged into the phone. The auto voice guided her through the messages. Yasmin kept getting stuck halfway through, pressing the wrong number and getting so flummoxed that she would hang up and start again from scratch. But finally, all the messages played, one after the other.

BEEP!

"Hello, Ms Pine. I am calling from Go Gettem PR to see if you'd like an exclusive day spa experience to thank you for your kind coverage of the bladder control TENAs in last month's issue…"

BEEP!

"This is Mary Raymond of 14 Evercrescent Avenue. I have a complaint for Felicia Pine and her band of miscreants at *The Woman's Standard*. There was a blatant typographical error in the astrological readings in the 29th November issue, 1941. In this context, the 'your' should be y-o-u-apostrophe-r-e. Not y-o-u-r. I expect an apology notice in the next issue…"

BEEP!

"Hello? Hello? My name is Betty Winters. I was wondering…if you're covering…Princess Elizabeth's coronation? I don't have a television…you see…and I don't trust them anyway. I've always relied…on *The Standard*…for those lovely pictures…you always publish. Hello? Sorry dear…I can't hear you…you'll have to speak up…"

BEEP!

Poor Betty Winters, thought Yasmin. She didn't keep up with current affairs. Elizabeth had been our Queen for many decades.

More messages came, faster than Yasmin could write them down. They all spoke so rapidly – except Betty Winters, who sounded like she was on a ventilator. Yasmin managed to write Betty's whole message, word for word. She paraphrased the rest.

She took a deep breath. Her big moment had arrived. She would need to take the messages to Felicia's office. Her very first interaction with Ms Pine in a work context!

She carried the A4 pad over to the glass office and knocked on the door. She felt the hairs on the back of her neck stand to attention. She reddened at the knock, imagining all work ceasing behind her as thirty employees stared from their desks. Of course, none of them did, but Yasmin was too terrified to check.

"Yes," Felicia said.

"It's Yasmin," she yelled.

"*Entrez*."

"Sorry?"

"It's French for enter," Audrey said, suddenly beside her. Yasmin flinched.

"Go away!" Yasmin hissed.

"Come in!" Felicia said.

"Okay."

Yasmin shook her head at Audrey, who put up both hands and backed away from the door. Yasmin opened it, and Deborah slipped through.

"Don't – ah..." Yasmin was left at the door, her mouth agape, watching Deborah checking out Felicia's office.

Felicia regarded Yasmin, her new office oddity.

"Don't what?" Felicia asked, frowning and following Yasmin's gaze.

Yasmin stood there like an idiot. Her confidence sank as Deborah straightened Felicia's framed photos hanging on the walls. Deborah paused at the large frame showcasing Felicia clinking champagne glasses with a man in a pinstripe suit. His moustache was so coiffed that it was almost a work of art. It curled beatifically before ending in two sharp points on either side of his nose. There were a lot of photos of Felicia with the same man, the same facial hair, just a different-coloured pinstripe suit and tie.

Deborah seemed captivated by the man's moustache.

Yasmin sent dagger eyes to Deborah.

Felicia looked behind her, then back at Yasmin.

"Is there a reason for you being here?" Felicia demanded, taking off her glasses and placing them on her expansive desk.

"Ah yes, Ms Pine."

Yasmin was transfixed by Deborah, turning the awards on

Felicia's bookshelf around so she could read the inscriptions. Deborah let out a little, "Oohh!"

"What?" Felicia asked, her patience shot.

"Oohh, what a lovely trophy," Yasmin said lamely.

Felicia glanced back to the glass-fronted mahogany case, which contained a large cup about the size of Yasmin's head. The 'Lifetime Achievement' trophy from the Australian Media Awards. The curve of its golden lip glinted in the sun and the light refracted straight into Yasmin's eyes.

"Will you tell me why you are in my office?" Felicia asked.

"I have some messages for you," Yasmin said, her hand shaking as she handed over the yellow pad of paper.

That's when Deborah perched herself on Felicia's desk!

Yasmin made 'go away' signals with both hands. Felicia caught her.

"Please stop that," Felicia said.

Deborah rifled through Felicia's in-tray of mocks and colour print-outs.

"Yes, please stop that," Yasmin hissed at Deborah, who gave Yasmin a 'stuff you' stare, lifting a sheet of paper into the air and theatrically dumping it on Felicia's desk.

Yasmin recoiled. What would Felicia make of the levitating paper?

Felicia frowned. "Damn air conditioning has two settings – 'freeze' and 'Antarctica.'"

Yasmin tittered in reply. "Yes, oh yes." She shut up at Felicia's stare. Felicia donned her half-moon glasses and read through the messages.

"What is this?" she asked, holding the paper out. "What kind of imbecile do you think I am?"

"They're your phone messages, Ms Pine."

"Don't bother me with drivel again. Out!" Felicia barked, shaking the paper at Yasmin, who retrieved the messages and backed out of the room quick-smart. "And close the door behind you!"

Yasmin grabbed Deborah's arm and pulled her out of the

office. Yasmin stood for a minute, feeling her eyes stinging as if they had been pricked with tiny acupuncture needles. She blinked away the inevitable tears.

She guessed she shouldn't have given Felicia that last message from Betty Winters. She had clearly been rambling.

∾

"I did it!" Yasmin said. "I lasted a whole day at *The Standard*. I didn't get fired!"

They rode the packed bus home, commuters jostling and pushing their way in, then out of the bus at each stop. The commuters stared at Yasmin's ghost-mothers, who'd made themselves visible again. Could they be a performance chorus travelling home after a matinee?

Yasmin didn't relax until they were back in her bedroom, after dinner.

They started a brainstorming session on ways to save *The Standard*. Deborah tapped out after they refused to stage a sit-in. She stretched out on a blanket on the floor in protest, snoring softly. Audrey drew birds-eye schematics of the office in the carpet with her finger.

"Their weak point is by the water cooler," she said, sliding her finger in a cross shape next to Felicia's door. "It's your best chance at infiltrating Felicia's office."

Nicole paced the room, her lab coat flapping.

"I can run you through a basic macro in Excel, and you can wow them with your proficiency tomorrow. Make up for today."

"How is any of this going to save the magazine?" Yasmin asked, throwing her hands in the air.

"We've got to concentrate on getting you through the week first," Nicole countered.

The clock ticked midnight, and her besties had proved to be zero help.

"I have no idea what to do," Yasmin conceded. "What chance do I have, if the all-powerful Felicia Pine can't turn things around? She's had over thirty years at the helm. Surely she would have figured out how to keep the punters happy by now?"

"Let's sleep on it. We might wake up in the middle of the night with the answer," Audrey said, laying herself out next to Deborah, taking a throw-pillow for herself. Nicole removed her lab coat and used it as a blanket.

Yasmin slipped into her nightie and collapsed into bed.

An elongated Felicia Pine stares at Yasmin from a towering height, jabbing a sharp nail into her chest. "It's all your fault," she keeps saying. "It's your fault for spilling to our advertisers who have all jumped ship."

Tasha appears at Felicia's side, and they start up in song, a duet from a bad-dream musical.

"You've single-handedly brought down Australia's longest-running women's magazine," Felicia croons. "Your friends have left you. And… we…hate…your…guts."

9

The next morning, at seven a.m. on the dot, Yasmin and her fairy ghost-mothers buzzed through the side door to WWC. She brandished her security card and gave Buckley a cheeky wave.

"Lovely morning," she said.

He scowled back.

The entrance gates gleamed in front of them, like the opening to a gold-laden cavern. Yasmin buzzed through the accessibility gate and held it open for her besties. She pretended to stop to consider something to account for the time lag while they pushed through.

"What coffee can I get you tomorrow?" Yasmin called over to Buckley, who scrutinised her as if she were a safe-cracking hoodlum.

He shook his head.

"Not a coffee drinker?" Yasmin asked.

"Look, lady. I'm not your friend."

"So hostile."

Nicole checked out his pecs.

"He's probably careful about ingesting fats," she whispered. "I'd say that makes him an espresso kind of guy."

"Hmmm…yeah," Yasmin said. Then realised that was a weird thing to end on. She closed the gate, and they piled into the lift.

They flounced into the office. Tasha was already at her desk, deep in sub-editing mode. She barely flicked her eyes away from the computer when Yasmin greeted her.

Erica's computer sported a colour wheel on its screen, so she had to be close by. Every other desk was full. Felicia's door stood ajar and, behind the imposing mahogany desk, Felicia sat, crossing lines through someone's article. Felicia's eyes flicked to her ringing phone, then back to her work. Then, after a few moments of ignoring her phone, she finally answered it.

"…then get it bloody done by five p.m. today, or you lose our business, for good this time!"

"Is Felicia always like this?" Yasmin asked quietly.

Tasha checked her watch. "You're in early."

"Yes, well. I used to be an Olympic-grade swimmer. So early mornings come naturally to me; all that training, staring at the black line…" Yasmin lied. But Tasha wasn't listening, so Yasmin asked, "Is it just me, or is Felicia angrier than usual?"

Tasha peeked furtively over her shoulder.

"She's pretty normal."

Felicia's 'normal' seemed as terrifying as a sheer drop off a cliff, so Yasmin busied herself with opening emails. Audrey pulled up an office chair, watching every click. She took notes in a notebook, which she hid every time someone looked their way so the whole floating paper and pen thing wasn't so obvious.

Yasmin wrote the words 'what are you doing?' onto a corner of one of the pages. She pointed at it, raising her eyebrows at Audrey.

Audrey wrote, 'I'm learning.'

Out of the corner of Yasmin's eye, she saw someone approach the desk at a power-walk.

"Disengage," Yasmin said, and her besties scattered.

Felicia Pine strode towards Yasmin like a catwalk model on a mission to assassinate Ralph Lauren.

"You. Whatever your name is," she said.

"Me? I'm Yasmin."

"That's right. Do you know shorthand?"

"Yes," she fired back. She absolutely didn't.

"Good, you're taking the minutes in the editorial meeting at nine a.m. Have Tasha add you to the calendar invite."

And in a flurry of Eau d'Hadrien and an earthy scarf, Felicia vanished.

Tasha had kept her head lowered during that exchange. What was that about?

"Ah, Tasha?" Yasmin said.

"I heard."

At ten to nine, Tasha and the rest of the editorial team had disappeared. Not entirely – Yasmin hadn't called the police, or sparked a woman-hunt. It was just that the floor had been vacated – except for Erica and the sales team – for some time.

Yasmin grew anxious. Tasha hadn't sent an invitation to her calendar. Yasmin didn't know exactly where she would find one, either.

She covered an inquisitive sweep of the office with a luxurious stretch. There weren't any calendars on desks, or pinned to the wall. How could Tasha send a calendar invite if there were no calendars to be seen? How would she find the editorial meeting?

She also didn't know what she would have to bring to the meeting. Paper and pen, naturally. But should she also bring her spreadsheet – the one listing all of the magazines and the various contributors? She didn't have anything else to show for her 1.2 days at *The Standard*.

At five to, panic started to set in. She was unprepared and was going to miss the meeting.

She considered asking the handful of sales reps who weren't already out on the road, but they were an exclusive and outgoing bunch who, quite frankly, scared her. They were the sorority team of the magazine.

Instead, she leaned over to speak to Erica. "Ah, hi."

Erica was laying a vast amount of copy next to a regal photo of Wills perched atop a polo horse. She had chosen a less-sheer blouse today with bold swirling print. Her deft stylus movements had an air of complete confidence.

"This had better be good," she said.

"Yes, sorry to interrupt. It's just that Felicia wanted me to go to today's editorial meeting, and Tasha must have forgotten to add me to the calendar. I'm not sure where it's held."

"How should I know?"

Great. Just great.

"Well, thanks anyway."

Yasmin grabbed her friends by their elbows and dragged them to a corner partially obscured by the multi-function photocopier.

"We're going to have to search all of the meeting rooms," Yasmin said.

"Agreed." Nicole limbered up, stretching her calves and shoulders. "It's faster if we split up."

"Good idea," Yasmin said. "Nicole, search the floor above. Deborah, the floor below. I'll stay on this floor."

"What about me?" Audrey asked.

"You can try and find the calendar in Felicia's office."

"Easily done. They trained us in infiltration techniques in spy school."

"Um, Felicia leaves her door unlocked, dummy." Deborah slapped Audrey on the shoulder.

"The meeting starts in five minutes! Go!" Yasmin instructed.

Deborah and Nicole slipped into the atrium. Audrey scuttled into Felicia's office, unnoticed by Erica. Yasmin strode in the opposite direction.

She craned her neck around the corner. The frosted glass panelling on each wall sat between knee and head height. She crouched down, attempting to identify the lower legs. Heels bloomed into shapely calves, but nothing identified them as Felicia or Tasha.

"Darn, darn, darn..."

It didn't bode well. If Yasmin showed up late to the meeting, Felicia might well kick her out onto the street. Taking shorthand was the first thing she'd asked Yasmin to do, and Felicia didn't seem interested in giving newbies second chances.

Yasmin came to the end of the hall, and the unidentifiable heels-and-calves hadn't revealed the correct meeting to barge into.

Audrey sprinted along the hall. Yasmin ran to meet her halfway.

"Where?" Yasmin asked.

"Follow me."

They raced to the Eleanor Gilbert Room, where Yasmin had attended her job interview. She had hoped the meeting was anywhere but there.

Audrey handed Yasmin a notebook and pen.

"Good luck," she said.

Yasmin discreetly opened the door. Felicia stopped mid-sentence, and every head swivelled, like a gang of meerkats. At least twenty staff sat ramrod-straight in high-backed chairs. At the head of the table, Felicia stood with her hands splayed on the desk, the epitome of ferocious power.

"I'm ah...sorry I'm late," Yasmin said in a stage whisper so as not to interrupt opening night of the Yasmin Tear Down Musical.

All the chairs were taken. Audrey invisibly followed Yasmin into the room. Yasmin spotted a pot plant in the corner, sitting on a plastic stool. She moved the pot plant to the floor, nodded an apology and sat. The stool's height left Yasmin peering upwards like a pre-schooler sent to the time-out corner.

"When people are late, it implies they don't respect me or my time," Felicia said, enunciating every word.

"I'm very sorry, Ms Pine. Of course I respect you," Yasmin squeaked.

"Are you contradicting me?" she spat back. "Because I know what being late means."

"I had an allergic reaction to the polyester in the chairs, and I had to pop to the—"

"I don't care."

"It won't happen again."

"Correct."

Yasmin caught Tasha's eye. Tasha innocently turned her attention back to Felicia, who started her tirade about profits and hooks and 'our readership,' at a pace Yasmin could never keep up with.

She opened the notebook and took notes as fast as she could, but she had no idea how to take shorthand, so she missed every sentence but the fourth one. She was so intent on taking notes that she hardly understood a single thing.

"You there, stop taking notes," Felicia said.

Yasmin started to write 'you there, stop taking...' before it sank in. Had Felicia addressed her?

Yasmin glanced up. Felicia was indeed staring straight into Yasmin's eyes.

"Ah, yes, Ms Pine." Yasmin absently fingered her magic penny, until she realised that Tasha was looking at her strangely. Yasmin tucked the coin back underneath the neckline of her dress.

Felicia eased into her chair, straightening the folder in front of her. She made a point of scrutinising all of them, in turn. And everyone – from the chief sub to the freelance contributor – sent their eyes to the floor.

"Why are we so unpopular?" Felicia asked the silent room. "Why is our circulation so dismal? It's because we've failed." She stabbed a finger on the boardroom table. "We've failed to stay relevant, we've failed to bring the next generation of readers with us. *The Standard* is no longer 'the standard' in women's lives. They can get the same information from a click-bait ad in just about any webpage you'd care to point at. Put bluntly, our readers – our die-hard fans who will fork out for every single one of our publications – are dying off. The millennials don't care, and you can be damn sure that if they don't care, neither will their kids. We've lost our entire readership."

She drew in a breath and stood tall.

"We need new readers, new blood, people who haven't subscribed to this internet thing, people who appreciate a physical copy of a beautifully designed, engagingly written magazine they can hold and feel and smell. People who want their celebrities in high-gloss, high-res. People who respect our editorial thoroughness. People who have trusted us for years, and whose mothers trusted us, and their mothers before them. We want to be progressive!"

She paused, then banged her fist on the table.

"So, no more of those blasted royal scandals! Our readers are sick of it! Nobody cares about the royals anymore – we're almost a republic for heaven's sake! Has anyone else got a decent idea for the 85th anniversary edition?"

You could hear a pin drop on the oh-so-plush carpet. Yasmin scanned the faces of the others in the room – they were all terrified.

"Well, then. I guess that's my answer. Just know, this week we'll weed out some of our *under-performers*." Her eyes fell on Yasmin. "We have to give our magazine the best possible chance of surviving the next issue. Because it could be our last."

She stood up, as did the rest of the room. Yasmin hurried to her feet, dropping the notebook that sat forgotten in her lap.

"And, one last thing. If nobody has a decent answer at the next editorial meeting, which, because you're a bunch of imbeciles, I might have to remind you is in *one week's time* – you're all fired."

And with that, Felicia Pine swept out of the Eleanor Gilbert Room, leaving a trail of perfume and horror-stricken faces in her wake.

10

They filed out and trudged back to their desks like pupils who had been whipped with the cane. Nobody spoke, each occupied with their version of what it would mean to no longer work at *The Standard*.

For Yasmin, it would mean the shattering of a life-long dream and the possible annihilation of her imaginary friends. She'd be unemployable once Felicia discovered that she couldn't take shorthand, had never worked in an office and had lied about her previous experience and references.

So far, Yasmin had the advantage that nobody knew about her many skill gaps and embellishments, which was thanks to Gargantuan Consulting's suspect vetting processes, and Yasmin's insinuation that she'd won the Walkley Young Australian Journalist of the Year Award. Soon the sheen would wear off, and she was terrified of Felicia finding out.

She decided to use her initiative.

"Ah, Tasha? Just wondering if you have some work you need help with?"

"You need to transcribe your notes from the meeting," she said. "And while you do that, you need to leave me alone and not ask any questions."

"Okay, thanks," Yasmin said brightly to help combat the

feeling that she was careening towards a figurative death. And where the heck had Deborah and Nicole hidden? They hadn't come back since the dreaded editorial meeting.

Yasmin sucked a yoga-worthy breath into her belly and spent a few minutes looking from computer to notepad.

"Ah, Tasha?" Yasmin asked timidly.

Tasha didn't hear, so Yasmin cleared her throat, feeling the muscles spasm. She was quite literally choking on her inadequacies.

"Tasha," Yasmin squeaked. And then let out in one long rush of breath, "what-program-do-you-use-for-transcriptions?"

"Word," she said, and Yasmin wondered if she'd just been given kudos in a hip kind of way.

When Yasmin didn't reply, Tasha rolled her eyes – at least Yasmin imagined she had. Yasmin could only see her from the eyebrows up.

"It's a word-processing program that you should know about if you were any kind of journalist."

She said it loudly enough for Erica to hear, which Yasmin found a tad mean.

"Oh great, thanks." Yasmin smiled apologetically at Erica. "Yes, I thought you meant it the literal way. Word the program. Got it."

Tasha must have shared a moment with Erica because they both giggled. Yasmin felt like the stupidest editorial assistant that Tasha had ever trained – so dumb in fact, that even Erica felt bad laughing at her.

She opened a Word doc and began transcribing her notes, but her scrawls from the meeting were even more confused than her memory of what was said. She tried to piece everything together, but nothing made sense.

'Circ numbers to 100k.'

'Imbeciles.'

'Relevant today?'

She stared at a paragraph of non-connected sentences in the Word doc, feeling indigestion grab hold. Maybe she should get the chop now. Perhaps she was better suited to a work environment with less responsibility. Should she let go of her dream of working at *The Standard* and let the company go under and her friends evaporate into nothingness? Maybe this kind of stress wasn't worth it.

Tasha popped her head over the partition. "There are some proofs to take down to Production," she said.

"What about the transcription?"

"They're holding the press. Do you have any idea how much that costs per minute?"

"Right. Proofs now, transcription later."

Tasha handed her an A3-sized yellow folder and Yasmin stuffed it with the proofs. A little thrill wavered down Yasmin's back as she realised this was the magazine before it was printed! She was in an elite club of those who saw it before it hit the shelves. For someone who usually hung out at her mailbox awaiting *The Standard* to be delivered each month, this was monumental. She held the package to her chest.

Tasha stuck a Post-it note on top of the envelope.

"Give it to Lynne. Basement level," she said. "Hurry back."

"Right. On it," Yasmin said, heading to the door.

She was making her way to the vestibule when she noticed her swipe pass magically floating across the room.

Yasmin sprang back and grabbed the pass from Audrey. She scanned her colleagues, her face flushing red. Only one person had noticed, and it was the girl at the lightbox, Louise, on the other side of the room. And, this time, she was wearing her glasses!

Louise had a quizzical expression and blinked a few times as if trying to clear her vision. She took off her glasses and then rubbed at her eyes. She removed a stuck eyelash from underneath her lid and replaced her glasses.

Phew! Yasmin was in the clear. She headed out to the lift area and, as she pressed the call button, Deborah and Nicole peeked from behind a display cabinet.

"Hurry up, you lot," Yasmin said.

The foursome piled into the empty lift. Yasmin pushed the button for the basement.

"So come on – your first editorial meeting. Spill!" Nicole said.

Yasmin told them of being late and then taking notes as best she could, but that she didn't know shorthand. That Felicia had said, if someone didn't come up with an idea by the next meeting, they're all fired. And how Yasmin probably wouldn't last that long anyway, because her notes were unintelligible and Felicia was well beyond having patience with her.

She leaned against the lift wall.

"So I might as well pack up now," she said.

Audrey smiled. "You said your notes weren't up to scratch?"

"That's an understatement."

She fished in Yasmin's pocket and held out her mobile phone. Yasmin didn't get it, until Audrey opened a recording app and hit the 'play' button.

"Nobody cares about the royals anymore – we're almost a republic for heaven's sake!" Felicia said. It was so clear that Yasmin expected Felicia to poke her head through the manhole in the lift's roof and fire everyone on the spot. Then it registered.

"I took the liberty of recording it for you," Audrey said with a grin.

"You blooming genius!" Yasmin hugged her.

"I must say," Audrey said, admiring the phone, "this pocket-sized spying device would have won us the war in record time."

The lift came to rest on the basement level, and the doors creaked open.

Dingy light filtered through from yellowing fluoro strips along the ceiling, onto a narrow walkway between tall cubicle dividers. The carpet showed several trails of thread at the ends, and large rips had been patched over with gaffer tape. The walls were made of cold concrete that gleamed slightly, as if damp.

They heard workers close by, tapping at keyboards or having frantic conversations on the phone, but the sound was dulled by the cubicle dividers.

It felt as if they were walking into a siege situation, with a sniper likely to pop over the nearest partition. It didn't quite feel safe.

"Ah, hello?" Yasmin said.

A forty-something woman in Target slacks and an ill-fitting blouse scooted her chair around the partition.

"Yes?" she said.

"I'm ah...from *The Standard*."

"'Bout bloody time. I've got Inksett on standby. We've got twenty minutes to get this puppy into a taxi out to Wetherill Park."

"Are you Lynne?" Yasmin asked.

"You've found me. It's never the messenger's fault, don't worry," Lynne said. "You new up there?"

"Yes, it's my second day..."

"I just won ten bucks."

"I'm sorry?"

"*The Standard* newbie comp." She shrugged. "It's a gift."

"Um, congratulations?"

Lynne took the proofs and tossed them onto her desk. She picked up a desk phone and dialled. While she waited for the receiver to pick up, she turned back to Yasmin.

"Come again soon. We're all hoping you guys pull out the big guns for the next issue. We need the jobs down here. This is a dying industry, my starry-eyed friend."

"We'll do our best..." Yasmin trailed off.

Lynne turned back to her call. "Garry. I'm standing at the taxi now. The proofs are inside. Hold off for us, will you, darling?"

Yasmin gave a little wave, unsure of how to best end the interaction. She was relieved when the lift arrived, and she rode back up with her ghost-mothers.

"That place was weird," Deborah said.

"Yeah, like an old war bunker," Audrey said. "And I've seen a few."

~

Back on the fourth floor, Audrey transcribed the notes from the meeting, listening through headphones plugged into Yasmin's phone. Audrey turned out to be a fabulous touch-typist, albeit a little heavy-handed with the keys.

She handed the chair back to Yasmin, who did a quick spellcheck and then emailed the notes to Tasha to look over. Of course, Tasha took less than a minute to come up with something to criticise.

"You should word this better, take out the ums and ahs. How did you even get all of those down? There's no shorthand equivalent."

"I was just trying to be accurate," Yasmin said. She decided to chance it and popped over to Tasha's side. "I was wondering if we could brainstorm. You know – ways to save the magazine."

Tasha huffed but swung her chair around to face Yasmin.

"We've tried absolutely everything," Tasha began. "We've run sweepstakes and spent our collective year's salary on television advertising. We've had celebs on the cover, fashion tips from top designers, *Masterchef* royalty writing exclusive recipes. Nothing seems to work. It's not just the magazine that's out of date – it's the whole industry."

"Well, you can't have tried everything," Yasmin said, hope tinging her inflection.

"We've got to find something exceptional that people can't get elsewhere. Otherwise, what is the point? We've done the same things, we've done different things. We can't seem to appeal to the new readers, and that's what we need to do. It's this elusive thing. Nobody cares."

"I care," Yasmin said.

"Do *you* have any ideas?"

Yasmin was so surprised that she answered truthfully. "Not a single one."

Tasha lowered her head. "I guess, enjoy this week then."

"We've only got one week?"

"Did you or did you not take the notes in that meeting? One

week to come up with an idea, or we're all fired. And Felicia doesn't make threats unless she can follow through with them."

Yasmin felt a stab of something – regret, maybe? – that someone else could have landed this job, and might have been good enough to save the magazine, her friends, and the whole damn company. How could she help if this talented team couldn't?

"Hurry up and make those changes I mentioned," Tasha said. "What does it matter – nobody in that meeting is going to mistake what was said."

"So I'll just email it to Felicia then?"

"And when you're done," Tasha said, "I have your first assignment."

11

"My first assignment!" Yasmin said excitedly. She noticed Tasha's expression: way too cool for that response. "I mean, yes, great. What do you need?"

"The horoscopes," Tasha said.

"Oh, sure. I can get the horoscopes for you. If you trust me with Divine Florette's number, of course!" Yasmin said, picking up her desk phone.

"No, you're writing them," Tasha said.

"But Divine Florette writes the horoscopes. She's written them for the last forty years." Yasmin put the phone down.

"'Divine Florette' is every editorial assistant who's ever worked on our magazine," Tasha said, turning back to her desk.

"You mean the stars – they're not real?" Deborah whispered with mock seriousness.

"They're only real if you're gullible," Tasha said over her shoulder.

"But I don't know the first thing about writing horoscopes," Yasmin said. "And our readers make decisions based on them. What if I tell people the wrong thing?"

"Oh, please. Don't tell me you rule your life that way. It's all down to the power of suggestion and being super vague."

"So what do I write about?"

"The usual. The only things that people care about: love, money, health. If you're stuck for something, throw in the promise of a new job."

"But...I'm not sure I can do that."

"Do you mean you're rejecting your first writing assignment?"

"No, not at all," Yasmin said, moving back to her desk. "I've got this. When do you need them by?"

"Eleven a.m."

Yasmin checked her watch. "But that's only an hour from now."

"Welcome to your first deadline at *The Standard*." Tasha tossed her the last issue. "For inspiration."

"I've read that – oof!" Yasmin said as Audrey elbowed her ribs. "I mean, no problem."

She knew what to expect from reading a horoscope, but writing one was an entirely different thing. Audrey scribbled on a pad of paper: "Love, money, health, work." Yasmin bent over the back issue, making notes as she went. And pretty soon she had the start of something.

"Here. What do you think?" Yasmin asked her ghost-mothers, who bent over to read.

You will face a challenge at work by Friday, so tread carefully. Honesty is the best policy, and you won't be happy until you come clean. If you get yourself into a bind, seek help from friends. Don't get into arguments, defer to those in power or you will face the consequences. Be willing to lean on others to get you through, and you will find the wisdom, passion and courage to be your best 'you.'

"You're good at pulling things out of thin air, that's for sure," Deborah said.

They made a few tweaks, then Yasmin handed it over to Tasha, who speed-read it.

"That's great. Now we need eleven more."

"I don't know the personality types…"

"So choose them at random. Have the copy on my desk in half an hour."

Yasmin sat back at her desk, appealing from Audrey to Deborah to Nicole.

"How am I going to get the other eleven done in half an hour?" she whispered. "That first one took me fifteen minutes!"

"Divide and conquer," Audrey whispered, handing a pen and some loose sheets of paper to each of them. "Deborah, you take Aquarius to Taurus. Nicole, we need you on Gemini, Cancer and Leo. Yasmin, take the last four."

"What are you going to do?" Deborah asked.

"I'll type them all up, starting with this," Audrey said, picking up Yasmin's first horoscope.

"Shouldn't I type?" Nicole said. "I wouldn't have the foggiest about making up horoscopes."

"It's just generalisations," Deborah said. "The worst possible version of what women supposedly worry about."

"I have the fastest typing speed," Audrey explained. "I'm pulling rank. Don't think; do."

Yasmin's adrenalin kicked in and she bent to scribbling. She didn't stop to think too hard, allowing her pen to fly over the page, dreaming up random details and vague references. Two other pens worked at the page, to all other observers writing miraculously in mid-air. But Yasmin sat between them and the greater office. Plus, everyone was too absorbed in their daily tasks to notice.

Yasmin was the first to finish the next horoscope and handed it to Audrey, who fumbled with the mouse, her cursor erratic at first, while she grew used to the touch. Her face was outlined in the backlight from the screen, a certain rapture on her features. She seemed completely at ease as she read from the sheet by her side and touch-typed.

Deborah was next off the blocks, slapping the paper down triumphantly. Nicole seemed to be having trouble, looking first to the ceiling, the floor and out the window.

"Just write anything," Audrey hissed, not missing a beat at the keyboard. She pressed each finger with force, so used to the heavy, manual typewriters of her day. But she soon got the hang of things.

"Do you have to type so loudly?" Tasha said from her side of the desk.

"Sorry," Audrey sang out before Yasmin could respond.

Yasmin coughed and cleared her throat.

"Sorry," Yasmin said. "I said that. Just then."

"There's no need to be dramatic," Tasha said.

Yasmin sent eyes of warning to her friends. They went back to work.

"Twelve minutes to go..." Yasmin softly counted down, tapping her watch as she scratched her pen across the paper.

Only six pieces of paper sat on Yasmin's desk, half of those typed.

"Eight minutes...."

With just as many pieces of paper.

"Five minutes to go..."

Nicole bent to her last horoscope.

"I can't read your writing," Audrey hissed, putting the final flair into a paragraph.

"Years of academia," Nicole said. "I can't write neatly *and* quickly. Which one would you prefer?"

"Neither," Audrey said, tossing Nicole's paper on the floor and ad-libbing. "Really winging it here, love."

"Two minutes!" Yasmin said, thumping her last page onto the pile and watching the second hand tick down on her wristwatch.

They crowded over Audrey, willing the words onto the screen. Audrey's fingers moved faster than rubber at a drag race. They watched as Audrey filled the page until she came to the very last word. She had finished all twelve horoscopes!

"Quick, Deborah," Audrey said. "Figure out which one is which."

Deborah closed her eyes and pointed to assign each of them. Audrey typed the headings.

"One minute to go!"

"Spellcheck!" Deborah said, too loudly.

"Silent spellcheck, please," Tasha said.

"Yes, of course, silent," Yasmin said, swatting Deborah on the arm.

Yasmin grabbed the chair and scanned the document, correcting all of the wiggly red lines, and some of the green ones too. Thankfully, Yasmin's fairy ghost-mother was almost ninety-eight-per-cent accurate.

"Print!" Audrey said, pointing to the button.

"Printing!" Yasmin said.

"Oh, for the love of God," Tasha said.

"Printer!" Audrey said, urging Nicole with her hands.

"Quick – thirty seconds!"

Nicole took off to the multi-function printer next to Felicia's door. Nicole picked the copy and ran it back to Tasha's desk, just as the clock ticked over to the hour.

Yasmin stepped to the side of Tasha's desk as if she'd just been to the printer herself. Their assembly line had been a success!

Tasha seemed surprised that Yasmin had finished. She picked up the paper, reading through, a frown dimpling her forehead.

"They're not long enough," Tasha said, putting them to the side. "Do them again."

"But the deadline…"

"I made the deadline up to see if you could deliver under pressure. Clearly, you can't."

"But that's not fair!"

"Fair has nothing to do with it. You need to step up or leave us to get on with things. Your choice." Tasha swivelled her chair back to her desk and picked up her phone. "Right now, I've got to organise the shoot for the cover for the 85th anniversary edition. I can't babysit you while you learn the ropes. If you can't even write the horoscopes, what use are you?"

Yasmin started to tear up. Tasha was right. What use was she? She was dead weight.

"Look, there's no use wasting more time on these," Tasha said, clearly stressing about her own work. "Just give them to Felicia."

Yasmin scooped up the copy and ushered her besties into Felicia's office. Felicia was out, and it was unclear when she'd be back. While they waited, Yasmin sat on the chair, while Deborah perched on Felicia's desk. Nicole leaned on the windowsill, and Audrey paced the room, a bundle of outrage.

"That Tasha will be our undoing," Audrey fumed.

Felicia breezed in. Yasmin stood. Felicia arched an eyebrow and eased into her executive chair. Yasmin pushed the copy towards Felicia's side of the desk.

"Tasha said I was to give these to you," Yasmin said, with a timid set to her shoulders.

"What's this?"

"My first assignment."

Felicia glanced over the top of her glasses. But there was no bile in Yasmin's words, only defeat.

"Hmmm…" Felicia said.

It was unclear how she was taking this.

As the adrenalin cooled, Audrey became a little defensive. She stopped pacing. Felicia was still reading the horoscopes.

"But it's good copy," Audrey huffed.

"No, it's not good copy," Felicia said, finally looking up. "It's not even fair or middling copy."

"No, you're right," Yasmin said.

"Do you think I am going to accept this from a Walkley award-winning journalist?"

"Oh."

"The writing's all over the place. It's as if a different person wrote each horoscope. It might just be the stars, but each one needs to have consistency, some common themes. Planets in retrograde. That sort of thing."

"I'm sorry, Ms Pine."

"Writing the horoscopes is the least important job we could have given you, and you've managed to mess it up."

"It won't happen again." Yasmin felt her face grow warm.

Felicia put the pages down on her desk and stood.

"You'll stay until these are finished. Don't come back until they're fit for the Pulitzer Prize of astrological projections."

"Yes, Ms Pine."

"And where are the minutes of the meeting?"

"I'm still preparing them for you…"

"On my desk before you go tonight too please."

Felicia's desk phone buzzed, and she held a finger up to Yasmin.

"Yes?" Felicia said. "I'm sorry to hear that, Tasha. Yes, of course, you head to the hospital. We'll handle things here."

Felicia hung up, seeming to be momentarily thrown. She tapped the desk absently and her eyes became unfocussed. Yasmin grew anxious – she hadn't seen Felicia in such a trance-like state before. Felicia glanced at Yasmin, sizing her up properly.

"Tasha's had a medical emergency in the family," Felicia said.

"That's awful, I'm so sorry," Yasmin said, feeling a pang of guilt for her. "Is there anything I can do?"

"The cover makes or breaks an issue, and this is our most important issue ever, in the entire history of *The Standard*," Felicia said.

"I understand."

"Yasmin, is it?"

She nodded.

"You'll have to step in and do the cover shoot," Felicia said. "Sandra Mobaski is due any minute."

"The…cover shoot?" Yasmin said, alarmed. "And not *the* Sandra Mobaski? As in, the Hollywood movie star?"

"Be sure that everything goes smoothly," Felicia said. "Keep Sandra happy, and don't stuff this up."

12

*Y*asmin slumped at her desk, trying to gather her thoughts. She felt overwhelmed, as if a semi-trailer of stress was barrelling towards her on the highway, and she couldn't move out of its way.

Audrey printed the email that Tasha had sent with the instructions for the shoot. Deborah raced to the printer to retrieve them. Nicole loaned Yasmin her clipboard, which seemed to be the obvious thing to take to a photo shoot. But the instructions failed to say where the shoot took place. Was that assumed knowledge?

"Ah, Erica?" Yasmin asked.

"Yes?"

"Where would you go if you were doing a cover shoot?"

"The studios are on the sixth floor. Take Ms Mobaski to styling first. Ask for Miss Rochford."

"I can't wait to meet Sandra!" Yasmin said, her fan-girl enthusiasm spilling over.

"First thing, don't call her Sandra. Second, check in with Roger in the car park. Ms Mobaski's driver will drop her down there."

"Thanks!" Yasmin scanned the intranet database and found the number for the car park. She dialled.

"Hi, Roger?"

"Speaking."

"Has San – I mean, Ms Mobaski arrived yet?"

"Her driver phoned ahead, and she'll be here in five minutes."

"Should I come down to greet her?" Yasmin asked.

"No, I'll just send her up through the service lift; she can find her own way."

"Really?" Yasmin asked.

"That was a joke. Yes, please come down and greet Australia's most famous movie export and escort her to her photo shoot."

"Oh. Sure, thanks." Yasmin felt her stomach kicking as if it housed a troupe of synchronised swimmers. She was about to meet her first real-life celeb!

Yasmin grabbed her handbag, her pass and Nicole's clipboard. She turned to Nicole who nodded her approval.

"Very professional," she mouthed.

Yasmin felt a thrill in her stomach as the synchronised swimmers began writhing in unison. She made her way to the lift with her friends in tow.

They rode down to the basement car park and exited to the concrete parking area that smelt of fuel and rubber. Yasmin had a flashback to her first encounter with Felicia in this very car park. She tried to ward off the imposter syndrome that the memory triggered.

Roger lounged in the small attendant's box. He wore the same white shirt and black tie as Buckley, although he didn't fill out his shirt quite as well. He was playing a game on his smartphone. Not a lot of action down here.

He stood up when he saw Yasmin, laying his smartphone on the counter.

"I'm here for Ms Mobaski," Yasmin said.

Roger blew air through his front teeth. "You're in for an interesting day."

"What do you mean?" Yasmin asked. "Is there something I should be worried about?"

"Here she is." Roger nodded to a sleek black stretch Hummer that had pulled into the drive.

The driver wound down her window and spoke to Roger.

Yasmin hovered behind, trying to duck down to see inside the car. Roger pressed the button to raise the gate, and Yasmin yelled through the window, "Welcome to *The Woman's Standard*!"

The car slipped through the gates.

"Great first impression," Roger said, waving her through the gate as well.

Yasmin bolted to the car, which made a left down the ramp and disappeared into the lower floor.

"Come on!" Audrey grabbed Yasmin's arm, and they all helped each other down the ramp and to the stretch Hummer idling in front of the lift.

The car door opened.

A deep hip-hop bass emanated from its interior – loud, intimidating and tribal.

Sandra Mobaski's tall booted heels came into view, revealing thick ankles and bulging calves. The hem of her skirt sat just below her knee – leopard print and loose. She slipped down from the height of the car to stand on the car-park floor, landing with a clattering of heels. Sandra stood in a flowing, red linen shirt, which covered her expansive middle. Oversized beads hung playfully from her neck.

Yasmin saw her face last – the beaming exuberance, that star quality. It was all about her eyes – they seemed to invite the gaze of others.

Yasmin and her friends approached carefully.

"Welcome, Ms Mobaski."

"What?" Sandra yelled above the hip-hop. Her driver shut the door, and the music dulled to low bass.

"I said welcome, Ms Mobaski," Yasmin said.

"Oh please, call me Sandra." She stuck out a pudgy hand adorned with funky rings.

Yasmin shook it. "Of course, Sandra."

"I was kidding about calling me Sandra," she said, glaring at Yasmin's rapidly sobering face.

"Oh, I'm so sorry...ah..."

"I'll give you that one, kiddo," Sandra boomed, chuckling and rearranging her skirt around her waist. "Let's go see Miss Rochford!"

"Of course, Ms Mobaski." Yasmin indicated to the lifts, but Sandra was already hobbling away, her boots doing some serious heavy lifting.

Sandra's driver gathered a selection of high-street shopping bags from the back of the Hummer and handed them to Yasmin. She arranged them on her arm, around her handbag and clipboard, and joined her besties and Sandra in the lift.

It was a squeeze, and, more than once, one of her invisible ghost-mothers bumped shoulders with the imposing star's figure. She frowned at Yasmin each time, and Yasmin apologised, rearranging the bags.

"Here we are!" she announced as the doors opened onto the sixth floor, directly into the impressive space.

The warehouse-sized room took up the entire floor. The large atrium was filled with clothes on hangers, shoes, fashion accessories and all sorts of feathery, sequinned props. Flanking the atrium on every side were white-screened studios, green rooms and blinking tech booths. Catina would love it here. Yasmin was impressed herself.

A petite woman approached, carrying an iPad and wearing a slightly alarmed expression.

"Ah, Ms Mobaski, welcome back!" she said, extending a hand. "It's such a pleasure to work with you again."

"Sweetheart, please. The pleasure is all mine." Sandra oozed a benefactor's confidence.

The woman indicated a feathered couch beside the green room. Sandra sat, resting her arms on the back of the sofa.

The petite woman grabbed Yasmin's elbow.

"There's no booking for this shoot," the woman whispered, a dangerous edge to her voice.

"I'm sorry, I didn't know about it either…"

"How the hell are we going to fit her in?"

"Felicia sent me," Yasmin said evenly. "It's for the cover of the

85th anniversary edition. So, I guess it's the most important shoot you have all day."

"Well," the woman huffed, consulting a schedule on a tablet. "We can bump Joseph Lamb. He can wait a few hours." Her fingers flew across the screen of her tablet. "And if we cancel Don Coward—"

"As in, the former Prime Minister?" Yasmin asked.

"Former is the word – what a fossil. Nobody cares, am I right?" She ushered Yasmin to one side, rearranging coloured bars on a scheduling app.

"I was told to ask for Miss Rochford?" Yasmin said as the woman deposited her handbag in a cupboard under an editing suite.

"Yes, of course. She's working with Amy Cartwright on *TV Exposé* at the moment, but we can pull her off that. I'll make the call."

She wandered away, dialling into her phone.

Yasmin took a breath, knowing that more experienced people were around her who seemed to know what they were doing. This could be okay. They were getting the star treatment. Who could say no to Sandra Mobaski?

Their star was engrossed in a game of Candy Crush on her phone, and so Yasmin discreetly joined her friends. They silently marvelled at the lighting rig above them, which was suspended within a huge metal cage. The edges of the studio curled up, making the whiteness appear to recede into infinity. Everything blew out, glowing slightly. Yasmin touched the wall to be sure they weren't floating in a white vacuum. They stood in the lighting of every Napisan commercial ever made.

A few minutes later, Miss Rochford arrived.

She was a lanky, svelte creature, swathed in a tight black dress with gold highlights. Her face was overly made-up, camera ready, with dense, thick fake eyelashes. When she spoke, her voice growled like a vintage Mustang fresh from a tune-up.

"How are we? I am sooo sorry I've kept us waiting," she said, pressing her hand to Yasmin's in a familiar way.

"Thank you for making yourself available."

"Don't even think about that, my darling," she said. "Now, what are we doing here for Ms Pine, hmmm?"

"It's the cover for the 85th anniversary issue of *The Standard*. We have Ms Mobaski."

"I love it, I love it," she said, touching the fabrics on a nearby hanger. "We're going to make her simply gorgeous."

"Fantastic."

"So what is the angle?" Miss Rochford turned her fake eyelashes towards Yasmin.

"Angle?"

"What's my brief? I can't work without a brief." Miss Rochford's eyelashes swept down in the most deliberate of blinks.

"Oh. Tasha didn't mention anything—"

"And where is Ms Mobaski's wardrobe, darling? I'm afraid we don't have anything on hand."

"Wardrobe? I don't know."

"Well, you find the brief and wardrobe for me please, darling, while I prep our star." Miss Rochford seemed a little put off, but remained professional.

Yasmin pulled out her smartphone, but she didn't know who to call. The only person who would help her was Erica, and Yasmin didn't know her number. So she googled the Warner Williams Corporation, dialled reception and asked to be put through to 'Erica, the designer.' When she explained that she was the new editorial assistant, the receptionist hung up.

Yasmin took the phone from her ear, peering at the screen. She'd definitely just been hung up on.

Panic settled until Audrey whispered, "Check the email."

Yasmin consulted the printed instructions on her clipboard, found the number of the designer supplying the wardrobe and found the link to the brief at the very bottom. Yasmin typed the link into her smartphone.

Miss Rochford moved towards the green room with Sandra in tow.

Yasmin felt her fingers shake. Sandra would not be one to wait around. Yasmin strode towards Miss Rochford and handed over her phone. Miss Rochford read the brief inside, noting the photos of the gowns to come, nodding thoughtfully, before discreetly handing the phone back to Yasmin.

"So," Miss Rochford said, clapping her hands together and heading to the green room. "Ms Mobaski. Let's make you the most fabulous you have ever been."

≈

To her credit, Tasha must have organised the wardrobe days ago because, ten minutes later, a young man pushed a wheeled hanger into the studio.

Yasmin and her besties watched the performance unfurl before them.

First, Miss Rochford laid out a selection of clothing and accessories for Sandra to approve or reject. There was only one rejection – the white linen shirt (Sandra didn't 'do' white) – and Sandra insisted on wearing her necklace in the first shot, rather than the glittery number that Miss Rochford had chosen. Miss Rochford signalled to the petite woman from before, and they all disappeared into the green room, followed by a hair and makeup artist.

Yasmin was unsure as to whether she should join them, so opted instead to peek at the activity inside, through the green-room door.

It took half an hour for Sandra to be made up for her first look of the day. She emerged, wearing a floating silk number, gathered around her midriff in ruffles. She seemed to hover over the floor, her hair amassed in a messy beehive, her face radiant – if more orange than normal.

"How do you like your Vera Wang, darling?" Miss Rochford asked.

"Oh, it's delicious!" Sandra replied, dipping her head with excitement.

"Nothing but the best for our star."

Miss Rochford held a steadying arm and helped Sandra traverse the room to the white infinity section of the floor.

We're not stuffing this up! We're not stuffing this up! I'm rocking the most critical cover shoot of any issue, ever, in the whole history of The Standard... *Maybe Felicia will give me a raise?*

As Sandra passed, Deborah leaned a little too closely towards their star. She stepped on Sandra's dress as it trailed along the floor.

Sandra stepped forward. Deborah's foot held the dress. Sandra took another step.

The awful sound of tearing fabric filled the air!

Yasmin grabbed Deborah and pulled her back off the hem, but it was too late. There was a gaping hole in the material, which revealed Sandra's lacy-briefed, dimpled buttock.

"Oh. Crap," Deborah said.

"I'm so sorry!" Yasmin covered for her, feeling her stomach drop all six floors to the street level below.

Sandra's neck flushed red until it met her orange makeup.

"How could you be so clumsy?" she demanded.

"This is a custom-made, plus-size Vera Wang!" Miss Rochford briefly lost her temper, then just as quickly, composed herself. "I am deeply sorry, Ms Mobaski. We will get you another gown."

"Plus-sized?" Sandra fumed. "Are you kidding me? I want to speak to Felicia."

Yasmin realised she was holding her breath.

"What have you done?" she whispered to Deborah.

13

*Y*asmin stood, frozen to her little patch in the studio. She watched Sandra Mobaski stomping back to the green room, while Miss Rochford followed, desperately trying to cover the gaping buttock-hole in the Vera Wang.

Yasmin rushed after them, not knowing how to make the situation better, but hoping like the blazes that Sandra wouldn't call Felicia. That would mean instant dismissal. Felicia had been looking for half of such a chance.

"Ms Mobaski?" Yasmin called after the train wreck. "I'm so very sorry, I'm the clumsiest person. It truly is a curse. Is there anything I can do?"

Miss Rochford glared at Yasmin before ushering Sandra inside and closing the door firmly in Yasmin's face. Yasmin's body shook a little. Her besties tried to gather around for support, but Yasmin flinched at Deborah's touch, and she waved them off.

"This is the most important moment in the entire history of *The Standard*," Yasmin hissed. "Everything is riding on this! And it's a catastrophe."

"I'm sorry, sister," Deborah said, seeming genuinely contrite.

"You three are banned from the studio," Yasmin said. "Go home. You're just getting in the way."

Yasmin ignored their hurt expressions.

"And you." Yasmin jabbed a finger into Deborah's chest. "You're not happy unless you're causing chaos. You're not my friend. You're my biggest problem."

Deborah's brow furrowed, but she stood her ground.

"I said, clear off!" Yasmin shoved Deborah. The shove surprised her as much as anyone, but she was too angry to care.

Deborah slouched out of the studio, while Nicole placated her, in an unusual show of solidarity. Audrey trailed behind.

Yasmin watched her friends go, feeling a black cloud of emptiness settle around her. Could this day get any worse?

The petite woman opened the green-room door and popped her head through. She beckoned for Yasmin.

"This is Sandra's phone." She handed over the gold-cased iPhone. "Whatever you do, don't give this to Sandra. She's trying to pull out of the shoot."

Yasmin took it and nodded her thanks. The woman retreated into the room. Yasmin caught a glimpse of Miss Rochford hefting Sandra into a brand new gown.

Just then, the gilded iPhone rang. A thrill of fear snaked up Yasmin's insides, but to her credit, she answered, her voice shaking.

"Sandra Mobaski's phone, Yasmin speaking."

"It's Crystal for Sandra Mobaski."

"Oh, hello Crystal. Ms Mobaski is preparing for her shoot and can't come to the phone."

"She can come to the phone for her mother," Crystal said.

"Oh, I'm so sorry."

What the hell was Yasmin meant to do now? She dithered for a moment before knocking on the door to the green room and letting herself in.

Sandra was now stuffed into a replacement gown and seated on the chair in front of the mirror. The hair stylist worked at the beehive with a hair dryer. The room was luminescent, from the globes ringing the mirror, to the mobile clothing racks, the commercial makeup kits and white towels.

Miss Rochford fussed about, presenting a few accessory

options, all of which Sandra dismissed. Her hair stylist liberally dusted hairspray and the petite woman checked things off her iPad.

"Ah, Ms Mobaski? I'm sorry, but it's your mother on the phone," Yasmin said, approaching carefully.

Sandra held up a finger, and all fussing ceased; the hair stylist, the petite woman and Miss Rochford sidled to the back of the room to give their star some privacy. Sandra took the phone.

"Yes, Crystal," she said. "You've simply got to get me out of this shoot."

Yasmin's knees seemed to weaken, and all eyes turned her way accusatorially.

"Ah, why is Ms Mobaski talking to her mother like that?" Yasmin squeaked.

"Because it's not her mother." The petite woman glared at Yasmin.

"Yes, thank you, Crystal. I think that would be wise." Sandra turned and glared at each of them in turn. She held her phone away from her ear and spoke to the room. "And my next call will be to Felicia Pine."

Yasmin had no idea what to do. So she sprang forward and grabbed the phone out of Sandra's hand.

"What the—?" Sandra gasped. Even Miss Rochford had the startled expression of a rabbit mid-highway in the dead of night.

"Ms Mobaski, please consider doing the shoot," Yasmin said. "I've never been the same since the operation, you see. It was my foot, it was caught in a garage door when I was a baby, and it's never fully recovered."

"What?" Sandra said, a little less combatively.

"Yes, I've had many surgeries, but it freezes up on occasion, and there's nothing I can do about it. I go completely lame and can't control where I'm stepping."

Sandra's mouth began to move. Then she thought the better of what she was about to say.

Yasmin pressed on. "So, you see, it wasn't deliberate. I'm deeply embarrassed. You are the brightest and best star that

Australia has ever sent to Hollywood, and our humble magazine would be perfect with you on the cover. Who better to feature on our 85th anniversary edition! I can't think of another person with the gravitas to pull it off."

The room collectively held its breath as they waited for Sandra's reply. She had a curious expression on her face, as if she'd just noticed where she was. She crooked a finger for her phone.

Yasmin handed it back, her heart thumping in her chest, her mouth suddenly dry.

"Crystal?" Sandra said. "I might see how the rest of the day goes. But be ready for my call."

Sandra hung up and turned to Yasmin. "I'm very sorry about your foot."

"Oh, don't worry about it. I hardly notice it now. Except for occasions such as this, of course."

Miss Rochford and the petite woman smiled encouragement to their star.

"Continue," Sandra said.

Everyone kicked back into their roles and fussed over Sandra until she was camera-ready. Yasmin watched from a discreet corner of the room, affecting a slight limp whenever she moved around.

Finally, Sandra was ready.

They moved to the infinity white area, with Miss Rochford on one arm and Yasmin a good few metres away. They sat Sandra down on a stool and gathered her gown just so. A photographer appeared and began snapping away. Sandra posed as instructed, and Yasmin could see that she was a true professional. Every pose seemed natural, yet elegant, and oh-so-composed. Yasmin peeked at the thumbnail preview screen on the camera and saw that the photos were nothing short of brilliant.

Just as Yasmin was starting to enjoy herself, Felicia Pine herself arrived.

"Crap," Yasmin said to herself.

"Sandra, my dear," Felicia crooned, arms open wide.

"Felicia." Sandra held for one last photo and then broke her pose.

The two women air-hugged around the gown. Felicia was careful not to touch Sandra's makeup or hair.

"How are you, dear friend?" Felicia said, her voice dripping like syrup over ice cream.

"Jet-lagged, of course," Sandra said, with a martyred air.

"I could book us for Catalina tonight?"

"I'll have to check with my agent."

"How is Crystal?"

"Cranky as always." Sandra's bosom shuddered as she laughed.

Felicia chuckled in reply. It was the first time Yasmin had seen anything but a scowl on her boss's face.

"I hope the shoot is going well?" Felicia asked, taking Sandra's arm.

Sandra hesitated, glancing at Yasmin. "Oh, what's a shoot without a little hiccup?"

"Oh dear, I am so sorry, Sandra. Is there anything I can do?"

"Yes. Fire that one," Sandra said, pointing at Yasmin, then grinning. "I'm just joking. Who can blame the help for being lame?"

Felicia flicked her eyes at Yasmin oh-so-briefly, then turned her full attention back to Sandra.

"So I'll leave you for your next look, shall I?" Felicia said, helping Sandra back to the green room. The entourage of helpers followed.

Felicia whispered something in Miss Rochford's ear as she passed, then disappeared into the lift.

Yasmin hovered nervously at the back of the room while Miss Rochford selected and fitted the next outfit.

The shoot dragged on for half the day. Finally, Yasmin's stomach gurgled so loudly that it interrupted a solemn silence.

"Girlfriend. I hear you," Sandra said from where she reclined on a soft duvet, rubbing her tummy. "What's the chances of a pastry or something?"

Yasmin checked the instructions on her clipboard and called for catering, which arrived ten minutes later – a tray of pastries and gourmet wraps, and a bottle of Moet. Not long after, a large bouquet of flowers arrived. Sandra admired the fragrant long-stemmed lilies and dancing lady orchids. She plucked the hand-written card from the centre.

"'My dear friend,'" Sandra read. "'Let's make history together. Felicia. Ps: I've booked us for Catalina tonight. We're flying in their sommelier from Melbourne; Jane is desperate to share her pairings with you. See you at 8?'" Sandra looked up. "Felicia knows how much I enjoy Jane's pairings!"

She licked her lips and handed the flowers to the petite woman, who whisked them away, presumably to deposit them with her driver.

That signalled the end of the shoot. Sandra waddled to the feathered couch and dug in.

Yasmin was so famished she could have eaten the whole tray by herself. She eyed the dainty puffs and soft camembert oozing from one of the wraps.

"Don't make me eat alone," Sandra said, waving her hand over the tray of goodies. "There's plenty for everyone."

Everyone picked up a morsel, even Miss Rochford, although she didn't take a bite. Yasmin, however, dug straight in and plonked herself next to Sandra on the feathered couch to better reach the food.

Sandra observed Yasmin tucking in.

"I like a woman who's not afraid to eat," Sandra said. She clapped Yasmin on the back. Yasmin almost inhaled a flake of pastry from her croissant.

"Why thank you, Sandra," Yasmin said, without thinking. Then she froze. Had she just assumed she was on a first-name basis with their Hollywood star?

Yasmin turned to Sandra, but her expression was pure hilarity.

"You're okay, kiddo," she said.

"Where's my extra-hot almond-milk latte?" Felicia said as Yasmin settled in front of Felicia's desk, having seen Sandra Mobaski off in her Hummer.

"I'm sorry, Ms Pine," Yasmin said. "I was a little distracted with the shoot..."

"And what's this I hear about a damaged Vera Wang?"

"Oh, that was an accident."

"A ten-thousand-dollar accident!" Felicia said. "It was custom-fitted especially for Sandra!"

"I'm so sorry."

"And now we can't feature it in the magazine, as we had promised to do. So where does that leave me, do you think?"

"I'm sure the gown can be repaired..."

"It will be out of fashion for Sandra's next visit. A total waste of time for Vera. It's an embarrassment."

Yasmin stayed silent, allowing Felicia her rant. Felicia leaned forward, all her concentration on Yasmin's reddening face.

"Consider this your first – and last – warning," Felicia said. "You're officially on notice."

14

*Y*asmin sat back in the belly of the office, surrounded by people who would soon be called her ex-co-workers.

At least, that's how it felt to Yasmin. The office suddenly took on a filmic sheen, like a perfect world that was too precious to touch, let alone live inside of. Voices seemed distant and phones had a musical ring, as if they were sound effects in a movie.

Audrey had returned to Yasmin's desk and was trying to console her. But Yasmin felt as if her mind had time-travelled into the future, and the decision to let her go had already been made. She knew her next stuff-up was only moments away. It felt impossible that she would last the day. She was on notice.

Panic started to pull at Yasmin's thoughts, and she fancied that her phone was ringing, and Felicia was on the other end, telling her to pack her things.

That's when Buckley and another large security guard burst into the office and quickly fanned out. Buckley spoke into a walkie-talkie, which he took from his hip. He pointed his colleague towards Yasmin's desk!

So this was it – Yasmin's final moments at WWC. She sat up straighter, as if that made a lick of difference, to prove that they couldn't take her self-worth. She grabbed her handbag and untacked the photos of her fairy ghost-mothers.

The guards turned at the next intersection of desks.

They headed, as if in slow motion, towards Yasmin.

Yasmin's stomach took a free-dive.

The guards ambled closer still, until they turned again. This time, away from Yasmin, and over to Erica.

They were here for Erica! Yasmin placed her handbag back, averting her eyes as Buckley scanned the rest of the office.

"It's time to go," Buckley said, holding out his hand.

"What?" Erica said, panic in her eyes. She gripped her stylus as if it were the only thing connecting her to the mothership, and she was about to be jettisoned into space.

"You've been let go," Buckley said. "You were sent an email."

"Felicia couldn't even be bothered to pick up the phone?" Erica said, panic raising the pitch of her voice.

"You should have packed up by now," Buckley said.

"I want to speak to Felicia!" Erica spat, like a cornered possum backed into a cage.

"Come on, now. You have to leave," Buckley said, keeping an even tone.

"I give you the best of my reproductive years, and now you're here treating me like a belligerent infant?"

"I'm sure these people have work to get on with."

"Oh, you love this."

"Actually, it's the worst part of the job."

"I work twice as hard as all of these bozos." Erica pointed to the rest of them in a sweeping gesture that finished on Yasmin, who reddened under the accusatory finger.

The other guard took her elbow – which was the last straw for her. She yanked her arm free and hit him.

"Let. Me. Go," she roared.

She grabbed the support beam next to her desk, interlacing both arms around it. Kicked off her heels. Wrapped both feet around the bottom of the beam. She looked like a rabid sloth up a tree.

Buckley moved towards her, placing a hand on her shoulder. But as soon as he did, she let out a scream fit to wake the deceased moguls of the publishing empires the world over.

"Workplace brutality!" she shrieked in an off-key operatic.

Buckley backed up, palms outwards. "Come on now, Erica. It's not dignified."

He moved to peel her hands from the beam, but she had interlocked her fingers, and she was stronger than she looked.

"No, you're right. It's anything but dignified." She stared defiantly.

There was a stand-off of sorts, with neither one backing down. Then Buckley nodded to his colleague, who moved to grab her feet.

"I'm being assaulted!" Erica yelled.

"What is this?" Felicia asked, appearing at her door.

There was a second of silence as every worker watched the drama unfold. Felicia's face was impassive, as if she were witnessing an annoying queue-jumper in line at a cafe, rather than the total emotional meltdown of one of her employees.

"Your muscle-monkeys are assaulting me in my place of work," Erica said, huffily.

"This is no longer your place of work," Felicia said. "You are currently trespassing on corporate property and in direct violation of the terms of your prior employment. You have been asked to leave the building, and you have failed to comply with that instruction."

"So pry me loose!" Erica said, a manic grin spreading across her face.

"I'll do no such thing," Felicia said, eying Erica's locked limbs. "I'll call the police, and you'll explain your criminal behaviour to a judge. And, all of the judges in this city are personal friends of mine."

Erica loosened her grip, the bluster deflating out of her. Buckley moved to one side, gesturing forwards.

"Come on now, you don't want a criminal record," he said kindly.

You could almost call him human.

Erica appeared small and frightened, her anger dissipating from the weight of the situation.

She untwined her arms from the beam and stood sadly at her desk, gazing at the design on her monitor.

Felicia glared at her. Erica picked her heels off the floor, and Buckley gently guided her by her elbow towards the atrium.

They approached the atrium door.

A banging distracted Yasmin.

It came from the other side of the door.

Behind the frosting, she saw the shadowed silhouettes of Deborah and Nicole. They were about to be crashed right into by two large security guards and a barefoot Erica.

Yasmin shimmied towards them and hung onto Buckley's arm as if pleading for sanity.

"Don't take her like this, please. Think of how much time she's put into the company."

In her peripheral vision, she could see Deborah and Nicole straining to hear, their ears against the door.

"She's being frog-marched out of the door, by two huge security guards!"

Deborah and Nicole pressed closer to the other side.

"Two big security guards coming your way!" Yasmin shouted.

The guards looked at her quizzically. Felicia watched with a face of thunder. Even Erica stopped struggling.

Buckley shook his head and smacked the door open right into Deborah and Nicole's faces.

Yasmin heard the crunch of tempered glass rebounding, followed by a slightly wet sound, like a giant fish slapping against a concrete floor.

Buckley caught the door on its ricochet back. The other guard reached to help Erica, who had fallen to the floor.

Nicole, in her shadowy invisible state, held her forehead. Deborah held a bloody nose. Yasmin watched the drips on the carpet follow Deborah as she wandered into the office.

Buckley also noticed the blood dripping – seemingly from nowhere, and in a beeline towards Yasmin's desk. He frowned.

"Police brutality!" Yasmin yelled, pushing the guards and Erica into the atrium, and shutting them outside.

Yasmin whipped her handkerchief from her pocket and held it against Deborah's invisible nose. Blood bloomed onto the handkerchief. Her co-workers seemed alarmed. She clenched the handkerchief as the blood dripped from her hand, from where she actually held Deborah's nose.

All attention turned to Felicia, but she merely nodded at a girl standing next to the water cooler.

"See if the new girl requires assistance," Felicia said. "You know where the incident book is."

The girl had flighty eyes and a tiny tattoo of a hummingbird curling up the back of her neck.

"Are you okay?" she asked.

"Oh yes, just a small cut," Yasmin said. "I should keep it above head height, you know, to stem the flow…"

"I'm the first-aid officer. Maybe I should take a look?" She seemed a little off-colour herself. It didn't seem that she had a calling as a first-aid officer.

"I'm okay," Yasmin said. "I just feel so bad for Erica."

"I know, right?" the girl said, dropping her voice. "She just bought that flat in Coogee. She's going to default now for sure."

"Oh, yes. That's what I meant too," Yasmin said.

The girl frowned. "You've been here, what, five minutes, and you knew that Erica had a flat in Coogee?"

"Oh, well. People are quick to warm to me, I guess," Yasmin said. She decided to chance it and held out her hand. "I'm Yasmin."

"Louise. You're the new editorial assistant."

Yasmin nodded, and Louise whistled sympathetically.

"Well, at least you'll have a few days here, hey? Better than nothing."

Yasmin still held Deborah's bleeding nose with her hand, to hide the true source of the trickling blood. They awkwardly waddled back to her desk. The rest of the office had slipped back to their work, too scared to under-perform for even a second.

"Are you sure you're okay?" Louise asked, flinching as blood ran over Yasmin's forearm.

"Could you point me to the first-aid kit?"

"I'll take you there. I have to fill out an incident report, in any case."

Louise led Yasmin to the kitchen and began unpacking bandages and disinfectant from a moulded plastic first-aid kit that hung on the wall. She sat Yasmin in a chair. Yasmin still had her hand held to Deborah's nose; it didn't seem like it would stop bleeding anytime soon.

"You might feel a little sting," Louise said as if she were talking herself into her first surgery, donning a pair of latex gloves. She turned, glimpsed the blood oozing from the handkerchief and turned back to fetch a bandage.

"It's fine, I'll do it myself," Yasmin said, grabbing the cotton balls. She handed a roll of paper towels to Deborah, who broke off a square. Louise frowned at the sound of the edges ripping free.

"What was that?" she asked in a panicked way. "Was that the sound of your skin…Oh my."

"It's okay. It's well known that cuts to the hand bleed more than anywhere else…" Yasmin said as Louise watched more blood dripping onto the floor on the other side of the table.

Blood miraculously dropping from about head height.

Oozing red rivulets from a floating, scrunched hand towel.

"Not good with blood?" Yasmin asked gently.

"No. I…it's all a bit stressful…never thought I'd have to… have to…"

Deborah dropped the roll of hand towel to the floor. Louise watched it magically land on fresh blood on the tiles. The sheets unravelled as the roll came to a stop at Louise's feet.

"I'm fine now," Yasmin said. "I was in the army reserve, you know, so I've done first aid. I think I've got it."

"Right." Louise stared at the bloodied paper towel. "You seem to be fine now."

"Yes, it's all very traumatic. Things sometimes look a bit wobbly, don't they?" Yasmin asked even more gently.

Louise peeled off her latex gloves, and dropped them on the floor, missing the bin. She couldn't take her eyes off the bloodied paper towel.

"I've seen post-traumatic stress before. In my unit," Yasmin said. "Happens all the time."

"I'll write up the incident report later," Louise said. "You seem fine now."

She backed out of the kitchen and hurried down the hall.

Deborah thwacked the roll of paper towel on the kitchen bench and swung up to sit on the countertop. She stemmed the flow of blood from her nose. The skin around it had swollen, already turning the colour of a smudged lead pencil. The bone bent slightly downwards, and her eyes were bloodshot.

How could Yasmin take an imaginary friend to the emergency department? How could the doctors treat someone without being made aware of their non-human state?

Deborah had to make do with the paper towelling, which quickly became drenched with blood. Deborah threw the sopping towels in the bin. Yasmin would probably be fired for creating a biohazard in the office kitchen. As if Felicia needed any more excuses.

"So that hurt," Deborah said, finally staunching the blood. She fished behind her ear for a joint, but thankfully she was out of ammunition for the day. Yasmin mopped the floor, cleaning the trail that wound around her.

"We found our way back," said Nicole, appearing at the doorway.

"And my nose found the flat of a door." Deborah sounded as if she had the mother of all colds.

"I'm sorry I said you were my biggest problem," Yasmin said, hugging Deborah.

"It's okay. I like being an anarchist, but only an arsehole would do that to you on purpose. I'm sorry." Deborah embraced Yasmin in a motherly way.

Tasha walked into the kitchen, glancing from the bin over-flowing with bloody paper towelling, to Yasmin hugging thin air.

"I'll get the cleaners to pop in?" Tasha said.

"Sure, thanks Tasha." Yasmin stood soberly. "I'm sorry to hear about your medical emergency."

"We're not that close," Tasha said. "I'm sorry you were hurt. That was nasty. Are you okay?"

"Yeah, just a cut. It bleeds worse than it is."

"You've got pints to spare then."

"They made me tough."

Tasha smiled, and it wasn't even forced.

"I'm sorry if I've been hard on you," she said. "There's no point in bickering. We've only got one crack at saving *The Standard*, and we need all the help we can get."

She couldn't quite look Yasmin in the eye, but it was the best apology she could muster.

"It's okay, Tasha," Yasmin said. "What can I do?"

15

*T*hat night, Yasmin blundered through a dinner of homemade pizzas, while her mother made small talk about some patient who'd camped out in the Ward B hallway thinking he was Mahatma Gandhi.

"That's mildly interesting," Yasmin said. "But I've never met the guy, and I have more pressing worries on my mind."

"Now that you're working, I want you out," Susan said, snatching up the plates and glad-wrapping the remaining uneaten slices of pizza. Yasmin knew she'd hurt her mother's feelings by the look of her tense shoulders. They practically touched her ears.

"I haven't even seen my first pay packet!" Yasmin sulked.

Catina's eyes were bright, savouring the drama.

"Young lady, you will respect me in my own home. I pay the mortgage and buy the food and keep you in clothes and electricity and internet. Hell, I even buy your shampoo. You're a twenty-four-year-old woman, and you finally have a job, so you'd better start searching the real-estate ads. I want you to move out by the end of the month."

Susan dropped a globule of fig and walnut ice-cream into her bowl, and retired to the living room to watch *The Bachelor*.

Catina hadn't been this happy since she'd received a standing ovation at the school play.

Yasmin pushed her chair back belligerently.

"Hey, wash up, loser," Catina said.

Yasmin ignored her and strode to her bedroom. She wanted to be alone with her friends.

"I'm so sorry about today. You especially, Deborah," Yasmin said.

Deborah sported a bright-pink band-aid over the cut on the bridge of her nose, and wads of tissue stuffed into each nostril.

"Don't worry about it, sister," Deborah said stuffily. "I can be a pain in the rear end."

"We've got bigger things to worry about," Audrey said. "The editorial meeting is the day after tomorrow."

Yasmin paced from the wardrobe to the bed.

"We have to figure out a way to save the magazine," Yasmin said. "Mum's one sullen outburst away from kicking me out of the house, and my career can't be over this soon. It's all I've ever wanted to do."

"Surely they wouldn't let you go, dear?" Audrey, ever the optimist, insisted.

"Were you in the same editorial meeting as me?"

"But your transcription of that meeting was flawless..."

"That's not her problem," Deborah butted in. "The whole company is about to implode. It's like they're running into a burning house and trying to save the dog."

"Instead of moving to a less fire-prone suburb," Nicole said.

"Exactly," said Deborah.

"I hope someone saved the dog," Audrey said, alarmed.

"But what do I know?" Yasmin asked, flopping on the bed.

Audrey pulled up the desk chair to sit on, Deborah sprawled on the floor, and Nicole paced the room.

"We need to consider this objectively," Nicole said. "Figure out what's worked in the past. Apply quantitative research to our data pools. I could use the climate-modelling program! It would need a few tweaks, of course..."

"We're not solving climate change," Yasmin said.

"What are you good at? What are your strengths?"

"She came top of her class at university," Audrey said.

"Yeah, on my forged transcript," Yasmin countered.

"Well then," Nicole persisted, "so she's good at fibbing? Pulling the long con?"

"That's not something to be proud of," Yasmin said.

"It means you're quick to think on your feet," Audrey said.

"And you have to be smart to make those things up," Nicole said.

"You're good at improvising and finding creative solutions to problems," Deborah said.

"But sooner or later they're going to find out I don't know anything," Yasmin said.

"Oh, just google it, honey," Nicole said. "Isn't that what all the kids do these days? Nobody knows anything anymore. It's quite sad."

"Fake it till you make it!" said Deborah. "I saw that on a billboard today."

"I am good at researching," Yasmin conceded.

They perked right up.

"Great!" Nicole said. "That's a fantastic start."

"And nobody knows the past issues of *The Standard* like you do." Audrey indicated to the ceiling, where all sorts of women, strong and unrelenting, gazed back.

"I guess not."

"So, let's start brainstorming!" Nicole handed Yasmin some butcher's paper and a black Sharpie.

An hour later, Yasmin and her besties lay exhausted on the floor of her bedroom, amongst a litter of highlighters and coloured Post-it notes. They had scribbled their ideas on paper, which they laid out on the desk.

Audrey stepped forward.

"My idea is a Friday-night drinking competition, which was the single biggest factor in winning the confidence of the French Resistance. You'll make friends in the office, and therefore form strategic alliances with those strong of spirit – or talented at imbibing them – as well as uncovering potential secrets to use to our advantage."

Nicole pushed past, holding an A4 piece of paper covered with active verbs.

"I've circled the words you most identify with," she said, before adding notes and figures furiously into a spreadsheet. "I've assigned a value to each of your responses."

"I hate to think of the analysis you'll spit out," Yasmin said.

"I say we roll the whole sheet of Nicole's analysis into a mega doobie and smoke our troubles away." Deborah grabbed Nicole's notes.

"Come on, help me out here," Yasmin said. "For real help, with some real suggestions."

"I don't know, hon," Audrey said. "I've been through some pretty tough times in my life. It doesn't seem that bad when you think about it. I mean, the whole world isn't under threat of anni-hilation by the Nazis, and your brothers and father aren't about to die at war."

"No, my father left me," Yasmin replied. She regretted it immediately.

"I was on my way to solving the biggest global threat humans faced in the twenty-first century," Nicole said. "It could have saved the entire world. So I'm not about to quit on you now."

"You guys have it so good," Deborah said. "No need for angry marches in the street. It's not like people are going to arrest you for what you believe in."

"In theory," Yasmin said.

"Well, you haven't been in and out of jail so you are free to have that opinion."

"I'm sorry, I don't know what to say," Yasmin said, depleted.

They sat for a moment in quiet contemplation. Audrey picked at the ends of one of her medals. Deborah twirled her rose-coloured glasses and Nicole persevered with her spreadsheet calculations.

"We'll really cease to exist if *The Standard* folds," Audrey said quietly.

"Do you think so?" Yasmin asked.

"What's your most favourite thing in the world?" Audrey asked.

"Receiving each new copy of *The Standard* in the mail."

"And when was the last time you read a back issue?"

"Preparing for my interview with Felicia."

"And before that?"

"Well I don't have to, because I know them all off by heart."

"So, not as exciting as reading a fresh issue, right?"

"Right." Yasmin frowned.

"So I'd be willing to bet, without a fresh batch of *Standards* arriving each month, suddenly our issues of magazines past won't seem so thrilling."

"I guess."

"Would it be fair to say that you might not read another *Standard* after it folds?"

"Maybe every now and again, for old times' sake."

"So all this –" Audrey indicated the pictures "– will be gone. We will stop being relevant to you. Ghosts feed off human energy, and if you're no longer directing energy to your magazines, we won't be able to survive."

"Our spirits inhabit your beloved *Standards*, so if you're not obsessing over them, what use are we?" Deborah said, a little unkindly.

"I can't lose you guys as well," Yasmin said. The thought hit her like a five iron to the gut, and her hand rested on her magical penny.

"We need to stay relevant," Deborah said, lying on the bed, throwing a tennis ball against the ceiling.

"And we need to appeal to the new generation of readers," Nicole said, pressing a button on Yasmin's laptop; the scrolling data appeared quickly and then disappeared, like fast-forwarded movie credits. She gave a disappointed 'ooh' at the final result.

"Look here," she said, pointing to a figure with an enormous set of decimals. "See, it's not so bad."

"Is the score out of ten?" Yasmin asked.

"Well, sure. Let's say that," Nicole replied, shutting the laptop.

Deborah continued to throw the tennis ball, and Yasmin found it annoying, it was arcing up and hitting the pictures taped to the ceiling. Deborah caught the ball, then threw it again. It was mesmerising, though. It allowed Yasmin time for her mind to wallow, thinking about how she was beaten. No – *knowing* she was beaten. That this was a stupid dream to have, that she should never have scored that interview, never discovered what could have been, what *she* could have been.

Deborah's ball hit the ceiling again with a dull *thud* and dislodged one of the pictures of Audrey. The photo peeled off the ceiling and floated down, landing softly on the quilt. Deborah stopped throwing the ball.

In the picture, Audrey held a shovel and wore practical pants, her blouse tied at the front. One leg rested on the lip of the trench she had dug. She smiled into the sun, and, around her, several Resistance soldiers hauled dirt out of the ditch.

"That's it!" Yasmin said. "We have to make you relevant, and we have to bring you to a whole new generation of readers!"

"That's what we just said," Deborah said.

"You're quite literally right," Yasmin replied, grinning. "I know how to save *The Standard*."

Deborah put the ball back on the desk. Audrey and Nicole pulled in closer.

"I'm going to have one of you featured in the 85th anniversary edition!" Yasmin said.

They seemed confused. Not quite the reaction Yasmin had anticipated.

"Think about it. Who do I know better than anyone in the real world? The three of you. You're all exceptional women from your time. You all helped shape what *The Standard* – and Australia – stands for. You've become a part of our modern consciousness without us even remembering!"

She appealed to her friends. But they still didn't get it.

"Okay, we'll start with Audrey. Where would we be if Hitler

had won? Where would we have been without women who fought right there, on the front line, to help the Allies to victory?"

Audrey smiled winningly, flicking her curls.

"And you, Deborah. You fought on the frontline too – for women's rights, for women to be able to participate in society just as men did. You spearheaded the feminist revolution in the seventies, started the women's marches of the era, demonstrated and were arrested for what you believed in."

Deborah, uncharacteristically, said nothing, just brought her hand up in a peace sign.

"And Nicole – you've won the Nobel Peace Prize! Your research could literally save the world. It doesn't get bigger than that."

"Technically the IPCC was awarded the Nobel Peace Prize, not me personally. It wasn't an individual effort..." But Nicole grinned. She took a step forward, her court shoes squeaking ever so slightly.

Deborah cleared her throat.

"Yes, but you have to choose now," she said, quietly.

"What do you mean?" Yasmin asked.

"There's only ever one person in *The Standard*'s feature article," Nicole said.

Her three friends either studied the floor or the black night out Yasmin's window.

"Which means," Deborah finally explained, "that you have to figure out which one you're going to pick. Which one of us are you going to feature in the anniversary edition?"

16

*Y*asmin could see her blunder, and she had that feeling in her stomach, a slight pulling sensation that told her she'd done something wrong. That feeling was becoming more prominent lately. Here were her three best friends in the world, and she was about to pit them against each other to see who was worthy of featuring in the anniversary edition. The one who would epitomise the best qualities of a woman – Yasmin couldn't choose between them. It was like asking a mother which of her triplets to send out for adoption.

"It's the only way," Yasmin said. "It's too perfect – and something only I can pull off."

"You'll have to hide it from your co-workers, especially Tasha," Deborah said. Her hair fell loose below her headband and seemed feathery in the downlights.

"You don't want Felicia stealing your idea," Audrey said.

"You're right," Yasmin said, delicately. "I will have to choose one of you, so I guess I'll hold a mock interview, see which one of you tells the best story."

"Hmph," said Deborah. "We all know who that will be."

"Do we?" Audrey said, her eyebrows arched. She shot Deborah a combative glare.

"The test isn't based on our achievements?" Nicole asked, touching her glasses, leaving a slight smudge on the lens. She wiped it clean with the hem of her lab coat.

"It's not a test," Yasmin said. "And I'm not sure what I'm after just yet. I'll know when the words present themselves."

"Who first?" Deborah pushed herself up off the bed.

"Nicole, Deborah, if you're sneaky you'll find some leftovers in the fridge. It's going to be a long night, so eat up. Just leave some for us."

Yasmin winked at Audrey.

Audrey sat in the desk chair. She smoothed her knee-length skirt and brushed lint off her brown uniform jacket. She checked the mirror as she pinned on her medals, perfectly aligning them with the top of her breast pocket. The metal clanked solidly, speaking of something more important than Yasmin had achieved in as many years on Earth.

Yasmin perched at the foot of the bed, notepad in hand. At the top of the notebook, she'd written: 'Audrey's Argument for Inclusion.'

Audrey noticed the heading, and Yasmin hastily rested her hand over the words.

"I don't mean…" Yasmin said, crossing out the words and tearing the page from her notebook. She scrunched it up and threw it over her shoulder.

"So," Yasmin began, "I know you were in England and France and all that and had a horrible time of things, and that you were a war hero who helped defeat the Nazis."

"That doesn't sound like a question," Audrey said.

"I want to know why you went to the war in the first place. You were needed at home, your mother was ill, and your father and brothers had already been deployed for the frontline. You had a household to run and a mother and siblings to care for. Plus,

Europe was the most dangerous place in the world. What made you go?"

Audrey peered at her hands resting in her lap. She interlocked her fingers and then let them slip apart again. Her medals clinked.

"I don't know. It was reckless, looking back. The world was turning evil with every passing goose-step. But I didn't leave Sydney to go to war."

"Oh?"

"I left on that steamer for London, for the adventure of it, and because I knew I wasn't supposed to. I was a 'young unmarried,' as they used to call us – un-chaperoned, free to do whatever I wanted on that ship. It was a gas."

Yasmin thought about that. How many young people had gone off seeking adventure overseas in Audrey's time – before transatlantic flights, Google maps and Airbnb?

Audrey shifted her head to one side.

"But it was a sort of selfishness, I suppose, that drove me out of Sydney."

"But you were anything but selfish. You put your life on the line."

"I fell into that, as part of the adventure-seeking. I didn't wake up one morning with the intention of single-handedly stopping the Germans. I ran away from a mundane life of servitude to my family. I shirked responsibility. And my family suffered for it."

"What did they think when they found out you were with the French Resistance?"

"Oh, they didn't know. I could never have told them – that would have put our entire unit in danger. I wired a few vague messages that alluded to nursing units. They filled in the rest."

Audrey had a far-away set to her eyes, as if the memory stood out clearly in front of her, right in the bedroom. "They only found out when I was awarded these blasted medals. Gave them quite a shock."

She fingered the medals: five round, two góld stars, a gold cross and a white cross. They were as impressive as any Yasmin had seen on Anzac Day.

"Do you regret not telling them?" Yasmin asked.

"I don't regret that. It was impossible for my family to understand, and gosh, I'd have shamed Mother by keeping company with all those unattached men! It was scandalous. No, the only regret I have – the biggest disappointment of my life – is leaving my beau in France, instead of staying on, seeing where things would have gone. I don't even know if he survived the war. Mother insisted I return – the war had ended – what excuse did I have to stay?

"I remember the last day we had together. He arrived late to lunch at the restaurant, and I drank one too many champagne flutes while I waited, and we fought. A real row. The waiter asked us to leave, and I remember the stark grey sky and the rain pelting on our coats in the cobbled street. We were soaked through in a few minutes, our skin steaming against the cold rain. We ran out of harsh words, and he just stared at me, this intense look of utter sadness on his face. And he kissed me."

Audrey put her hands to her mouth and closed her eyes. She sat very still.

"I've never been kissed like that since," she said.

"You were married, weren't you? After the war?" Yasmin probed.

"Yes, my husband, Bill. Oh, I had affection for him, of course I did. I wouldn't settle for an unhappy marriage. But that passion in France – well, I guess it was young love. Maybe we only get one of those each lifetime."

Audrey let her breath in slowly, filling her up, and then out again. And there was real weight in that breath. The weight of lost love.

Deborah chewed on a carrot stick as she sat on Yasmin's bed. The sound irritated her. Deborah noticed and put the carrot on the table. She sat at the desk, hands fidgeting, feet tapping to some unheard music.

"So, Deborah. What drove you to fight for women's rights?"

Deborah's eyes flashed as she settled into her chair.

"At the time, it seemed like the most important cause in the world. I couldn't understand why other women weren't interested. All my friends were women – why wouldn't we fight for our rights? But most didn't want to rock the conservative boats they all sailed in. The seventies were a time of prosperity. They saw that they had it better, economically, than their parents had."

"And did you?"

"We sure did, sister. At that stage, each generation outdid the last. It seemed like the natural order of things, like it would continue that way forever. Most of my friends were happy to have decent-paying jobs; I was the only one prepared to have a criminal record to fight for what I believed in."

"Which was equal pay for equal work?"

"That was meant to be the beginning. I didn't think we'd get quite so stuck at that stage."

"I guess that inaugural march was the culmination of a lot of organisation behind the scenes. Was it your greatest achievement for the cause?"

Deborah shifted in her seat, and Yasmin allowed her time to settle. Deborah's eyes went to the floor.

"No, the march was badly organised – we had hardly any megaphones, except the ones the teachers had borrowed from their schools. The banners were simple. We didn't have a unified message. The rabble was sporadic, and some of them didn't know exactly why we were marching."

"But the marches have continued every year, since then." Yasmin scribbled some notes, frowning. "You started something huge."

"Yes, marches are great for sending a sense of outrage, a sense of purpose through the group. But then it doesn't translate into real change. People take it too far, get arrested; hate groups target the marches, and they get a bad name. But it did highlight the changes we had to make, and after a few years, parliament listened."

"What made you decide to devote your life to the cause?" Yasmin said, glancing up from her notes.

"Honestly? I didn't know it was a life-long dedication. I thought it would be over in a few years, tops. But even now, women are still fighting to be safe from violence and to participate in life just as a man does."

"Was it worth it?"

"I guess so." Deborah thought for a moment. "But I also sacrificed so much. I never married, never had kids of my own. When I was younger, I never thought I wanted kids. But as you get older – I guess biological forces kick in."

"I don't understand. You fought for women to have more options than just having kids and raising a family."

Deborah nodded almost thoughtfully as she searched for the words.

"Being a woman means having the ability to create life. I was never about one or the other – career or family – because that denies us choice. Not every woman wants kids, but most do. A woman shouldn't have to feel like she's choosing between two opposing aspects of her life."

"People have always surrounded you," Yasmin said. "So many people believed in the cause that you created. They loved you for it. That wasn't enough?"

Yasmin sat back in her chair, surprised. If that many people loved her, she would surely be the happiest person on earth. So many friends! Deborah had mobilised thousands and inspired a whole generation.

"Most of those people were anonymous," Deborah said, her hands fidgeting. "They didn't know me, not really. They didn't connect with me, you know? I remember sitting in a squat in Redfern after that first march. And there were women everywhere – wearing jeans and tie-dye, smoking pot, putting garlands of flowers on each other's heads, chanting slogan after slogan. The whole house hummed with hatred, with bile. There was no love for each other there, only hate for their oppressors, for men. I started a division – one camp of women thought we went too far, and our camp thought we didn't go far enough. The word 'feminist' became a dirty word to most. And, rather than feeling close to these women, to my kindred spirits here on Earth, I felt disconnected.

"The squat crawled with women that night, coming and going, and joining or leaving that swell of sound. It was the swell of hate. And I felt, more than at any other time, that I was adrift, you know? That my cause had become bigger than me and outgrown my childish notions of what we could achieve. And I didn't feel like a single woman understood."

Deborah's eyes went to the floor, and she suddenly seemed vulnerable. Yasmin had never seen this side of her friend before. She let Deborah continue.

"I needed intimate relationships with people who knew me well, who didn't want to rub against my sheen, to be hangers-on, to worship me. I'm human, and I always yearned for that closeness with someone – I just never met the right partner at the right time."

Deborah trailed off, a sadness descending.

"Everyone eventually went home to their husbands, boyfriends, girlfriends, children, parents. Part of them forgot why they marched at all, and they resumed their normal life, back to cooking the meals and cleaning the house and staying silent at the dinner table. Things didn't change right away.

"I remember, at the end of that first march, that my biggest disappointment was not having a family of my own to go home to. My home was a squat in Redfern that had just been trampled through and left ratty, just like my relationships. And I'd never felt so alone."

Nicole settled into Yasmin's desk chair and adjusted her lab coat. She pushed her glasses up her nose.

"I've heard some incredible stories so far," Yasmin began, "but

I'm sure yours will take the cake. You've achieved so much and been recognised with one of the highest honours – the Nobel Prize. How did you feel when you stepped out on that stage?"

Nicole took a heavy breath, rent with deep frustration.

"Well, technically I'm not a recipient of the Nobel Prize. To set the record straight – I'm just a lead author of several of the papers that made up the IPCC."

"I'd call that a technicality…"

"It's embarrassing to say otherwise."

"The IPCC – that's the Intergovernmental Panel on Climate Change?"

"Yes."

"Okay," Yasmin said, "but how did it feel?"

"I felt weighed down. I heard everyone clapping, and all I could think was, 'They might be dead in twenty years if I can't stop this thing.'"

"This 'thing' being climate change?"

"Absolutely."

"Well, if anyone can beat it, you can," Yasmin said, grinning. She saw a pleading in Nicole's eyes. Yasmin hadn't thought this interview would go the way it had.

"At this rate, nobody's going to stop it," Nicole said.

Yasmin edged her shoulders back, imbibing a sense of positivity that neither of them felt. She scratched some illegible notes on her notepad. When she glanced up again, Nicole stared out the window at the branches of the jacaranda tree bobbing in the wind. Its purple bell-shaped flowers peppered the green. She was restoring her faith in the world by turning to nature.

"So what do you think was the turning point, when you twigged that science was your calling?"

"I had a choice of specialisations at university. I had a particular love of microbiology, studying life at a cellular level. It was simple, contained. It was a saturated field but held the promise of me staying in Australia with friends and family. Then a colleague convinced me to consider working in the emerging field of climate science; it was on the fringe back then, and I figured out pretty quickly that I had a real chance in that field because it was new – there was less competition. I could become an expert with way fewer years under my belt. And, back then, I guess ambition won. The move was purely strategic, not altruistic."

"But, would you have chosen differently if you had your time again?"

"I don't know. I could have led a quiet life, been less in the media spotlight. I felt intense pressure, like it was all up to me. That I was the one who had to save the world. It was a curse, in every way imaginable. I felt like if I failed – if the work failed – then I would be letting down a whole generation – heck, a whole species. If I couldn't communicate the science clearly enough, if I couldn't get enough people to listen? Well, I'd doomed humanity. It was a huge burden."

Yasmin sat back, stunned.

"I had no idea you felt that way," she said, reaching to take Nicole's hand. "I'm sorry, I just knew about the glitz and ceremony. I didn't think—"

"Thankfully there's enough distraction to keep me from imploding each day." She grimaced. "I try not to think about what it would mean if we failed."

"I'm totally going to start recycling my plastic bags," Yasmin said.

"It's the least you can do." Nicole grinned back.

Yasmin imagined Nicole accepting an award on a stage that few women had graced before, knowing that her life's work was probably not nearly enough. Yasmin realised she would never work as hard as Nicole at anything in life.

Yasmin observed her friend with renewed respect. She wasn't just some stiff in a lab coat. She cared – to the detriment of her happiness.

"I guess trying to convince a world blind to the ticking bomb has its downsides," Yasmin said.

"It does make for some broken-record conversations," she replied.

"So what would you have done differently, if you had your time over?" Yasmin asked again.

"I would have studied microbiology at Sydney University."

Yasmin took her time in asking: "And what would that have meant for you?"

"I could have led a small, quiet life. I could have been mildly successful in the scientific community and anonymous to the rest of the world. I could have saved my face from the TV cameras and the newspapers, and the bile of Allan Jones on Talkback. The climate sceptics wouldn't have mailed death threats to my home. I would have written books that nobody apart from die-hard scientists would read. I might have presented a few papers internationally, but I'd stay mostly at home, with friends and family. And none of them would be jealous of my exposure or think that meant I had it all together when, inside, I was struggling to keep my head above water. I was a rock for everyone else. Literally everyone. I felt like I didn't have anyone. I needed someone else to be a rock for me."

Yasmin thanked her ghost-mothers, who were much quieter than usual, their bluster dispersed. Yasmin was good at interviewing people: without meaning to, her besties had revealed their greatest regrets in life, and Yasmin realised for the first time that they were human, just like everyone else. That just because they had achieved things in life, it didn't mean they were exempt from the human condition, or feelings or fears. That they wouldn't have liked their lives to have been different. Even an archetype of a woman, confined within the pages of a women's magazine, had struggles and burdens and a life nobody ever imagined.

And now Yasmin felt the weight of responsibility on her shoulders. How would she choose between her ghost-mothers? How could she claim one more worthy than the other? And would they still speak to her after her decision?

She stepped out of the bedroom, leaving her besties within.

She paced along the landing, running her hand over the railing. She moved past the portraits of Catina and herself as kids, when they were chubby and innocent-eyed.

With her face set, her feet ceased pacing. She stepped back into her bedroom.

17

*Y*asmin and her friends were up early the next morning, grumbling from a lack of sleep, heading to work on a mostly empty bus. Yasmin was eager to arrive at the office at the same time as Tasha.

The threesome seemed subdued, not nearly as excited to accompany her to work today. Deborah openly sent death-stares Audrey's way whenever their lines of sight crossed. Audrey seemed to slip into a state of reflection, hardly noticing her surroundings and almost getting off at the wrong stop. Nicole, positively jumpy, started at each honking horn and every squeeze of the brake.

Yasmin hadn't felt much like talking either, in case she gave anything away.

Her besties turned invisible at the revolving doors to WWC, and they made it through the security gates and up to their floor without incident. Yasmin felt a little lighter than last night, as if she were coming to the end of the flu: her chest wasn't quite as constricted.

"One way or another," she whispered as the lift came to rest on the fourth floor, "this will be settled tomorrow. I'll put you all out of your misery."

They pushed through into the office.

Tasha, already installed at her desk, was strangely frozen, editing, mid-sentence. Her finger pointed to a line on her computer screen, as if she'd fallen asleep halfway through, but with her eyes open.

It was the first time that Yasmin had seen her in this state; she usually ploughed through each article, subbing it ready for publication. She seemed to have a defeated air to her shoulders and didn't hear Yasmin approach.

"Morning," she said, and Tasha jumped in her seat. "Sorry, didn't mean to startle you. Are you okay?"

"Of course," Tasha said, but it was clear she wasn't.

"You know," Yasmin said, as her besties settled in grumpily around the desk, "I'm very good at giving other people advice. Pretty bad at taking my own advice, but I've heard that other people find it useful."

Tasha seemed reluctant to share. Yasmin rounded on her side of the desk, offering her sympathetic presence. Was she going to have to cheer everyone up today? Tasha let Yasmin stand there for a minute or so.

"I don't know what to do," Tasha finally said.

"About what?"

"About Felicia. I don't know how to stop her from firing me."

"What do you mean?"

"I don't have any ideas. We've tried everything already. It's now a rapid, inevitable slide into recycling bins and rubbish tips. Everything we've worked for—" She broke off, seeming to snap out of it. "I guess all we can do is keep our dignity."

"I wouldn't polish your resume just yet," Yasmin said, patting her on her shoulder.

Tasha turned, suspicious.

"Why is that? You're too happy. Yesterday you were miserable." She stood up. "What do you know?"

"Nothing," Yasmin said vaguely.

Louise pushed through into the office, and Yasmin waved. Just a small twitch of the hand, enough for Louise to dip the merest incline of her head. Had Yasmin made a work friend?

Felicia emailed asking for her extra-hot almond-milk latte, so Yasmin popped down to the cafe and returned, depositing the takeaway cup on her desk. Felicia hardly looked up, much less said 'thank you,' and Yasmin didn't linger. She headed straight over to Louise's desk.

"Hi, um, Louise?" Yasmin said.

Louise seemed surprised but approachable. "What's up?"

"I wondered, do we have an archive section?"

"Sure do. Second floor, behind circ." She lifted an eyebrow. "Why do you need the archive section?"

"I just wanted to check a few things."

Louise sat back, contemplating Yasmin, who gave a cheery wave. She picked up a notepad and pen and discreetly ushered her besties to the lift well.

Level two appeared pretty much the same as *The Standard*'s level, with an atrium at the lifts and frosted glass doors leading inwards. Yasmin swiped her card and ushered them all through.

The interior, however, was decidedly less glamorous than the floor they'd come from. It was configured in a telemarketing set-up, with each desk occupied by a worker wearing a headset. There was the chatter of a pre-prepared script, which each worker read from their computer screen. The gist of it was: would they like to subscribe to the next six months and receive the 85th anniversary edition before it hit the newsagent's stands? Yasmin hoped a few customers replied with a resounding 'yes.' From the telemarketers' demeanour, however, they were trying to push a pile of rocks up Mount Kosciuszko. Each time they were hung up on, they dialled again, making the next call, and the next.

Every desk was stripped bare of personalisation; every worker a temp, and every one of them wretched. You had to respect their unfailing hope in the face of adversity.

One dim corridor led off towards the bathrooms, then continued, hugging the inside of the building. A couple of overhead lights had blown, and another flickered. This was not on the tour – nobody came this way. Felicia wouldn't frequent this hallway without putting in a complaint to maintenance.

Yasmin knew she was in the right place.

"I don't like it down here," Audrey said. "Reminds me of our bomb shelter."

"Or the way to the men's loo at Rusty's," Deborah said, crinkling her nose.

"There's an air of the tunnels underneath campus," Nicole said. "We were stuck down there once when they evacuated the library."

A small sticky-taped sign pointed towards the archives room. Yasmin found a tiny opening in the low light, flanked by a stout old post box, its red paint crumbling onto the carpet. She ran her fingers across the letter hole of the post box, and some of the stiff paint stuck to her fingertips.

"Why are we here again?" Deborah asked.

"I can't very well use your obituaries," Yasmin said. "I'm gathering other supporting documentation."

Yasmin and her friends entered the room, which was at the front of a much larger, cavernous warehouse-like space. Inside, the gloom deepened. At the front desk, a forty-something-year-old lady sat hunched, her face lit by the computer screen in front of her. She was deep in her work and didn't notice them approach.

"Uh, hello?" Yasmin said quietly so as not to startle the lady.

"Yes? Are you lost?" Her voice was gravelly and her breath reeked of nicotine, even from a good couple of metres away. She was like a nocturnal creature, evolved to thrive in low light. She blinked and stood up behind her desk, and Yasmin tried not to breathe in the wafts of her breath.

"If you're looking for circ, they're back the way you came," she said.

"No, I'm looking for you," Yasmin said with a smile.

She waited while this sank in.

"Well, you've found me!" Suddenly, the woman morphed into the most jovial human Yasmin had encountered at Warner Williams Corporation. "What do you need?"

Back at her desk, Yasmin upended the cardboard box, spilling the loot and historical intrigue across the white surface. Her besties helped her sort through it all, picking out useful records.

She'd found a stack of memorabilia from the three ladies' eras and began sorting them into piles. She picked out film negatives, sheaths of brittle magazine pages, various memos, internal documents and newspaper clippings.

"See the way the light hits my medals here," Audrey said, indicating a particularly flattering film negative.

"Yes, that's a good one," Yasmin conceded.

"Look here," Deborah said, pointing to a magazine cover, "there's a halo around my hair as if some higher consciousness has touched my shoulders."

"That's my favourite of you…" Yasmin said.

"The night I accepted the Nobel Prize." Nicole picked up another picture, in which she stood on a large stage, while the room applauded in a standing ovation.

"I would have been so proud," Yasmin said.

Tasha popped her head over her partition, clearly annoyed.

"When you've stopped talking to yourself," she said, "I have some actual work to finish." She spied the artefacts spread out across the desk. She frowned. "What are you doing?" she asked.

"I'm checking out other applicants for your job," Yasmin said. She noticed Tasha's despondency and took pity. "I'm just getting some inspiration."

"Well, do it silently, please?" Tasha was back to irritation mode.

Were they no longer friends?

Back in her bedroom, Yasmin's mind raced with ideas, facts and figures as she scrawled notes. Deborah perched on the desk, trying to catch a glimpse. Yasmin pulled her hand over the notebook.

"Oh, come on. It's been all day. When are you going to tell us?" Deborah whined.

"Yes, dear," Audrey said. "Fair's fair. You never shoot a soldier in the back."

"I can't take much more of this," Nicole said.

The three of them jostled closer to Yasmin, and soon they were pushing and bickering, and the din was as loud as a crowded party in a can, and getting shriller by the second.

"Stop!" Yasmin leapt to her feet, scooping up her notebook. "I've made my decision. I'll tell you right now, but you have to calm down."

"You have?" Deborah said, letting go of Nicole's lab-coat collar.

"Yes," Yasmin said.

"Well, don't leave us hanging," Nicole said, straightening her glasses, which had slipped in the altercation.

Yasmin opened her notebook and took a calming breath.

"I've got a handle on which of you to feature in the anniversary edition. It's been a difficult choice, but I know I've made the right one."

"We will respect your decision, Yasmin," Nicole said.

"Suck up." Deborah punched Nicole's arm.

"Ow!"

"Shush, the both of you," Audrey said.

"And, tomorrow," Yasmin continued, "I'll present my ideas to Felicia, and my decision will be final."

Yasmin closed the notebook, her face beaming. "Ladies, take a seat."

18

A new day at the office.

Yasmin had emailed Felicia earlier that day, asking for five minutes of her time. She'd replied curtly, "Get me a salad and a bottle of kombucha."

Yasmin's ghost-mothers were in their most excellent invisible disguise mode. Nicole rubbed Yasmin's shoulders, Deborah hummed the old sit-in favourite, 'From Little Things, Big Things Grow,' and Audrey fussed, touching up Yasmin's eyeliner. Yasmin noticed Louise frowning at the magically levitating eyeliner pen, and slapped it onto the desk.

Louise squinted, putting her glasses back on. Yasmin waved, and Louise turned back to her computer.

Tasha had her headphones in, and everyone else languished in freak-out mode. Not one person paid any mind to Yasmin or her invisible crew.

"So do you feel one-hundred-per-cent prepared?" Nicole whispered.

"No." Alarm tinged Yasmin's reply. "I'm not one hundred per cent about anything, especially where my job is concerned."

"Don't freak her out," Deborah said. "Just chill."

"Make sure it's a clean extraction, you know," Audrey offered, "in case guts start to fly."

"You're not helping right now."

Yasmin took a steadying breath, plucked a few photos from the archive box, and headed to Felicia's office.

She hooked a brown paper bag over her arm. It had fancy twisted-board handles and contained a salad from the most exclusive, gluten-free, raw salad bar she could find. In one hand, she held the photos and nervously rolled the bottle of kombucha in the other. Her besties hovered.

"We'll wait outside," Nicole said, "to give you some privacy."

Yasmin took a deep breath and exhaled like she had done that one time she tried meditation. She couldn't further delay the moment. It was time to be brave.

She knocked gingerly on Felicia's door with the cap of the kombucha bottle.

Too quietly.

Felicia hadn't heard.

Yasmin rapped again, louder this time, trying to imbue the confidence she didn't feel.

"Yes, yes," Felicia said. "*Entrez.*"

And there Yasmin stood in Felicia's office for what could be the last time. Yasmin closed the door behind her, leaving her besties on the other side, jostling for eavesdropping positions.

In here, with no means of escape, Felicia's perfume overpowered, as did her manner. Yasmin smelt the musty kale in Felicia's salad and the hint of lemon in the recently shampooed plush carpet.

Yasmin squinted as a shaft of sunlight glinted off Felicia's lifetime-achievement award.

"Yes?" Felicia barked, still bent down, marking proofs. She added an aggressive strike through a section of copy.

"I...ah...brought your lunch," Yasmin said, handing over the salad and the kombucha. Felicia didn't look up from her mocks. Yasmin couldn't see the copy for the red pen.

"Yes, yes," she said, indicating the desk.

Yasmin plonked Felicia's lunch next to the in-tray. Felicia moved her attention to the salad.

"I...have..." Yasmin began, her voice sounding tiny.

"What is it?" Felicia asked, poking the salad with the wooden fork.

"Kale with grilled chicken, ancient grains and raw vegetables," Yasmin said.

"I don't mean the salad. What do you want?"

Yasmin faltered. This was not going well. She glanced nervously at the framed photos on the wall, of Felicia and the sharp-pointed moustachioed man. Why were there so many of those photos?

"I have an idea. For the 85th anniversary edition," Yasmin blurted out.

"Oh goody." Felicia marked a particularly forceful line through an entire page.

"I was thinking, there are these three women, from previous eras. They've all been in *The Standard*, and I thought we could run a little, romp-through-history-type feature."

"How much protein did they stuff into my salad?" Felicia asked. "Who do they think I am, a bodybuilder?"

"I...ah...have dug up some research. On the women."

"What women?"

"Well, there's Audrey Elizabeth Stewart. She was thirty in the year 1950, the year she was featured in *The Standard*. She joined the French Resistance in northern France during the Second World War to help deliver an airdrop of supplies, including guns and ammunition. She tried, unsuccessfully, to head up the Resistance movement, and instead became their chief infiltrator and saboteur. She made it onto the Gestapo's most-wanted list."

"So she's good at war, at a time when that would not have been acceptable for a woman. Tell me why our readers should care?"

Yasmin placed one of the archive photos of Audrey onto Felicia's desk.

"She eventually helped the French Resistance defeat the Nazis and win the Second World War. She received several medals, our most decorated female war veteran. Most of her medals had never before been awarded to a woman. Then or since."

Felicia reluctantly leaned over, straightening the picture of Audrey shaking hands with the Prime Minister, receiving her medal for bravery.

"Nice hat," Felicia said.

"I feel you're entirely missing the point," Yasmin said, but Felicia wasn't listening.

Yasmin felt a pain start in her solar plexus but pressed on, placing Deborah's picture on the desk.

"Then there's...there's...Deborah Reece. The unwitting face of the women's movement in 1970. She organised the largest women's march in Australia. She wrote the book on feminism shortly afterwards and became Australia's pre-eminent expert. She campaigned for equal pay. And it looks like we owe her now."

Felicia leaned in close.

"Do you see any men in my office?"

"I don't remember seeing any on this floor, exactly..."

"So how do you know I'm paying them as much as you?"

"That's not the point..."

Felicia stabbed a kale leaf.

"How can they have the nerve to charge twenty dollars for a slab of chicken and a head of kale?"

"There's also Nicole Cook, who won the Nobel Peace Prize for her ground-breaking work on climate-change modelling."

Yasmin smoothed out Nicole's picture on Felicia's desk. Felicia grew preoccupied with a smear on the side of her coffee cup.

"Her work was instrumental in forming our understanding of climate change today."

Felicia frowned and leaned closer to the stain, rubbing it with her finger.

Yasmin persevered. "She could very well help save the earth from total annihilation."

"Some people say it's not man-made, you know, this climate change stuff," Felicia said.

"I'm sorry," Yasmin said, in a tone that indicated she was anything but. "Am I boring you?"

Felicia acknowledged Yasmin for the first time, who felt bright-red humiliation creep up her neck. She shook slightly.

"Boring me, no," Felicia said, surprised. It was clear that nobody had spoken to her this way before. It didn't bode well.

"I'm sorry, Ms Pine," Yasmin said, eyes downcast, "but I think that we need to make *The Standard* relevant again, to the younger generation."

"I agree." Felicia pushed her glasses up on her nose. "But I fail to see how reeling out these geriatrics is going to appeal to a younger audience."

Yasmin gently pushed forward the photo of Deborah at the front of a raging crowd, arm extended, fist bunched, with everyone screaming behind her. Pure, fierce energy.

"Deborah started the revolution, and it is currently winding backwards. If we don't remember the fight we've had to get where we are, we risk losing everything to the patriarchy. That goes for all kinds of social justice, not just the women's movement. Maybe it feels to the younger people as if we're heading back into the dark ages, as if everything we've gained is about to be lost."

Yasmin tapped the photo of Audrey, crouched behind a wall, rifle in hand.

"This is a reminder of the darkest days in humanity's living history. It reminds us that complacency against evil means surrendering to war. To the younger generation, it feels like we're slipping along the road towards global nuclear war, and I don't know about you, but I don't want to see that. We won't survive."

Yasmin pushed the picture of Nicole forward. Felicia leaned in. Yasmin spoke with more confidence now.

"And this one, Nicole, reminds us that we have to work together if humans are to survive at all. We're facing the largest challenge the world has ever had. Humans are the cause of climate change. She reminds us to consider science and facts, rather than fake news and personal opinion, to stop us from destroying ourselves. Climate change is something the younger generations get and are extremely concerned about."

Yasmin paused, but Felicia merely regarded the photos.

"Hmm," she said eventually.

"We have to remember our past to see our way through the future. War, the break-down of social fabrics – hell, even climate change. You'll be dead when we're left to figure out the answers to the mess you've left us. We have real problems to solve."

Yasmin moved back from the desk, trying to quell the red rash that had moved from her neck to flush her cheeks.

"*The Standard* needs rebirthing, a resurrection of the ideals and values we used to have. A rebooting of *The Standard*'s relevance to our young readers of today. And these are the women to do it."

Felicia studied Yasmin. Shook her head. Started to poke her salad again. Put her fork down.

"So you think other people are as passionate about these issues as you are?"

Yasmin sniffed. Stood up straight.

"I think they're the most important issues that people should be passionate about. We've got real problems to solve, and we feel powerless. Give us back our power. Give us hope."

Felicia observed Yasmin, the corners of her mouth lifting slightly. She covered the almost-smile by inserting her straw in the kombucha. She sipped daintily.

"And which of these women are we featuring in the anniversary edition of *The Woman's Standard?*"

"All of them."

Felicia considered this. "But we only ever write about one person in the feature article."

"That's not negotiable," Yasmin said. Felicia raised an eyebrow and pushed the salad away. The meeting had taken a dark turn.

"So how did you come to choose these women in particular?" she asked.

"They spoke to me," Yasmin said without thinking.

"We do not use clichés in this office."

"No, I mean they stepped out of the page and spoke actual words to me."

There was a pause.

Darn, Yasmin thought. I almost had her.

Felicia couldn't just unhear this conversation. Yasmin had revealed too much. Her mind raced ahead and contemplated how long it would take before security pried her from her desk.

"I've already said you're on notice?" Felicia asked.

"Yes," Yasmin squeaked.

"Good," Felicia said, a dark flash to her eyes.

Wait – what? That meant that Felicia didn't need to give any more warnings before she fired Yasmin.

Felicia indicated the door. Yasmin grabbed the photos of the three women and stumbled from the office, all bravado leaving her faster than a jet lifting from the tarmac.

19

*Y*asmin's lip trembled as she fumbled her way to her desk chair, feeling consumed by humiliation and embarrassment. She tried reasoning with herself: she was paranoid, the whole floor hadn't just downed tools to watch her cross the room.

She lay her forehead on the desk.

Darn, darn, darn!

She turned her head to the side and opened her eyes. Yep – they were all staring at her.

Double darn!

Yasmin felt the pressure of Tasha's palm on her elbow. Yasmin burrowed her forehead into the desk, willing it to bury her in the plywood. Her face felt inflated, as if she was a pufferfish.

"What the heck did you just do?" Tasha asked gently.

"I think I'm fired," Yasmin squeaked.

"Tell me everything. I'm usually a good judge of this kind of thing."

Yasmin lifted her head. Tasha handed her a tissue.

"You didn't predict Erica's demise." Yasmin wiped her sweaty, blotched brow.

"Oh, please. I called it before you even started working here."

Yasmin covered her head in her hands. She needed time to

recover. She needed to get out of the office. She fanned herself, feeling fresh sweat drip over her temple.

"I've got to get out of here," she squawked, standing up. Then she noticed every person at every desk turned her way, staring at her meltdown. And beside her, invisibly, Audrey, Deborah and Nicole, open-mouthed, in a state of shock.

What Yasmin wouldn't have given for the privacy of her bedroom. Her friends drew in closer, as close as they dared while respecting Tasha's personal space.

Then Tasha did something unexpected. She placed her arm around Yasmin's shoulder. And when Yasmin unwound from her folded, prone position, Tasha's expression wasn't catty, or vindictive. She seemed genuinely concerned. At least, Yasmin thought that's how her expression read. She was a little too freaked out to know for sure. She started to hyperventilate.

"Deep breaths," Tasha said, rubbing Yasmin's back, just like Nicole usually did. Yasmin calmed a little. She still shook slightly from the adrenalin.

Tasha handed Yasmin another tissue, and she dabbed the sweat on her forehead, temple, and upper lip.

Tasha dropped her voice to such a practised whisper that Yasmin's ghost-mothers had to lean in to hear.

"Tell me everything, and I'll let you know if you're in trouble or not."

"Oh, I know I'm in trouble."

Yasmin gave Tasha the cliffs notes, leaving out the actual pitch. She forced herself not to react to her besties. She didn't sugar-coat it, because, what was the point of sugar-coating anything now? She had lost her job; she had nothing to lose. And when you're that desperate, opening up to a colleague doesn't seem so bad. She could even help Tasha's career; if Tasha heard precisely how Yasmin's downfall occurred she would know the traps to avoid. If nothing else, Yasmin ensured Tasha's survival.

She convinced herself her actions were altruistic. And that made her feel a little better.

When she had finished, she sat back in her chair, untacking the photos from the partition. She felt congested, right at the back of her throat. She took some deep breaths but felt herself losing it. And when she had finally stopped shaking, she felt the deepest sadness overtake her, as if she were falling into a pit with Tasha standing at the mouth, all the way above her.

The loss she felt was complete. She'd blown it. She'd lost her job – the job she'd dreamt about since she was a child, that had brought her fairy ghost-mothers to life. She'd let them down. She felt the loss of her besties the most, and her stomach grew painful, a deep ache.

Yasmin didn't notice her magic coin on its chain, glowing and growing warm.

"Yeah," Tasha said. "You'd better pack up your desk." She stood up, when something caught her eye.

Tasha wore a curious expression, like someone not believing what they're seeing. As if she'd realised the laws of physics didn't entirely apply as she thought they did. Not as she *knew* they did.

Yasmin jolted out of her misery and followed Tasha's line of sight. It landed to the right of her desk, over to where…

Holey moley! Right to where Audrey stood, her hand outlined in sparkly silver. Yasmin watched as she lifted an embroidered handkerchief to one eye. Yasmin held her breath for long enough to feel her heart pause.

Audrey's hand sparkled, the same way it had the first time she'd come to life in Grandma's magazine.

Tasha stared at the exact spot of Audrey's hand. And Yasmin knew, as well as she knew that birds fly and confetti falls to the ground, that Tasha could see Audrey!

Yasmin held the glowing penny with one hand and grabbed Audrey with the other. Yasmin hauled Audrey towards the atrium.

"Just going to grab some air!" Yasmin shouted over her shoulder, gripping Audrey tightly, grasping her silvery sparkling hand to hide the glow. Everyone stared, pointed and made little 'ooh!' noises. Definitely a turn for the worse.

Yasmin and Audrey crashed towards the lifts. The door to the office closed behind them in an exaggeratedly slow way, as if taunting them, every worker craning their necks to catch one last glimpse of the crazy lady and the mysterious floating hand.

"What's wrong, dear?" Audrey asked as they waited for the lift. It was so slow! Why was everything in slow motion today? Yasmin snatched the hankie and wrapped it around Audrey's glowing hand.

"I just blew my nose on that..." Audrey finally noticed the sparkle. "Oh, my."

"'Oh my' is not the freaking start of it!" Yasmin hissed.

The lift *dinged*.

The doors opened onto a mousey man in a pin-stripe suit, his oiled and styled moustache ending in two points. The man from the photos in Felicia's office! He was someone incredibly important in Felicia's life, and now he was witness to Yasmin's meltdown. Her career prospects sank deeper into the metaphorical quagmire.

"Don't tug so hard," Audrey complained as Yasmin pushed her into the lift.

"What was that?" the mousey man said, with surprise and a touch of disdain on his face. He stepped out of the lift.

"Sorry, I don't know my strength," Yasmin said, smiling apologetically and jabbing a finger at the button for the ground floor. The lift doors clicked shut.

"Pretty soon you'll sparkle all over," Yasmin said as they rocketed towards the lobby. "And do you know what happens then?"

"No, what happens then?" Audrey asked.

Yasmin thought about the only scenario that came to mind on the spot. It involved several scientists prodding Audrey with needles and one particularly cruel doctor wielding a surgical saw. Yasmin shook her head, trying to clear the sound of the screech from her mind as the saw descended onto Audrey, who was strapped to a table...

"The men of science," Yasmin said.

They sped through the foyer and out onto the street where

they flagged a cab. Yasmin tried to hide Audrey's arm, which rapidly became sparkly too. They climbed into the back seat. The taxi driver didn't even look at them, already concentrating on the next lane of city traffic, waiting to pull out.

"Where are we going?" Audrey asked.

"You tell me, lady," the taxi driver said, merging into the next lane without checking his blind spot. The neighbouring car honked its horn, swerving back into another lane. The taxi slid on through.

Yasmin told him the address and asked him to take the City Westlink. There would be less traffic that way.

"Well, we're going to die before we get there," Audrey said. Yasmin hushed her, and for the first time, the taxi driver flicked his eyes to the rear-view mirror.

"Your friend want to drive?" he asked.

Audrey sparkled top to bottom now. She was luminescent in sepia-tones, her face and clothes washed out – straight out of a black and white photograph of old.

Yasmin yelped. What would the cabbie make of Audrey?

"Ah, no, she didn't mean anything by it," Yasmin said. "She's...from somewhere else."

"Yeah. Somewhere without manners," the driver said.

"Invisible!" Yasmin whispered, wiping her brow. Between the glowing coin against her chest and the heat emanating from Audrey, it was steamy in the back seat.

"I can't," Audrey said. She closed her eyes again and strained, but she remained visible, shimmering with a silver light over the top of her browns and yellows.

They pulled up outside Yasmin's house. She paid the driver, and he wished them a good day. He hadn't properly seen Audrey or noticed her magical sparkles. Cabbies must get sick of looking at passengers all day. Yasmin imagined they could have been a flotilla of blow-up penguins and he wouldn't have noticed.

Yasmin checked for neighbours, realising that school had finished not long ago. The area was full of mums and dads driving their kids home, pulling into driveways close by. The older school kids were passing in rowdy knots, boisterous and shoving each other.

"Quick, let's go," Yasmin steered Audrey towards the house. "You can't be seen."

Yasmin fumbled with the keys. Audrey turned and waved at a neighbour, who was pulling into their driveway. The neighbour waved, winding down her window.

"Hello there, Yasmin. Who's your friend?" She took in Audrey, outlined in silver waves that undulated around her form. The neighbour wound her window back up and hurried her pre-school-age children into the house.

"Hey, what are you dressed as?" a boy called out as he sauntered past.

"I'm a real woman," Audrey replied, quite happy with herself.

"Freak!" a high-school kid yelled, his shirt untucked.

Audrey seemed lit up like a bonfire on cracker night.

Yasmin opened the front door and they bumped into Catina.

"I'm so sorry…" Audrey said.

"Who is your weird friend?" Catina asked, stepping back. "What's wrong with her face?"

"Catina, this is Audrey." And then she whispered an aside: "Straight from Comic-Con."

"Well, guess you've got to go all out if you're entering cosplay," Catina conceded, a little impressed. "The uniform has that authentic touch. Where'd you get it?"

"Cos-what?" Audrey said, perplexed, as she righted herself.

"We're…ah…going to work on her next outfit."

Yasmin dragged Audrey upstairs into the bedroom and then placed her hands on Audrey's shoulders.

"Stay here," Yasmin said. "Don't leave my room until I get back."

"Back from where?"

"Work."

Yasmin rocketed out into the street, flagging another cab on the next block. She had to rescue Deborah and Nicole.

20

*B*ack in the office, Yasmin couldn't find Deborah or Nicole. She checked the cracks between desks. The pot plant next to Felicia's office. She filled a paper cup from the water dispenser so she could peer at the wall behind to check they weren't hiding there.

Everyone in the office was working hard, their heads lowered. Yasmin had been relegated from the main show. Louise happened to glance across as if Yasmin was some oddity at the zoo caught out in the wrong enclosure – a platypus stranded in the faux savannah with the flamingos.

At least Grandma's penny had stopped glowing and was no longer as hot as a car bonnet in the summer's sun.

"Some magic trick," Louise said.

Yasmin flinched as if someone had just pinched her arm. "What?" she said defensively.

"The magical, floating, sparkling hand. Have you always been interested in cheap parlour tricks?"

"Oh that – yes, I'm auditioning for a new show. It's a cross between *X Factor* and *MasterChef*. We have challenges, and I had to create an optical illusion…"

"I think I saw two more of your illusions on the second floor. They were terrorising circ."

"Really?" It must be Deborah and Nicole. "Ah, how long ago was that?"

Tasha joined them at the water cooler and topped up a paper cup. "Where have you been?" she asked.

"I had to go back home for more lighter fluid," Yasmin said. "It's an all-day show, so I have to prepare…"

Louise seemed unconvinced.

"Did I, or did I not, say to check with me before leaving the office?" Tasha said.

"Sorry, Tasha," said Yasmin.

Tasha arched her eyebrows, dropped her spent paper cup into the waste bin and moved back to her desk.

Yasmin yearned to salvage today, to start again. And if she couldn't do that, she'd do what Erica hadn't – leave with dignity and give the rest of the girls something to hope for.

Yasmin jumped on Seek to browse other jobs. Probably bad form, but she hardly cared now. She'd just opened a particularly depressing job ad, for work as a dishwasher in a pizza joint, when an email popped into her inbox. It was from Felicia, addressed to the whole floor.

Emergency Editorial Meeting. Eleanor Gilbert Room. Ten minutes. Attendance is compulsory.

Felicia wouldn't want Yasmin there. Part of her wanted to rebel, to pop along anyway. To see the faces of her co-workers as Felicia threw her out on her derrière. Part of her wanted to attend the freak show, to be finally outed as a pathological liar who performed random acts of magic in her spare time.

Five minutes later, the exodus to the Eleanor Gilbert Room had begun. Yasmin guessed nobody wanted to be late. Pretty soon she sat alone on the floor, amongst the abandoned workstations, a strange, echoey feel to the space, as if she was the last person left on an earth populated by white desks and screensavers of cats wearing clothes.

She stood up, making sure everyone had left. This was her chance to find Deborah and Nicole.

Felicia's door snapped open and out she strode: an eagle and a lioness rolled into one. She moved with a fluidity, gliding on heels so high that any reasonable person would break an ankle with their first step. Felicia waltzed by Yasmin's desk, stopped, and turned around.

She sized Yasmin up, her head to the side. "I don't tolerate tardiness."

She turned towards the Eleanor Gilbert Room.

Did she mean for Yasmin to come to the meeting? To fire her in the most public of ways, as a warning to the rest of her employees? Of course she did. But saying 'no' to Felicia Pine would be complete career suicide. Even worse than telling Felicia what she really thought.

She followed Felicia into the boardroom. All the chairs were taken, but Yasmin preferred to stay standing anyway. It was like organising a date just for coffee, rather than dinner: she knew she didn't want to sit through two more courses after she'd been given the chop. She'd leave the five dollar note next to her untouched latte and get the hell out of there.

Yasmin slumped against the back wall. She slipped her hand into her pocket, feeling the weight of her phone.

Felicia stood at the head of the room.

"So I've tasked you all with coming up with ideas for the 85th anniversary edition," Felicia opened, glancing at each of her employees. She rested her gaze on Yasmin, who discreetly pushed record on her phone.

Someone coughed. Another shifted slightly in their chair, which creaked like cracking bones. Tasha sat in the seat next to Felicia, her eyes riveted, as a fanatic might worship her priest.

"So far, the response has been disappointing," Felicia continued. "In fact, I don't think there's been a single idea good enough to save us from folding. Except one."

Surprise filtered through the editorial team's expressions.

Tasha's eyes went to the table, the picture of humility. So she'd presented something to Felicia, too.

Felicia's voice lost the dangerous edge. She almost smiled. It was a close thing.

"I had lost all hope until my idea came to light. I thought of it while walking my Pomeranian. You know how inspiration hits, like a bolt of pure energy from the sky, illuminating things that were previously dark. And my idea is just that illumination. It's going to save our magazine, our jobs and the whole damn company."

Stunned workers began to clap. A few turned to each other in surprise. Tasha seemed a little crestfallen, but that could be expected when the boss stole your idea and presented it as their own.

"So what's this idea?" Louise piped up.

Felicia smiled dangerously. Yasmin almost expected a forked tongue to flick out of her mouth. Instead, she snapped a presentation onto the wall behind her. The woman by the door dimmed the lights.

The Powerpoint came to life – it revealed a picture of a woman, in black and white, wearing a smart uniform and an ancient headset, twiddling dials on a wireless receiver. It was a picture of Audrey!

"This saboteur infiltrated Nazi forces and worked in the French Resistance, helping to thwart countless attacks and ultimately helped us win the Second World War. She is the most decorated woman in the entire Australian force. She reminds us of humanity's darkest days, that we can't be complacent in the face of the current threat of nuclear war. We need to keep those in power in check. We need to fight against evil. We need to ensure humanity's survival."

She pressed another button on her laptop; a second picture popped up – a slightly washed-out colour photo of Deborah, at the front of a crowd, her fist in the air, rallying the women's movement.

"This activist started the largest women's rights march in

Australian modern history, fighting for equal pay for equal work. And now that revolution is currently being wound backwards. We have to be vigilant for all social justice, to not rewind the inroads we've made. To let people know they have a voice."

She pressed another button, and a picture of Nicole popped up – on the stage, accepting her medal.

"And this scientist won the Nobel Peace Prize for her contribution to our scientific knowledge of climate change, and how to stop us from obliterating human existence. She reminds us to turn to science – facts and not fake news – to save humanity, something the younger generation gets and is extremely concerned about."

Felicia pressed another button, and the screen showed all three women in the same slide.

"These women will be the three stars for our 'Women Through the Ages of *The Standard*' feature. I want us to reboot their story. I want us to show the younger generations of Australians just what we can achieve, through the experience of people who've been there before, facing somewhat impossible odds. That women persevere and improvise and band together when the going gets tough. That we're not going to give up – either on our world or on this magazine. Because it's do or die for *The Standard*. We need to work together – all of us – to make this issue a success and bring hope and inspiration to our next generation of readers."

She sat back in her seat, watching the reactions of her employees. Tasha seemed surprised. This had blindsided her. It had blindsided Yasmin, too. So, Felicia liked Yasmin's idea?

"Ah, Felicia?" Yasmin said quietly.

"Yasmin," Felicia countered, like a general sizing up a rogue soldier.

"That's my—"

"Are you about to contradict me in any way?" Felicia demanded.

"I...ah –" Yasmin remembered Jane from Gargantuan Consulting's parting words "– think it's a great idea."

"Excellent. Lights, please."

The woman by the door flipped on the lights.

"Now, this is our lead feature, something to spark hope in our youth. I expect you all to carry on with your general assignments, but I want everything in the magazine to tie back to this feature. To have its essence. We have to be bold to survive in the new world that we live in. We have to be exceptional."

"What about Sandra Mobaski's piece?" Tasha asked.

"We'll still run it, but further back in the issue. These three women are our top priority."

Felicia beamed at everyone except Yasmin. Tasha seemed a little shell-shocked.

"Ladies." Felicia snapped her laptop shut, dismissing them.

Yasmin held back outside the door to the meeting room, watching the team disperse. Where did this leave her? Felicia would at least have to ask Yasmin to share her research before she left. Then again...How had she obtained the photos she'd used in her presentation?

Felicia glided out of the meeting, the last to leave, and breezed right past Yasmin, without acknowledging her. The rest of her team had a good head start.

Felicia turned back, almost as an afterthought. "Yasmin, when these women *speak* to you again, do let me know."

And then she whisked away, her scarves floating behind her as she strode the halls, which she commanded with such power and ease.

Did this mean that Yasmin wasn't fired?

21

*Y*asmin sat at her desk, thumbing through the box from the archivist, finding the exact photos that Felicia had used in her presentation. She held each one up to the fluorescent light as if she imagined things. But there they were. How?

Tasha popped her head over the partition. Yasmin could see that, on the shaved part, her scalp seemed to have gone slightly red.

"I ah..." she began. "Sorry to interrupt."

"You're not interrupting." Yasmin fanned the photos out on the desk.

"I wanted to apologise," Tasha said, leaning forward and dropping her voice. "I saw you bring the photos back from your meeting with Felicia. I thought they might mean something to her..."

So the rat had outed itself. Yasmin felt a twitch tease at her eyelid. But then she realised how Tasha might have unwittingly helped strengthen her case.

"You really shouldn't have done that," Yasmin said, pleasantly enough. She didn't want to overdo it. "I guess this means you owe me one."

"Of course," Tasha said, relieved. "Name it."

"When I think of something I'll let you know."

Tasha sank back behind the partition. Owing Yasmin would not have been on her agenda when she woke up this morning.

And – just like that – the citrus, basil and ylang-ylang of Felicia Pine's perfume wafted over them.

"Yasmin," she said, heels clipping briskly into her office.

Yasmin followed. What else could she do?

Yasmin shut the door behind her and sat in front of the enormous desk. She tried not to play with a caught thread in her skirt. Her magical penny slipped into view, through the neckline of her dress, and Yasmin tucked it back underneath. It was no longer glowing.

"So we're going with the 'women from magazines past' idea," Felicia said, closing a folder of proofs and signing a front cover sheet. She slid the folder to one side.

"Thank you," Yasmin said.

"Why are you thanking me for my idea?" Felicia said, pointedly. "We're not going to have a problem, are we?"

"Of course not." A shot of fear travelled up Yasmin's spine and out of her tear duct. She blinked, her eyes stinging.

"Good. So share with me everything you have on these women. I'll get Rachael in to brainstorm our angle and write the piece. You can interview the ladies. Tasha will sub it."

"Oh," Yasmin said.

"Are they all still alive?"

"Yes," Yasmin said without thinking. "I mean…"

"Are they alive, or aren't they?" Felicia said impatiently.

It was half a lie. Yasmin's ghost-mothers were more alive than they were supposed to be.

"Yes," Yasmin said. "They're still kicking."

"Good, so I want you to track them down, get them to sign the usual release forms, and set up some interviews."

"Interviews…oh my." How the hell would she pull that off?

"We'd like to showcase them in their own homes, of course. It's what our readers most strongly relate to. Celebrities in their own spaces: a private peek into the lives of those who are otherwise unattainable."

"I...ah...don't think that's going to be possible," Yasmin said. She didn't say 'because each of them lives in my bedroom.'

Felicia frowned. "Well, presumably they all have to live somewhere?"

"They're camera-shy."

"Nonsense. You haven't even asked them yet."

"I'm sure they're too old for that sort of thing anyway..."

"You will take Libby with you. She's our best photographer. Oh, and we'll send the ladies a list of questions to help them prepare. We'll get better answers that way, while still feeling off the cuff."

"But I've never..."

"I'm sure your wealth of interviewing skills at *The Guardian* will help enormously here. Your Graham Inquiry piece was on the money. How you ever made him confess to money laundering – on tape no less – well, I have to admire your genius. Get going – we're on a deadline here."

Back at her desk, Yasmin panicked. She'd lost Deborah and Nicole, and she had to interview all three of her ladies in their own homes. But her ladies were ghosts, hadn't aged a day beyond thirty, and their own homes happened to be Yasmin's bedroom.

Most perplexing, Felicia thought Yasmin was some interview ninja. Interviewing someone in the safety of her bedroom was one thing, but now there were the added stakes of feature copy on the line. She'd fudged her experience, which added up to zero. The potential to stuff this up was higher than an orbital satellite.

What the heck would she do?

Tasha swept around the desk, concern etched on her forehead.

"Did you get fired after all?" she asked.

"No, but I might as well have," Yasmin said.

"Why's that?" Her eyes widened. "Did you insist that the feature was your idea?"

"I didn't," Yasmin said. Tasha was on her side now, right? "I can't even take credit for it."

"Take that as the highest compliment Felicia could ever give you. Try not to wallow in the empty, fathomless depths of zero recognition." Tasha tried to hold back a hiccup.

"You say that like you've been in my shoes before. But I don't know what I'm going to do. I'm going to have to interview these women…"

"That's amazing!" Tasha beamed with genuine happiness. Then it must have sunk in that she wouldn't interview them herself. "Good for you."

"I have no idea what I'm doing," Yasmin said.

"Are you kidding me? Your article! I didn't know that about you when you first started. But it was pure genius."

"That's what they're saying – pure genius." Yasmin laughed but it came out strangled as if she'd swallowed it halfway down. She took some more deep breaths. "So time to pull in that favour."

"What do you need?"

"A crash course on interviewing etiquette. As in, I know how to interview someone…"

"Of course."

"Just, ah, not how *The Standard* does things."

"On it." Tasha disappeared behind the divider, tapping away at her keyboard. "I know how it is – it doesn't matter how experienced you are, there's always quirks between each organisation."

"One last thing, where are the release forms?" Yasmin said casually.

Yasmin found Deborah and Nicole in the hallway, camped out behind a display case of golden awards that *The Standard* had won over the years. The awards were crowded into the case, almost as shimmery as Deborah and Nicole, who had also *appeared* for everyone.

They looked as if they were about to skip a dimension or two on their way to a distant planet. They did not appear altogether human and yet they somehow were. Deborah had retained her seventies' washed-out polaroid colour. Nicole's sheen was over-glossed as if she'd been dipped in lacquer. They didn't fit in. They would generate too many questions that Yasmin didn't have the answers to.

"What should we do?" Nicole asked, peeking from behind the display case. Deborah acted way more chill, strutting down the hallway. She threw her hands out in sharp bursts, sending out luminescent electrical charges in waves from her fingertips.

"Both of you, go home now. You remember the way to the bus stop?"

They did.

Yasmin spied a clothes rail with a box of accessories on the lower tray. She lifted two pairs of over-sized sunglasses and two headscarves. Deborah and Nicole put them on. Now they looked like celebrities who were trying to avoid the paparazzi. Yasmin was banking on the fact that nobody ever really saw another person in the city. Everyone was too engrossed in their own drama.

Yasmin gave them some money and instructions on buying a travel card. She told them to be unobtrusive on their way out of the building.

Back at her desk, and with the help of Tasha, who was pretty cool about it all, Yasmin armed herself with three release forms and the interview style guide. The style guide read twenty pages thick, but Yasmin felt familiar with the types of questions asked and the themes for the stories, as she'd read so many *Standards* in her time. Plus, the three ghosts and Yasmin knew each other intimately. So the actual interviewing could be fine.

What drove a dagger into Yasmin's guts, and then twisted said blade around from side to side, was the thought of the photographer. How would she get three random ladies to pose as her women from 'magazines past?'

Nicole would have been pushing forty-nine and heading towards the peak of her career. Deborah would have been seventy-nine, and probably needed a walking stick to attend marches these days. And Audrey would have been turning ninety-nine this year! Where would she find someone who had lived for almost a century?

Yasmin watched Audrey take a compact from her handbag and dust foundation powder onto her cheeks.

Foundation powder. That triggered something. A thought, the seed of an idea. What was it exactly? Where had she seen face powder recently…?

And then she remembered, and it sparked a plan.

It involved trusting one other person with her career, and therefore her life. She had to let them in on her little secret.

"I'm going out," Yasmin told Tasha.

"You've already taken your lunch break. You were gone a full hour," Tasha said. "I don't know what it was like at *The Guardian*, but nobody takes lunch at *The Standard*…"

"It's an emergency," Yasmin replied, grabbing her cardigan from the back of her chair. "It's about the interview."

Tasha remained impassive. Her threshold for Yasmin's stupidity was wilting.

"I'm calling in that favour," Yasmin said.

"You already called it in…"

"Oh, come on, that was nothing. Something you would have done for any new recruit…"

"Not true. Usually, I don't help new recruits at all."

Yasmin smiled her most disarming smile, picked up the archive box, and rested it on her hip.

"Listen, is it worth losing your job over?" she asked.

"Aren't you going to wait for Libby? She's just grabbing her gear."

"I'll take Libby next time. For now, I need to set a few things up."

"Fine, fine. I can't believe the fate of WWC rests on your oh-so-tall shoulders."

Yasmin tossed over the photos that Felicia had used in her presentation.

"You could help by finding the negatives for these."

Yasmin headed out of the office, into the lifts, and out the foyer, nodding to Buckley on the way. She hoped like hell they weren't monitoring her swipe pass. Tasha was right – that excursion home with Audrey earlier today was a massive break from the office. But, with Tasha covering her back there, could she pull off the biggest con of her life?

22

The driving rain leaked into the bus and dripped down Yasmin's back. The humid summer storm outside was stifling and the driver cranked the air conditioning in an attempt to de-moisten their mobile tin can.

They lurched around a corner, and the passengers held tight as the bus leaned heavily to the side, sending commuters into each other.

Arriving home, Yasmin shook her umbrella in the hall and headed into her bedroom. Thankfully, all of her ghost-mothers had made it back. They stood in front of her, real people except for their odd appearance.

"So what now?" Nicole asked.

"I need time to think," Yasmin replied.

"Precious little of that going around," Deborah said. "I overheard Tasha saying we're going to print in a week."

"Well, we need time to find older actors and scout out homes as suitable locations for the photo shoots. Prep them on their characters, have them memorise their back story. Find something other than cash – which I don't have, as I haven't been paid yet – to bribe them with so they're happy to pretend to be old versions of real people..."

As Yasmin went through the list, every component seemed

impossible. She didn't have the time or funds to start up her little theatre group for the aged.

"And don't forget they can't be too famous in their own right, so people recognise them from a banking commercial..." Nicole said.

"What about the real us?" Audrey asked, quietly. "Surely Felicia could read our obituaries in *The Standard* and know we've passed on?"

"I've removed all of the references of the obituaries from the archives," Yasmin said. "So hopefully she won't twig."

"You're going to be found out," Nicole said.

"No – this will work," Yasmin said.

"Catina must know old people? Actors, I mean?" Deborah said hopefully.

But, when Yasmin asked her sister, Catina most certainly did not know people like that.

"Who in their right mind would pretend to be someone else, another living human, for a magazine spot? They're actors, not rent-a-mums! You can't even pay them," she said. "Plus, I don't know any actors in that age range. All my friends are from drama at school."

Right, so that was Plan A aborted in the space of a few seconds.

"I'm sorry I didn't believe you were real, by the way," Catina said, prodding each of the ghost-mothers in turn. "You guys have got some funky colour palettes, that's for sure."

"If I can't figure this out, I'm screwed," Yasmin said. "Forget working at *The Standard*, forget saving it from folding, and forget —" Yasmin choked up.

"What?" Catina asked.

"My fairy ghost-mothers...If the magazine folds, they will cease to exist. Everything's riding on this."

"You've backed your way into a no-go zone," said Audrey

"It would have been easier if you were normally dead, rather than ghosts..." Yasmin said, and from the hurt in Audrey's eyes, immediately regretted it. "No offence, Audrey, but you're knocking on a hundred."

"Ninety-nine," Audrey corrected.

Catina frowned, trying to concentrate.

"I think I might have something," she said. "Back in a sec."

She left the room.

Yasmin face-planted on the bed. She closed her eyes and breathed into her pillow. Her breath came back hot.

"If it's not a website of unknown geriatric actors, I don't think it will help," she mumbled through the pillow.

Catina returned holding a small glass bottle with a screw-cap lid, like nail polish. She held it up as if they should know the secrets held within.

"What's that?" Deborah finally broke the silence.

"Deborah, how old would you be, really, in 2019?" Catina asked.

"Really, really old?" Deborah said.

"She was thirty in 1970, so that would make her seventy-nine in 2019," Yasmin said.

"Hell," Deborah said, shaking her head. "I'd look older than Bob Dylan."

"What about Audrey?" Catina asked.

"I would have turned ninety-nine this year, like I said," Audrey piped up.

"So, that would make Nicole forty-nine?"

Catina unscrewed the bottle, pulling out the brush attached to the lid. Just like clear nail polish.

"I refuse to conform to society's version of a castrated woman," Deborah said, shying away from the tiny bottle.

"Just...let me do something," Catina said.

She brushed the clear liquid on Deborah's skin at each side of her eyes. She brushed some more in the space between her eyebrows, all across her forehead and at the pinched edges of her mouth.

Deborah recoiled when Catina tried to paint her décolletage.

"You've been intimate enough with my face, leave my cleavage out of it," Deborah snapped.

Yasmin wasn't sure what Catina was up to until the clear liquid began to dry. A curious thing started to happen to the painted parts of Deborah's face. The liquid creased up, forming wrinkles in her skin!

"Oh wow. That could work," Yasmin said, moving closer to Deborah, peering at her face.

"What?" Deborah said, checking herself out in the mirror. "Man, I'm ancient!"

"It's genius," Yasmin said, hugging her sister. They pulled away, a little embarrassed.

"For once I'm grateful my sister is a drama student," Yasmin said.

"Is that a 'thank you?'" Catina grinned.

She tried her magic bottle on the other two, with similar results, and the three of them crowded around the mirror, checking out their new look. They contorted their faces into exaggerated expressions and play-acted at being old ladies. Catina directed their 'performance' and gave them notes on how to make their movements more authentically aged. Of the three women, Audrey took to her new role the most naturally.

"It's the same as going undercover for an operation," she said.

Yasmin started mentally checking off things as her plan began to pad out.

"We'll have to borrow some wigs."

"I can score some from the props department at school. And we will need a few bags of sand to add a tummy and a larger derrière to Nicole."

"Why am I the one who's porked up?" Nicole said, offended.

"Because you've spent your life sitting in front of a computer at the lab," Catina said gently.

"That just leaves the little problem of our homes," Audrey said.

"But we'll just use yours," Deborah bounced on the bed in a sprightly way that belied the age of her face.

"You don't think that Mum would notice something's astray, like, I don't know – a whole photo shoot going on in her living room? She'd take credit for the decor before you could say 'prawn salad.'"

"What about Airbnb?" Catina offered.

"Expensive," Yasmin said.

"Won't you, like, lose your job if you can't pull this off?"

"I most certainly will."

Yasmin thought about it, trying to visualise the last forty dollars in her bank account, mentally calculating three full houses for a full day's stay. Forty dollars wouldn't even cover one night in a single room of any one of the homes she'd need.

"We could use the studio at the office," Audrey said. "That would work out fine."

"Too risky," Yasmin said. "Miss Rochford would see through your disguises. We need you in a different environment so that Libby is less likely to suspect. Actually, Airbnb is the perfect solution. Catina, how soon can you borrow those wigs?"

"I can check them out tomorrow, after class."

"Great, I'll book us a house. We'll have the photo shoot the day after tomorrow." Yasmin picked up the bottle of clear wrinkle-maker. "And we're going to need a substantial amount of this."

Yasmin snuck downstairs and found her mother's purse resting on the kitchen bench, right beside her keys. She was about to pilfer the credit card when her mother ambled into the kitchen, holding a glass of wine. Yasmin whipped her hand out of reach and feigned innocence.

"Oh, there you are," Susan said, kissing Yasmin's cheek.

"Mum, I'll start on the salad," she said, pulling cherry tomatoes from the fridge.

Susan eyed Yasmin suspiciously. "Don't forget to set the table." She wandered into the living room to relax in front of the television.

Yasmin dumped the entire punnet of cherry tomatoes into the spinner and handed it to Catina.

"Here," Yasmin said, giving her a little push to the sink.

"I'm your chef now?" she asked.

Yasmin rested her finger against her lips and headed towards her mother's purse. She checked around the corner – Susan was watching old episodes of *Game of Thrones*. Yasmin waited for the inevitable battle scene and slipped the credit card out of the wallet. Catina watched, shaking her head.

"She's going to cancel her card when she sees the transaction on the bill," she said.

"By then it won't matter."

Yasmin headed upstairs and breezed into the bedroom. Deborah spun 'Foxy Lady' on the record player, Nicole scribbled on a clipboard in the corner and Audrey wrote a diary entry on flower-printed paper.

Yasmin ignored them all and slapped open the laptop. Half an hour later, she'd booked an Airbnb a couple of streets away. She snuck downstairs before *Game of Thrones* finished and slipped the credit card back into her mother's wallet and grabbed the bowl from Catina.

She innocently tossed the salad as her mother trudged in. "Mmmm. Smells about ready," she said, taking the chicken kiev out of the oven. "You took a long time to make the salad."

"You haven't heard about the latest listeria breakout? I washed every lettuce leaf individually."

"There's listeria in the lettuce? Throw it out then."

"It's fine. I was thorough."

"You didn't set the table like I asked."

"Sorry…" Yasmin quickly set the table.

Susan eyed Yasmin.

"Expecting guests, are we?" she asked.

"What? No, of course not," Yasmin said.

She realised she'd set the table for six places.

23

*Y*asmin left her besties at home the next day – they were no good to her, now that they were visible to everyone. She left them listening to Johnny Cash and eating croissants pilfered from the pantry. They seemed happy enough. It wasn't the first time they'd been stuck in her bedroom all day, waiting for her to come home.

She slithered into her chair at work at 7:35 a.m., which earned a greasy from Tasha.

"You're late," she said, with an inflection that could be sarcasm, or it could be the honest, painful truth. It was a close call.

"I've scored the interviews with the original women," Yasmin replied, watching Tasha's face transform into pain again – definitely pain. Yasmin could tell that Tasha wished she could conduct the interviews.

"When?" she asked.

"Tomorrow. I've lined up all three of them. We'll make a day of it, you know. We'll go to Audrey's house to make it less effort on her part. We don't want to tire her to death."

"And when were you planning on sharing your schedule with me?" Felicia said, standing beside Yasmin, having snuck up on her again. This wasn't how she wanted to tell Felicia!

"Ah, sorry, Ms Pine. I just got in. I was going to check my emails and then come and tell you."

"Emails can wait," Felicia said. "My office, please."

Felicia strode to her office, and Yasmin followed. Felicia offered her a seat, and sifted through Yasmin's carefully curated research notes – in which the three ghost-mothers were very much alive, and all references to their deaths had been erased.

Felicia grilled Yasmin on the logistics of the shoot and the questions she planned to ask in the interview. She wasn't happy with Yasmin's response.

"You're probing too far," Felicia said. "It's not an exposé. We're not *The Guardian*. We want to celebrate these women's lives, not denigrate them."

"You're right. It's *The Standard* – we don't do hard journalism here," Yasmin said.

"And what kind of journalism do you think we do?"

"I don't know…fluff pieces?"

Felicia leaned back in her chair, her features hardened. Yasmin persevered.

"I'm sorry, Ms Pine, but *The Standard* publishes stories on women – highly accomplished women at that – in their homes, showing off their domesticity, commenting on their choice of wardrobe and how well they've raised their kids and supported their husbands. It's just not relevant to the younger readers, because that's not what life's like for them."

Felicia's lips thinned. Yasmin felt less sure of herself.

"And what do you propose?" The edge of Felicia's voice sawed through Yasmin's already sapling-thin confidence.

"Show these women in their natural environment, not just in the home. Get them doing things, being something. These are women who changed history! Don't show them taking scones out of the oven."

"What's wrong with scones?" Felicia said. "The smell of fresh-baked scones is one of life's pleasures."

"For both of us, yes," Yasmin said. "But I'm not most twenty-four-year-olds."

"I wish you were. It would make things much easier."

"So, beyond baking, think about what these women accomplished, why they're famous. Have the photos match the energy of those accomplishments. Show our readers what it takes to be a real woman."

What had Yasmin just said? She'd already booked the Airbnb for a total cost of $480 plus GST!

"I still want to start the shoot in the women's houses," Felicia said. "It's what our current reader expects, and we can't afford to turn them off. They're the last thread to save us from insolvency. But if the ladies are up for an excursion, let's get them out of doors, taking us through the places that shaped their youth. Maybe pop in on their childhood homes. Oh, and see if you can get Audrey with that bomb shelter she built. If it still exists. If not – find another backyard that still has a bomb shelter in it. There will be one somewhere in Sydney."

"Thank you, Ms Pine."

"Oh, and I'm doing the interviews," she said, flippantly, sorting through Yasmin's doctored research notes. "I feel like getting back into the ring. You've already laid the groundwork, so we have a solid base to work from. I'll run the shoot."

"Oh," Yasmin said.

So they had to pull off the charade in front of Felicia too?

Back home, Yasmin was freaking out. Getting it right in front of Libby was one thing but in front of Felicia Pine? Nothing got past her, not even microscopic enzymes. This gig just got a whole lot shakier.

Catina had done a fantastic job on Yasmin's ghost-mothers' makeup, although the wrinkle smears glistened in certain lights. Catina had to put so much on Audrey that her face looked like a glossy, sunken football. Yasmin cracked up the first time she saw her. But then Catina dusted some foundation over the top, hiding the shininess.

"Right, done," Catina said, helping Audrey into her wig.

Yasmin turned. A forty-nine-year-old, a seventy-nine-year-old and a centenarian-minus-one stared back.

Audrey wore a long skirt and a long-sleeved blouse with a cardigan and neat pearls over the top. Her short-haired wig was composed of wispy, curled white hair. She wore a pair of black orthopaedic shoes.

Deborah had kept her original hair, but Catina put through streaks of grey at the roots, reminiscent of regrowth. Her locks flowed down her back over a bright-green top. She wore a low-slung necklace that ended in an upbeat flower pendant.

Nicole had her hair up in a bun. She wore a sleeved crew-neck t-shirt over the top of her loose-fit jeans, canvas boat shoes and a floppy summer hat. Catina had placed just the right amount of padding around her bum and thighs.

"Brilliant!" Yasmin said. Audrey scratched underneath her wig, which lifted a little off-centre. "Don't do that, Audrey. Pretend like it's real hair."

"It itches," she said.

"Places everyone!" Catina said.

The fairy ghost-mothers lined up. Nicole waddled, giving measure to the sandbags of faux fat on her bum and thighs. Deborah remembered to slow her gait but remained agile enough. And Audrey limped, slightly unsteadily. Catina handed Audrey a walking cane, which she leaned on for effect.

They waited for Yasmin's response.

"We've found our stars," she said.

She thanked Catina profusely for her time and effort.

"Now," Yasmin said after they were all seated, and Audrey had removed her wig, "we need to make the following things – some buttons and placards for a women's rights protest march, historically correct for the year 1970. Nicole, we need to source a graduation gown and cap, and your Nobel Prize. And for Audrey – we need your medals and a backyard with a bomb shelter in it."

Catina nodded at each of them, except the last request.

"That's going to be tricky," she said.

"Or not," Audrey said, stepping forward and resting her wig on the bed. "I might know of a place."

"Good," Yasmin said, and she couldn't have been prouder.

They spent the rest of the evening making placards and buttons and taking staged photos of Nicole in her graduation gown and mortarboard. Audrey polished her medals.

The next day, Yasmin went to work as usual. She snuck the archivist's box downstairs and handed it off to Catina, who waited on the street outside.

Yasmin waited for instructions back on the fourth floor at WWC. Felicia sat inside her office with the door closed.

At nine a.m., Felicia crooked her finger at Yasmin, and they rode the lift down to her limo in the basement car park. Libby joined them there.

Felicia, Libby and Yasmin sat in the back seat, going over the logistics of the day, as the driver sliced them through the city traffic and out into the suburbs.

Yasmin was relegated to Felicia's assistant – in a clear demarcation of power – and Felicia consulted with Libby over the shot list she needed. Libby knew where the power lay, and she agreed with everything Felicia said, remarking on the brilliance of each suggestion.

They arrived at the Airbnb house – single-storey, federation-style, with a rose garden out the front and a long driveway leading down the side. Just like the photos on the website. The painted fence was somewhat faded, and the gutters were long overdue a clean, so it had a lived-in look. Yasmin couldn't have scouted a better location.

"Go on ahead and announce us, will you," Felicia said, standing on the curb, shading her eyes from the sun.

"Of course," Yasmin said.

She headed up the path and rang the doorbell, sneaking a peek back at Felicia, who yabbered to Libby in her superior way. Everything was going to plan, until Audrey answered the door. She picked at her wig nervously.

"Will you go inside?" Yasmin hissed at her, nice and low so

Felicia and Libby couldn't hear. "You're supposed to be an invalid."

"Sorry," Audrey said, giving a little wave to Felicia. Felicia waved back, all botoxed smiles.

"Where's Catina?" Yasmin asked.

"She's in the kitchen, making coffee…"

Yasmin thrust the framed photos at Audrey.

"Give her these to dress the set with."

Audrey hurried away.

"You're meant to be ninety-nine years old, so show the weight of those years!" Yasmin reminded her in a stage-whisper. "And where's your cane?"

Yasmin shut the door and headed back to Felicia.

"Her nurse will be here shortly," Yasmin said.

"I must say, she's more sprightly than I had imagined," Felicia said.

"Oh yes, she's quite active in the mornings, but by lunchtime, well, her joints freeze."

"I'd better head inside to set up." Libby hoisted a tripod and a large camera bag onto her shoulder and let herself in.

"Well?" Felicia said. "Announce me, will you?"

24

*F*elicia stood in the heat, her enormous sunglasses hiding her aggravated demeanour.

"You said we would have them in their own homes. This is one home."

"Well, it's less tiring for them all this way. Honestly, we don't want Audrey to travel. So everyone's coming to her."

"She wouldn't have to travel. *We* travel to the other houses."

"This could be like a reunion special. As if the three women were meeting for the first time at a dinner party."

"Our readers need to see their personal spaces. Kitchens and living rooms and so forth."

Yasmin smiled back angelically. "Nicole's house is being demolished, she's putting up a kit home. And Deborah's house is being sprayed. For rats."

Felicia's lips set hard against each other.

"Let's start with Nicole!" Yasmin said breezily, guiding Felicia through the front door.

They set up Nicole in the study, the mid-morning sun slanting onto the large desk in front of a floor-to-ceiling bookcase. Libby approved of the quality of light and set up her kit.

On the bookshelf, they'd placed the staged graduation photo, its faded colours accentuating Nicole's far-away look. Her expression implied that Nicole contemplated a future of academic prowess. In reality, it had been taken at two a.m., and she was dog tired. Next to the photo, they'd framed the newspaper clipping showing Nicole shaking hands as she accepted her Nobel Prize.

It was perfect.

"So I'm going to record our interview, but just ignore the camera and the phone – we're just two people talking," Felicia said, setting her phone in the middle of the desk. Felicia sat on one side of the desk, with Nicole on the other.

"Yes, I've done my fair share of press, it's okay," Nicole said, scraping her chair painfully on the hardwood floor.

But she hadn't done her fair share of press at her current age of thirty. And she was nervous as hell. Libby snapped a shot and Nicole flinched.

Felicia noticed, but merely said, "Ah, Libby, will you take a seat for a moment?"

Libby sat on an Ottoman in the corner of the room, resting the SLR on her legs. Nicole adjusted her chair again, seemingly uncomfortable like she couldn't quite get the distance between her torso and desk right.

Catina, wearing her mother's blue nurse's uniform, carried a tray set with a porcelain teapot, sugar bowl, milk jug and dainty teacups with saucers.

"Tea, Doctor? Ms Pine?"

Nicole shook her head, and Felicia helped herself to a sugarless, black tea in a china teacup painted with pink roses. She set the cup and saucer on the desk, the steam distending softly in the natural sunlight.

"So, Doctor Cook. You're our preeminent climate-change scientist in Australia. I imagine that climate science was not as well received when you first began your career?"

Nicole relaxed a little, taking a deep breath.

"No, it was more fringe then. It hadn't been verified by the global scientific community in the way it has today."

"What drew you to such a fledgling area of science?"

"I guess I had a gut feeling that the science was right, that human intervention had massively interrupted the natural order. It certainly warranted more investigation. I was hoping to be proved wrong – we all were – and I was certainly hoping that the more alarmist of those in our community were wrong. It turns out, not one of us went far enough."

"And, going back further, what drew you to study science?"

Nicole told them, and they saw so clearly the year seven girl with the long braids, sitting in class, absorbing everything her high-school science teacher said.

Nicole lit a Bunsen burner, smelling the strike of the match and the pungent escaped gas, watching the heat of the blue flame lick the bottom of the wire gauze, which supported a bubbling beaker of chemicals.

Her teacher lit a small strip of magnesium. She watched it combust in a bright white flame – and then it disappeared. It was thrilling – like watching the flash of the creation of the universe. That was the moment Nicole knew she wanted to be a scientist. She wanted to understand the questions of the universe. Science would help her answer them.

Nicole studied hard for her biology class, and even harder for chemistry. Her bedroom was adorned with sticky notes covered in formulas, pasted behind her bedroom door, above her desk, on her mirrored wardrobe.

She ran to the mailbox, pulling out a large cream envelope with her final year results. She celebrated with her family, holding her results above her head, relieved tears streaming over her face.

She packed her Daihatsu Charade with boxes and her suitcase. From deep in suburbia, she waved to her parents and boyfriend, watching them in the rear-vision mirror as she drove away down the leafy streets. She saw the streets recede behind her – the houses turning into vacant blocks, turning into farmland as she left Sydney behind.

She entered the small country town of Bathurst, parking her car and striding along the college halls with her bags. The bare brick walls of her tiny room hemmed her in as she set her bags down and felt that she had never been so happy.

She led a study group in the library and tutored younger students through their exams – while she aced her own. Her parents visited for her graduation, taking cheesy photos as she threw her mortarboard in the air.

She drank cheap wine with her flatmates, hosting house parties in the backyard, setting the fire pit alive with flames in the winter. She worked for hours at the modelling computers in the lab, running figure after figure, making calculations.

She taught a lecture theatre full of students, marked papers, and worked towards her doctorate.

She addressed a large conference, the spotlight picking her out on the podium. She grew frustrated at the impassive faces in the audience – they didn't realise the impending danger. Nicole felt impotent to effect real change.

Night after night, Nicole was the last to leave the lab, her glasses reflecting the computer screen as she ran the numbers. She was shocked at the results she saw. She triple-checked them. Her colleagues' sombre faces reflected the gravity of her research as she presented her findings.

She advocated for change and was interviewed by the media, who failed to report the seriousness of her findings. She was called a hippie and the worst slur of all – a greenie.

Nobody cared – at least that's how it felt. There was talk of action, but no policy. She was just another leftie do-gooder trying to erode the Australian way of life.

She bumped against the prickly power of politicians and business-men, people with vested interests in discrediting her. She was appalled at the bile of the climate denialists – some of them scientists too – and the blatant inaction by their government.

She worked with various teams and was put forward to contribute to the IPCC paper. She was asked to be a lead author. She boarded a plane, to a city thick with traffic and shouts in Italian. She was the youngest scientist there, working tirelessly in committees and round tables, docu-menting and fact-checking. So carefully constructed were those reports.

And then, the defining point of her career. She stepped out on stage, with her colleagues, to a standing ovation, to accept the medal for the Nobel Peace Prize. She celebrated with her co-authors. They felt like they really could change the world.

. . .

Felicia sat back, impressed. Nicole had done so well. Libby snapped a few discreet photos as Felicia wound up the interview.

"So what would you say is the single biggest accomplishment in your life?"

"Most people would expect me to say the Nobel Prize," Nicole said, a distant tinge to her expression. "But really, my biggest accomplishment was moving to Bathurst. I became an adult, standing on my own two feet, living away from home and supporting myself through my studies. I deliberately chose a place out of Sydney. And it was where I decided to devote myself to climate science. I found out who I was there."

Felicia probed again. "And who are you?"

"I'm just like anyone else," she said. "I want to save humanity from itself, but unlike most people, I have a tangible way to do so. I wish people would listen."

Felicia eased back in her chair and scribbled a few things on her notepad.

"Thank you, dear," Felicia said, holding out her hand. Nicole stood up and shook it.

Yasmin watched Nicole's sandbags of 'flesh' move from her bum to her hip. She slipped in beside the chair to shield Nicole's misshapen bulge.

"What are you doing?" Felicia asked.

"The hornpipe. It's just something we do," Yasmin said, grabbing Nicole close and jigging on the spot. With her spare hand, she straightened Nicole's sandbags, which now safely sat by her butt cheeks, where they belonged.

"I apologise for my assistant," Felicia said – was she blushing beneath her foundation? Yasmin had managed to embarrass the one and only Felicia Pine.

"Oh, we're like old friends." Nicole laughed, slapping her sandbags.

25

*F*elicia made her way to the covered veranda next.

Deborah sat on the step to the backyard, puffing away on a joint. She stubbed the roach out on the brick steps to the house, just as Felicia joined them.

"Ah, Miss Reece." Felicia held out her hand, and Deborah shook it.

"Call me Deborah," she said, exhaling a lungful of smoke that blew back into Felicia's face.

"It's a pleasure to meet the instigator of modern women's liberation," Felicia said, frowning as she fanned the smoke.

"Am I not what you were expecting?" Deborah asked, with just a hint of defiance. Felicia blinked but otherwise kept her face impassive.

"Oh dear, Deborah, take a seat inside..." Yasmin said, deflecting Deborah's animosity. "And Ms Pine, make yourself comfortable."

They moved into the dining room and sat at the long table made from a single slab of knotted pine.

Felicia noticed the walls strung with women's rights propaganda posters. A bunch of the slogan buttons rested on the dining-room table.

"We've dressed the set, so it looks like Deborah's house," Yasmin said.

Felicia nodded her approval.

When they settled, Felicia began. The shutter of Libby's camera clicked as she worked.

"So, Deborah, what sparked your fascination with women's rights?"

Deborah began.

She edged along the halls of her high school on that first day of year seven as the sound of students' feet echoed on the linoleum. Lockers lined one wall, their dull metal doors slamming as students rushed to their next class. Deborah made way for the older students who seemed as grown as adults.

Deborah sat at the front of classes that year, too afraid to speak up. But she joined music class and began singing lessons. She had a fair voice – it wasn't Grammy-ready, but she sang in the chorus of the end-of-year musical. Her singing lessons opened her diaphragm and gave her permission to bellow her scales.

Deborah had found her voice, and the next year she stood at the front of a ragged group, facing off with the older year nines on the oval at the back of the school, fighting for their turf. She stacked rings on each finger and slammed her fist into Damon's face. Blood bloomed on his cheek. He hit the grass, muddying his white school shirt. The year nines gave Deborah her turf back.

When she reached year nine herself, she sat behind the sheds at recess, her back to the painted brick wall, smoking cigarettes stolen from her mother's purse.

She marked The Hill as her undisputed territory. She scrawled her gang's manifesto on a torn sheet, making photocopies in the library. She handed them out – full secrecy on pain of death. Even back then, people followed her. She stood as the leader of her ragged group and led them in and out of scrapes.

She sat outside the Deputy Principal's office, holding a tissue to the cut above her eye. Half-listening to the Deputy berating her for brawling like a brat. He told her how she'd never make a good wife, how she would destroy her future, how she would be lousy at bringing up kids. But above all, the Deputy point-blank said she should have let the boy win.

Deborah didn't think that was fair. He was weaker and amoral, and a tattle-tale – the worst trait of all. Why should he have won the fight, just because he was a boy?

Deborah lounged in the library, marking obscenities in the margins of a book of Fairy Tales. She hid the book in her bag and snuck past the librarians to show her friends.

She learned to smoke pot on her first day of university, egged on by long-haired youths in flares and tie-dye shirts. She waved socialist banners and painted the walls of the Women's Room in rainbow colours – a room that she had fought for.

She found free love in the arms of one man, and then another, finding them to be insipid, rather than antagonistic. And she knew that this was the time, the only time there might ever be, to raise a revolution.

Deborah organised a sit-in, and they held hands in a circle of peaceful protesters.

Deborah watched black and white images from America, following the marches and resistance that cropped up. Their anger fuelled her own.

She addressed a large gathering in the quadrangle. The female staff stopped to listen. She handed out flyers and burnt candles at peaceful protests, ignoring the jeers of passing men, shoving and cat-calling. The women were unmovable in peaceful defiance.

Deborah watched her male colleague at the office empty out his yellow pay envelope and was shocked at the scattered notes and coins on the table. She looked at her much thinner yellow envelope as he spun his coins and downed his beer.

She formed the Women's Action Group with a bunch of friends. She rallied on campus. The unarmed, shoeless students faced off a line of police, resolute in riot gear.

She told her fellow students about the pay gap they would face once they graduated, how they couldn't apply for certain jobs, how their career was over the minute they were married or became pregnant.

She dropped out of university and moved into a squat in Redfern. She made toast in the morning under the griller, boiling tea in a saucepan on the stove. She shared her breakfast with members gathered in the dilapidated living room. In return, they made placards and stuffed envelopes with her new manifesto.

Deborah stood at the front of a crowd of thousands in Hyde Park. She led the protesters in the largest march of its kind. Women from all walks of life swelled the ranks, holding placards. Deborah's slogans echoed off the office buildings in George Street.

A neo-Nazi threw an egg at her face, and it made the Sydney Morning Herald *the next day. Deborah's egg-stained face became the image of the revolution.*

The politicians on the nightly news grew nervous about their female voting constituents.

Deborah pored over research as she wrote her book. The book. The one that defined a movement and would be handed down from mother to daughter.

A heavy-breathing stalker on the phone, during dinner, threatened to kill her. The police officer told her that she was wilful and had brought the heat on herself, that there was nothing they could do.

The bookstore cancelled her launch at the last minute, amid 'security concerns.' Deborah remained to turn the guests away herself.

She sat alone in a squat, sifting between the hate mail and fan mail. The fans were outweighed by the bile.

It seemed like the start of the revolution that would change the world forever.

"And it's a good thing you started the revolution," Felicia said, jotting down notes while she talked.

"Hear hear, sister," Libby said, snapping a final shot of Deborah, who swelled with purpose.

"If only I'd lived to see it," Deborah mused.

"Lived to see what?" Felicia asked.

"The Bill. Equal pay for equal work."

There was a pause as Felicia thought.

"It was passed in 1984."

"What?" Deborah said, picking a piece of tobacco off her lip.

"The Australian parliament finally passed the Sex Discrimination Act in 1984," Felicia said.

"I think what she means," Yasmin interjected, "is that we're still waiting for that law to be passed in practice, rather than theory."

"Oh, yes," Deborah said, putting on her most serious face. "I meant, the Bill has been passed, sure, but equality? Well, we're still waiting on that."

Felicia nodded thoughtfully.

"It did feel as if the whole world would change, that we could never go back."

"Cheers to that," Deborah said, raising her imaginary pint glass.

"And thank you, Deborah!" Yasmin said, imaginary cheersing with them all.

Felicia shook Deborah's hand, and Yasmin steered them down the hallway to their next interviewee.

Once Felicia was out of earshot, she pinched Deborah's arm on the tender part just above her elbow.

"Ow!" Deborah said, grabbing her elbow. "What was that for?"

"What do you mean you would have liked to have seen it?" Yasmin hissed. "You were alive in 1984, remember?"

"I forgot. It's a lot to remember. The truth of what happened and the lie of what we're saying happened."

"You are seventy-nine years old," Yasmin said. "Act your age."

"You act yours first," Deborah said, flicking her the bird and slamming the screen door on the way to the backyard.

And Yasmin saw it – that flash of defiance, the impossibly bright spark of passion. The Deputy Principal had seen it, as had the policeman who had come about the death threats.

It represented the most dangerous thing there was, both then *and* now.

It was the spark of revolution.

26

*Y*asmin left Deborah in the garden; she was still in her rebellious mood.

Yasmin composed her flushed features, ushering Felicia and Libby down the hallway, turning off into the larger living room. A Turkish rug lay on the floor beneath an ancient, brown leather couch. On it, Mrs Audrey Elizabeth Stewart sat, a crocheted rug warming her knees, her wig slightly off-centre.

Catina checked the watch pinned to the pocket of her mother's borrowed nurse's uniform and motioned to the couch against the wall.

"Would you like a seat, Ms Pine?"

"Thank you." Felicia sat elegantly with her knees together, her back ramrod straight.

"Audrey, may I introduce Felicia Pine," Catina said, enunciating every word as if Audrey were hard of hearing. She leaned in, trying to catch each word. Bless her little acting skills! "She'll interview you today for *The Standard*."

"Wonderful magazine," Audrey said, folding herself back into the lounge.

"Thank you," Felicia said.

Libby snapped the legs of her tripod into place and fitted the SLR on top.

"What a large camera," Audrey said. Libby smiled at her. "I can't get used to the newfangled gadgets these days."

"Of course," Felicia said.

"Except for computers. I love computers," Audrey said, scratching under her wig, which slipped slightly over her forehead.

"Wig," Yasmin whispered. She patted her on the head, as a friendly granddaughter would.

Audrey discreetly adjusted herself. Felicia fiddled with the recording app on her phone and didn't notice.

"Oh, you have a computer?" she asked.

"Not me. But Yasmin has one," Audrey said. "Sometimes in her room we—"

Yasmin burst into a coughing fit.

"Oh yes, Audrey. You mean the photo I showed you of my computer?" she said.

"Oh yes, the photo." Audrey recovered, bashful.

Felicia tapped record on her phone with the merest hint of scepticism in her expression.

Audrey leaned forward, entranced.

"We didn't have these types of things when we were taking dictation at secretarial school."

"No, I suppose you didn't," Felicia said, smiling. "Would you tell us something about your early life?"

And Audrey did.

Her eldest brother dared her to climb to the top of the Jacaranda tree at school. She fell and broke her wrist on the asphalt, but still pulled herself up on the Jacaranda the next day, plaster cast and all. She sat on a high branch with her legs swinging as the boys called her names.

She snuck into the sick room at school, stealing all of the mercurochrome. The entire school went a week without adding red stains to their scrapes and bruises.

When she turned eight years old, her mother woke her at 5:30 a.m. to make her brothers porridge. Audrey wiped her sister's running nose and rushed through her homework at the kitchen table. Audrey's mother taught her French from the homeland as they pegged washing on the line.

She played with her brothers in the backyard, shooting marbles and play-acting at being soldiers.

On one rainy day she dropped her books, splashing them into a puddle. Her teacher whacked the cane across her fingers. She held in the tears, watching the red welts grow.

She shook hands with the Principal on her last day of school at fourteen, hatted and gloved.

Audrey deliberately made mistakes on her typing tests at secretarial school and set the matron's wastebasket on fire. The regimental matron rapped her hand with the edge of the ruler in front of the whole school. She soaked her welts at home in a bucket of iced salt water.

Audrey – yet another 'young unmarried' – began work at Prescott and Sons, an accounting firm in the city. Mr Prescott patted her on the rear at the end of each working week, but she continued to turn in faultlessly typed pages.

She listened on the radio as war broke out in Europe. She kissed her father and brothers for the last time, watching their brown uniforms disappear into the streets while neighbours shouted well wishes from their front porches.

Audrey snuck a portion of each paycheque into a glass jar under her bed. She wiped more noses and made more breakfasts.

She packed a suitcase with clothes and her glass coin jar, booking passage to England. She stepped onto the steamer as if it was a new world, filled with sumptuous dinners and dashing young passengers.

She dined at a table full of well-travelled young hopefuls. She listened to tales of daring rescues and lucky escapes. She fell for a young Frenchman in uniform returning to his unit in France.

She danced with the Frenchman, letting him light her cigarettes. They took walks on deck late at night, watching the stars recede behind the turbulent wake of the steamer.

They hit bad seas, and Audrey heaved into a bucket in her cramped cabin.

She took shore excursions with her Frenchman, amongst the humid tropics and dank ports. He said the White Cliffs of Dover could be the gates to heaven itself.

Wearing a borrowed veil, Audrey stood next to the Frenchman, smart in his uniform. Her friends threw rice that caught in her veil like sprinkled pearls.

They boarded the ferry to Calais, then made their way to Paris, stepping along the Champs-Élysées, sipping cheap wine from shallow flutes. They danced to swing jazz and ate at restaurants with white tablecloths, breathing in swirling cigarettes and perfumes.

They yearned for the excitement of war as the thrill of the wine dissipated.

Audrey worked for the English-language newspaper in Paris, typing up reports and handwritten stories. She sobered at the news being wired in from Poland.

Audrey watched the newsreels at the local picture theatre. She didn't need to know French to understand the images she saw – the mass graves, the whiff of cremations. The Nazis' horrific advancements.

She snuck a defector into their apartment – the first of many. As he drank onion soup, the skinny boy's eyes were huge in his sunken head. He woke in the night screaming.

She rushed underground during each air raid amongst bundled citizens with a single suitcase, wondering if they would ever return home.

Audrey boarded the ferry again, moving into London's East End. She walked up the stairwell of the active service building, resolving never to merely write about things again. She resolved that now was the time for action. She scurried underground as the searchlights picked out approaching German bombers.

She dressed in her uniform and started training as a spy, rigging traps, crossing electrical wires and tapping at a signalling machine. She lay on her belly in the mud, under obstacles on the firing range. She clinked glasses with the men at the end of a long day's instruction, drinking the hardest of them under the table.

She parachuted back into France to meet up with the French Resistance, groups of which were holed up in small towns. She met the ragged Resistance fighters, who laughed when she relayed her orders. She grabbed a pistol from her belt and shot a pigeon in a nearby tree, *watching it drop dead to the ground. She told tales in French over pigeon stew that night.*

She manned the radio into the early dawn, listening to mostly static through the headphones. She snuck through the forest, nabbing supply drops parachuted from London. She signalled back to confirm stores of guns, ammunition, food, and basic comfort items.

She watched her troupe's faces fall when a raid by the Germans shot four of their men and smashed the radio. She broke up their quarrelling, knowing there was no way they could radio London for supplies.

She snuck into a party at a nearby German officer's house, pretending to be one of the high-society guests. She approached a German officer, cool beneath her sweat, flirting with him until she'd gained his confidence. She found her way to the basement, letting in her fellow resistance friends to pilfer the radio from under the very noses of the enemy. They rode back, heroes, to their new French Resistance headquarters.

She was the last person standing at their celebratory feast that night; the leader of the French Resistance had passed out on the floor beside her.

She scouted the camp in the earliest hours of the morning before the rest of her troupe had woken. She opened a card from her husband, stifling sobs as she read out the poem from the first man she had loved.

She hid behind a concrete wall, her De Lisle Carbine in hand, as the German bullets bit into the dust at her feet. She stitched a man's arm back together. She ran low behind a brick wall, throwing a grenade at a German sentry. She shot an SS soldier and broke another's neck.

On the day the Germans surrendered, the townspeople who had survived came out to celebrate. She hugged her Resistance fighters as the town toasted with foaming bottles of beer and sweet wine. The townsfolk spat on the surrendered Germans being led out of town.

Audrey's eyes fixed on a distant point out of the window.

"I lost my brother and Pa-Pa. And many Resistance Fighters," she said.

"I'm so sorry," said Felicia.

"And I never saw my husband again. I don't even know what

happened to him. I remained in France after the war to try and find him. But he never came home."

Felicia reached out and touched Audrey's hand. She sniffed minutely, then took a deep breath, regaining her stoic posture.

"I killed a few Germans," Audrey continued, "but I never felt bad about a single one of them. Because I knew this was more than the most terrible war that had ever been waged. I knew that if the Germans won, that was it for humanity. We were fighting a very particular evil."

"And thank God we won," Felicia said.

"God had nothing to do with it," Audrey said, fingering a gold cross on a chain around her neck.

After a respectful silence, Felicia prodded: "Would you show us the bomb shelter that you built with your siblings?"

27

*Y*asmin paled at the mention of the bomb shelter – she hadn't been able to find one at such short notice.

"Ah, it's time for Mrs Stewart's medication," Yasmin said. "It makes her very sleepy, and it will be dark by the time we get to her bomb shelter…"

"Nonsense," Felicia said, "there's plenty of time for Mrs Stewart to take a nap."

"This has been delightful. I'm having so much fun!" Audrey said, tilting her head. Her wig unpicked from the bobby pins and slipped askew. Yasmin tried to get Audrey's attention. Libby snapped a few more photos before realising her subject was akimbo.

"Ah, maybe we could ask your nurse to come and freshen you up?" Libby said, without much tact.

"Oh, this?" Audrey said, prodding her wig. "I forgot I was wearing it."

"Yes, because she actually has no hair!" Yasmin said. The proclamation ricocheted off the walls.

Audrey went bright red with the effort of keeping quiet. She was used to exploiting her feminine wiles, unhappy with the insinuation that she was bald as a newborn baby.

"I do have quite a lot of hair actually," she said, scratching sulkily underneath her wig.

"Please excuse my assistant," Felicia said icily.

"I...ah...am going to get the other ladies in here, you know, for a group shot," Libby said.

She shouldn't have bothered.

Deborah stood in the middle of the hallway, ripping her protest banners into small pieces and spraying her confetti about. Nicole clutched the framed photo of herself on stage, accepting the Nobel Prize, looking miserable.

"Nobody will listen," she muttered.

Deborah slapped Felicia's shoulder. Tea sloshed right out of Felicia's cup and across the front of her dress.

"I'm so sorry." Yasmin quickly dabbed at the tea stain with her handkerchief.

"Tell me," Deborah said, "you guys are rolling in dough up there on the exec floor, am I right?"

Yasmin mentally face-palmed herself. Deborah's eyes shone, oblivious to her lack of tact.

"I beg your pardon?" Felicia said, standing up.

Nicole shied away from Libby, holding the photo of her accepting the Nobel Prize. She seemed so saddened by that photo, the epitome of humanity's failure.

"Just let me take one last photo of you with that frame..." Libby said.

Nicole backed away into the wall, and both sandbags shifted to the side – it looked as if her entire butt had manoeuvred to her thighs. Yasmin heard the rip as Nicole hit a snag on the door frame. Then the softly trickling sand hit the floorboards. A little pile gathered at Nicole's feet, forming a perfect pyramid.

Audrey chose that exact moment to scratch under her wig, which then slipped sideways.

Felicia scanned from Audrey to Deborah to Nicole. She was beginning to realise their charade. The three women had done well but needed more practice at this acting gig.

"Well, I think we're all exhausted…" Yasmin said, ushering Deborah and Nicole to the hallway.

"Wait," Felicia said, and her tone indicated zero funny business. "You're not who you say you are."

Felicia peered closer at Deborah's shiny faux wrinkles and bloodshot eyes. She scuffed her shoe over the piles of sand accumulating at Nicole's feet. Audrey's wig, like Newton's apple, fell off and splayed across the floor. Audrey's thick, curled locks poked out from under the constraints of her head stocking, luscious and brown, in their damp-set prime.

"You're all pretending to be the women," Felicia said. "None of you is real. What do you think you're pulling here? Who are you?"

"They are the real deal," Yasmin said softly. Pleading.

"Rubbish!" Felicia roared.

Yasmin had seen her mad before, but this was dialled up to apocalyptic meltdown, like Mad Max and Furiosa's offspring on the day the world blew its top.

Libby snapped some new photos of the three women as their half-disguised selves.

Last of all, Felicia laid her eyes on Yasmin.

"You," she said. "You've orchestrated a full-scale deception."

"Ms Pine, it's not what you think. These are the real women from past issues of *The Standard*. It's them, in the flesh!"

"They most certainly are not!" Felicia roared.

She might have had a point. Nicole held her deflated artificial fat bags at her side. Deborah danced to the music in her head, in darting movements a seventy-nine-year-old Jane Fonda would be jealous of. Audrey rubbed at her cheek, sending sheets of wrinkles flaking onto the floor.

"What is this farce? We can't use any of it!"

"But everything's done now, and we've worked so hard…"

"We cannot deceive our readers. How dare you?" Her cheeks reddened.

Catina popped her head around the door, smiling sweetly. "Anyone for a top-up of tea?"

"I do not want a bloody tea!" Felicia roared. And then to Yasmin. "Explain yourself."

"Their accomplishments are real. Our readers need to remember; it's their way into history that people can relate to—"

"Ah, Felicia?" Libby said, holding out her phone, which was opened to a googled webpage. "The real Audrey Elizabeth Stewart was in *The Standard* in 1950 – this is her obituary!"

All eyes swung to Audrey, who slipped on her wig and sat, with force, on the floor.

"And no centenarian-minus-one is *that* nimble," Deborah said, slapping a women's lib sticker onto Audrey's chest.

"And the others?" Felicia asked.

Libby's fingers swiped and tapped, but Yasmin stepped forward.

"They all featured in the obituaries."

Felicia glanced from Deborah to Nicole. Deborah grinned as if she'd won Anarchist Island.

"So you would have us take pictures of women who are actually dead?" Felicia regained her composure, and her inner rage was even more terrifying. Her eye started to twitch. "How do you think that would make *The Standard* look? And how do you think it would make *me* look when it's revealed that I interviewed women who are *actually dead*!"

Felicia stared at them in turn, and Yasmin shivered with unpleasant chills.

"Who are you?" Felicia asked, her voice trilling.

"Ms Pine, maybe we should reconvene..." Libby said, gathering her kit.

Felicia gathered her handbag, and Libby packed up her gear. Felicia stuffed her compact into her bag with such force she nearly punched right through the material.

"Libby, get Tasha. I need legal on the phone."

"Felicia, please, it's still the story of the decade..." Yasmin said.

Felicia rounded on Yasmin, digging a shellacked fingernail into her chest.

"You're most definitely, unequivocally fired!"

28

*Y*asmin didn't remember much about the hour following Felicia storming out of the Airbnb, crackling with bile. Her besties removed their costumes, and Catina made another pot of tea. Yasmin held a cold cup in her lap. Someone removed the props and placed the furniture back where they'd found it. Audrey washed up, and Deborah picked up all the joint stubs she'd left in ashtrays and glasses around the house. Someone led Yasmin to the couch, where she now found herself sitting.

Everyone stared at Yasmin with varying degrees of sympathy. Even Catina appeared to be devastated.

Yasmin began to bawl. She wasn't much of a crier, but when she did let go, it was the water show of the century. The burning hot tears coursed along her cheeks and mingled with snot. Her eyes screwed up and her entire face stung. She tried to talk but the syllables jumbled. She couldn't take enough breath; it felt as if she would die from sobbing. The ache in her chest spread out to her arms, which felt as heavy as a front-loader washing machine.

She felt the least attractive she'd ever looked. She didn't cry like a movie star, in that controlled, tear-dripping way, her forehead crinkled just so. Rather, she looked like an astronaut who'd removed her helmet in the crushing atmosphere of a strange planet. Her features squished together as if under extreme pressure.

And at that moment it felt like she was the most distressed person there had ever been, or ever would be. Nobody else could feel in as much pain.

She'd lied to gain employment. She'd been exposed as a fraud. And she'd orchestrated her boss into a situation where her lies and fraud were beyond a doubt. She'd embarrassed Felicia and could have destroyed her reputation.

Yasmin doubted she'd ever find work again, not even in a cafe serving mail clerks, let alone within the hallowed halls of the publishing world.

All her dreams had been flushed down the toilet. And she only had herself to blame. It wasn't Nicole's or Deborah's or Audrey's fault that she created them and made them into solid beings. It wasn't their fault that Yasmin's imagination doomed them to their current age, and form, and lack of era-appropriate appearance. And it wasn't any of their faults that Yasmin had lived so many lies that she'd allowed fakery to become second nature. She'd tried to deceive everyone, to her own ends.

Her world had gone to the dogs, and Yasmin had nobody to blame but herself.

Audrey clicked into practical mode, and brought Yasmin a towel to wail into. Deborah, rather unhelpfully, started singing various women-power chants, telling Yasmin that now was not a time for sorrow; it was a time to get angry. And Nicole just held Yasmin's hands in hers, unable to right the obvious wrong paths taken.

Yasmin felt slightly better when Catina laid a sympathetic arm around her shoulders. It was the first real sign of emotional support they'd had as sisters – perhaps ever. It felt so foreign. Yasmin breathed in the scent of rosebud conditioner in Catina's hair and felt her heartbeat through her t-shirt. She had Mum's hands, Yasmin noticed. She found that comforting.

Catina had also worked hard. Yasmin hoped they never found

out about her involvement, that the experience didn't stain her future. This was the kind of thing to kill careers.

"I'm so sorry," Yasmin sniffed, wiping her streaked face with the towel, leaving it blotchy and red. Her eyelids were quickly swelling, and she knew that by nightfall they'd be as bulbous as tennis balls.

"No, dear. We're sorry," Audrey said kindly. "What an awful job we did."

"I think I did okay," Nicole said.

"No, we were pitiful," Deborah said.

A smile tugged at the corner of Catina's mouth. She wrapped her arms around Yasmin, and they sat there, rocking slightly from side to side. The hotness left Yasmin's head, and an ache began behind her brows.

"I'd say acting is not any of your fortes," Catina said. "Except maybe Audrey. If it wasn't for the fiasco with your wig falling onto the floor."

"And not being dead would have helped too," Deborah said.

That dampened the mood. Audrey turned away, pretending to examine her wig. She dabbed at her eyes. She didn't want them to see.

"So, what now?" Yasmin asked, the first words she'd spoken since the floodgates opened.

Home was the only place left to go, so they packed up the Airbnb, and Yasmin left the keys under the fake rock at the very end of the garden, as instructed by the owner. They stepped into Yasmin's hallway.

Susan yelled from the kitchen. "Where the hell have you been? I didn't slave over a hot stove all evening for you to miss dinner."

She appeared in the hall, and Catina moved to placate her. Yasmin couldn't deal with her mother right now.

"And who are these people?" Susan demanded as Yasmin's ghost-mothers trudged up the stairs.

"They're nobody," Yasmin said.

She saw the hurt on her ghost-mothers' faces, but it felt true. They were just her imaginary friends. They were nobody to anyone but Yasmin.

"What, are you starting some club in your bedroom now?" her mother asked, supremely annoyed.

"No, Mum. Just leave it!" Yasmin bristled.

Catina, bless her sisterly socks, led their mother back into the kitchen. Yasmin continued up the stairs following her threesome and threw herself face-first onto the bed. She didn't have any tears in reserve; she felt drained of all fluids, her head pounding. She felt too awful to bother with a Nurofen.

Yasmin rolled onto her side and stared at her reflection in the mirrored wardrobe and hated herself more with every scowl.

Her friends didn't know what to do, so they just sat with her, waiting for her to come good. Yasmin didn't think that would happen anytime soon. She wasn't sure she'd come right ever again. She felt the antithesis of good, and maybe this would be her new eternal state. Her punishment for lying her way into a job and then deceiving her boss by presenting three ghosts of women as older versions of their real selves. All in the name of a worthy story.

She was a supremely crappy journalist.

Yasmin sat up in bed after darkness had fallen outside. And now, instead of giving into despair, Yasmin grew angry as hell. Why hadn't she come clean at the very outset and admit that she had no experience as a journalist? Why did she lie on her resume and then deny it point-blank on so many occasions after that? Why did she keep up the charade, getting herself deeper and deeper into the lies until she believed them herself, until the lying was who she was?

How could she think that nobody would find out that her fairy ghost-mothers were dead? That nobody would look up their obituaries? That their families wouldn't come forward?

If the feature had turned out to be the best *The Standard* had ever done, did that justify all the lies?

Yasmin lay back on her bed, and her besties settled in for the night. But sleep eluded Yasmin. She became aware of the one thing that wasn't going to forgive her – her conscience. It felt as foreign as a splinter beneath her scalp, needling away as she tossed in bed.

She lay awake for an hour or so until the neighbourhood settled and the moon was high enough to shine into her bedroom – a blue, judgemental light. Yasmin leapt up, pacing back and forth. Her besties unfurled from sleep, watching the angry energy.

She snapped on the desk lamp. Her shadow appeared evil in the light thrown against the wall. It elongated over the room, and the women in the magazine clippings on her ceiling seemed afraid. They were right to be.

She stood on the bed, swiping magazine posters from the ceiling. First, an advertisement for Ponds soap, with a natty jingle written beside the smiling, beautified woman. She tore at the ad for perfectly starched dresses; the youthfully healthy lass taking Bile Beans; the elegant pearls of the Odorono deodorant patron with a dapper man on her arm. Yasmin snatched the slim beauty wondering at diet pills and silken sheets and sanitary pads. She ripped up the article on liposuction, and Nicole Kidman posing in an Akubra hat. The luscious lashes promoting Max Factor mascara.

Yasmin ripped them all to tiny strips.

She even clawed at the photos of Audrey in her uniform, operating a radio; Deborah at the front of the protesting crowd, hailing through a megaphone; Nicole at the podium of a great lecture hall, with slides containing formulae and diagrams behind her.

Yasmin tossed the torn pages onto the bed and fell to her hands and knees, ripping and scrunching and tearing each page to tiny, damning confetti.

Her ghost-mothers watched, appearing a little paler than usual, but they didn't interfere. And when Yasmin's rage had subsided, she gathered up the shreds of her former infatuation and stuffed them into a bin liner snatched from her desk drawer.

She tied up the ends and stuffed the huge, soft bag in the corner beside her antique wardrobe.

Her besties stood around, trying to calm her. Yasmin reached into Deborah's pocket for her lighter.

"Hey!" Deborah said.

She smelt the lighter fluid at the familiar *ttch* as the flame flickered. Yasmin dangled the lighter over the bag, mania etched on her face.

"That's enough," Nicole said, stepping in and grabbing hold of the lighter. "Do you want to burn down your house too?"

"Yes," Yasmin said.

"Well, it won't help you," Nicole persisted, handing the lighter back to Deborah. Deborah made a show of shoving it deep into her pockets.

"You're right," Yasmin said. "Nothing will."

29

*Y*asmin slept well past midday the next day, dreading opening her eyes into true consciousness, unwilling to face up to yesterday's events – as in, the ending of her life as she knew it.

Okay, so Yasmin might have been a little dramatic there. But sleeping to midday, while hiding from reality, encouraged nightmares that recurred, over and over.

She can't tell why the spider is chasing her, or why it's morphed to human-size, or why it has Audrey's face. The Audrey-spider whispers, far too low for human ears, and Yasmin doesn't understand.

She is stuck in a loop. Each time she travels closer to the u-bend of the sink, then is shot back up to peer down the drain. On what seemed like the hundredth attempt, Yasmin feels the smack of the pipe on her bum, and the Audrey-spider screams at her like reverb.

"Make it right."

Yasmin woke with a jolt, frozen with fear, her legs too heavy to move. Her eyes watered, her breath coming in pants. And the real

Audrey hovered over her, concern on her face, but not because of her dream.

"Do you know what to do?" she asked.

Yasmin wasn't even sure she was awake.

"Yes."

∿

Yasmin carried the archive box under one arm, with her research notes piled on top. She had her besties in tow for their last trip to Warner Williams Corporation. Yasmin couldn't very well add 'stealing the only archival copies of the history of *The Woman's Standard*' to her list of crimes.

The foursome was grim, and Yasmin had instructed her besties not to put on their makeup or costumes but to come as is. Let the world see who they were.

Besides some sideways glances on the bus, nobody noticed. Even the bus driver was preoccupied with setting his little box to record the next zone of ticketing. And Yasmin appeared so grim, so utterly defeated, that nobody bothered with quips or derision.

As they entered the foyer, her old nemesis, Buckley, headed straight their way.

"I've been expressly told not to let you back in," he said, hands on his walkie. "Got to say, that doesn't surprise me."

"Buckley, my man!" Yasmin said, smiling at his humourless face. "Is that a new goatee?"

He put his hand out to stop Yasmin. She held out the box, innocently. "I'm just returning these to Archives. You can come if you like."

He slid his walkie from his belt. He pressed a button and spoke into it.

"Ah, Roger? Got a little assignment for you." And then to Yasmin: "I'll have to escort you through, I don't trust you. Plus... I've always wanted to see if Archives exists. I heard it was boarded up years ago..."

"Really?" Yasmin said.

215

Buckley glanced at Audrey, Deborah and Nicole who were more than a little conspicuous.

"Nice costumes," he said.

Ten minutes later Buckley had traded with Roger, and he and the four women shared a lift to the second floor. To his credit, Buckley didn't stare at Yasmin's ghost-mothers. They wouldn't have been the weirdest things to come into the building.

"I heard Archives keeps copies of every memo ever sent," Buckley said.

"It's a stunner," Yasmin said, trying to keep the irony out of her voice.

"And the crone who runs it curses anyone who crosses her," Buckley said, more school-boy excited than security conscious.

The lift *pinged* as it came to rest on level two, and Yasmin waited for Buckley to buzz them through. They headed past the telemarketing team and through the dank, almost-abandoned corridor. They arrived at the little door at the end, with the red, crumbling, painted post box next to it. Yasmin knocked, and the archivist's gravelly voice bid them enter.

"After you," Yasmin said, waving Buckley in front.

He stepped through, marvelling at the cavernous shelves, the stink of dust, the historical greatness of the place.

"Wow, this is a crap heap," he said.

"You got it!" Yasmin said, and slammed the door, with the archivist and Buckley on the other side.

Yasmin pulled the heavy old post box in front of the door. It was so heavy that it held the door shut, and Buckley was trapped. They heard the thud of his shoulder hit the door, and the post box's flap shuddered with each heave. But it held firm.

They heard Buckley radio through to Roger. Yasmin picked up the archive box and twirled a finger at her besties. This ship was turning around.

Audrey caught on first and grabbed the research from the top of the box, holding it under one arm. Deborah peeked further down the corridor, waving them ahead. Nicole moved as if she wished the walls would devour her, but brought up a half-decent rear guard. And Buckley's shouts grew dimmer with each hurried step towards circ.

They passed back through telemarketing without any of the downtrodden customer service reps noticing. Their collective script-reading created too much of a buzz for Buckley's commotion to be heard.

Yasmin and her friends slipped into the lift, and Yasmin repeatedly pressed the call button. When the elevator finally arrived, they piled in, just as the other lift came, and Roger popped out, scanning frantically for signage. He spied their lift closing. Moved towards the closing doors. If he caught them, it would all be over.

Yasmin jabbed at the button. The ancient lift squeezed shut, in slow-mo.

"Wait...do you know where Archives is?" He leapt for the doors, and – just before they bumped to – put his hand in the gap. The sensors twigged. The doors opened again!

He sized them up. Recognised Yasmin.

"Where's Buckley?" he demanded, pulling out his walkie-talkie.

"Come in here and find out, sweetie," Audrey said, sashaying forward, her hips pointing towards him.

The strange woman in fancy dress completely threw him.

"Sorry!" Audrey kicked the back of his knees. He dropped to the floor. She karate-chopped his hand, and he dropped the walkie-talkie. She scooped it up and grabbed Yasmin.

"Come on!" She roused the team, and they dashed from the lift, leaving the hapless Roger groaning on the floor inside.

Audrey led them to the fire stairs. They burst through and clattered up two floors of echoing concrete steps. She sure could hotfoot it in a pair of sensible heels.

They burst out onto the atrium of the fourth floor.

"Wait," Yasmin said, holding the others back. She headed over to the frosted entrance when a shadow of a person passed behind. She knocked on the door, hefting the archive box to her chest.

"Courier," she said. "You have to sign for it."

The shadow returned and opened the door to reveal themselves: it was Tasha!

"Oh, thank God it's you," Yasmin said.

Panic flashed across Tasha's face.

"You can't be here," she said. Then she noticed Yasmin's besties in all their natural glory and backed up a little. Yasmin used her retreat to push gently through. And now she had the attention of the entire floor. Every fearful face turned their way.

Behind them, the lift *dinged* and Roger limped out, holding his knee.

"Grab those women!" he said, hesitating when he spied Audrey.

Yasmin's former colleagues raised quite the hullaballoo, not quite knowing how to react. Audrey lunged towards one of the copy-editors, who stifled a scream.

Felicia's door opened. Silence dropped as if someone had upended a fish tank over the floor. Everyone wanted to see how Felicia would handle Yasmin. The security guard moved forward and grabbed Audrey's arms.

"I'm sorry, Ms Pine," Roger said. "These women have infiltrated the building, and then this one assaulted me. And they've taken Buckley hostage." He tightened his grip, staring at each of them, inviting a reply.

"No, we just sent him on an errand to Archives," Deborah said.

"Ms Pine," Yasmin began politely. "I'm sorry to drop in unannounced. But I wanted to talk to you about something important."

"Haven't my lawyers been explicitly clear?" Felicia said.

"We have one thing to say to you, and then we'll leave," Yasmin said, stepping forward, flicking her hair back. "Please, I promise to never bother you after this."

"It's all right, Roger," Felicia said. "I want to hear what she has to say."

She waved them into her office, glancing at the odd-looking women.

Yasmin ushered her friends through first. The not-so-hushed

chatter rose behind them. Tasha must have wondered what trickery they were managing now.

Yasmin was back in her favourite career-wrecking office, facing off with a royally annoyed and supremely influential magazine editor.

"You don't work here anymore," Felicia said, sitting straight down and leaning back in her executive chair, her piercing eyes humourless.

"Yes, you're right," Yasmin said, pausing respectfully.

"You put me in an impossible position. You almost destroyed the reputation of the magazine. It's been running for eighty-five years for God's sake! Not to mention my reputation as editor. Never have I seen something so brazen, so potentially damaging and down-right illegal."

"I understand."

"You lied on your resume. We called your reference, and he turned out to be someone called Jerry who works at a fish and chip shop, not *The Guardian*. You're no journalist."

"Yes, I did lie on my resume."

"So what are you doing here, opening up fresh wounds? I should march your lying arse to legal myself."

"I agree with everything you've said, Ms Pine. I misled you and your staff, and I lied about my experience. I tried to deceive you, misrepresent who these women were," Yasmin said evenly.

Yasmin's ghost-mothers weren't fearful of Felicia. Just curious to see what would happen next.

"You won't have to see me again," Yasmin said, "but please still run the story. Don't use the photos from the shoot, use these."

Yasmin heaved the archive box onto Felicia's desk.

"The women's obituaries featured in *The Standard*, they all passed on, tragically, at the age of thirty."

Felicia eyed the obituaries resting on top of the pile.

"The women's accomplishments are real, their stories are real," Yasmin said. "I just hacked the way I went about reporting it."

Deborah stepped forward and placed Yasmin's research notes on top.

"It's true, this is our lives, as it happened," she said.

"I'm sorry, but why are you all so faded looking, so drained of colour? And you –" she pointed to Nicole "– are positively glossy."

"I saw them in past issues of *The Woman's Standard*," Yasmin began, "and they did speak to me, just like I told you. They became the only people who listened when I talked back. They were alive to me. And now, they're alive for others too."

"Don't be so clichéd, Yasmin."

"It's true. I'm finally done with lying. I'm ready to face whatever ramifications there are. But first, I wanted to tell you the truth."

"Right on, sister," Deborah said, giving Yasmin a satisfied nod.

Felicia watched Yasmin, pity in her eyes. Yasmin dreaded Felicia's pity more than her rage.

"I can't believe any word that comes out of your mouth," she said. "You do understand that?"

Yasmin felt the bottom drop out of her stomach, felt her breath catch sharply in her chest. She felt sad for all the things she could have done but didn't. And she felt sadder for the things she shouldn't have done, but did.

"These are my fairy ghost-mothers," Yasmin said. "Spirited from the pages of *The Standard* fourteen years ago."

Felicia stared as if Yasmin had grown a Pinocchio nose. She reached her hand to her telephone.

"I've had quite enough of whatever…this…is," she said.

Yasmin felt a deep sadness overcome her, as she thought about the best friends she'd ever had. How losing them was now inevitable.

Felicia's eyes flicked off Yasmin for a moment. She frowned, observing something just over her shoulder. Yasmin turned, and her fairy ghost-mothers were aglow, just as they had been when Yasmin first saw them in the magazines at Grandma's house, and again in her bedroom when they had become three-dimensional. And even that time in the office when other people began to see them. Their shimmering halos surrounded them in fuzzy light – gold and red and silver.

Felicia's mouth dropped open.

"What kind of magic…" she asked.

"It's my friends materialising whenever life gets real," Yasmin said, lifting the glowing penny from beneath her neckline. She held the coin aloft, which was hot to the touch.

"I don't understand," Felicia said, backing her chair towards the window. "It seems like a fire hazard. Make it stop."

"I can't," Yasmin said. "I have to make this right."

30

*H*er besties were aglow, stunning and shimmery and as wonderful as they'd ever been.

"What happens now?" Felicia asked, eyeing the magic before her, crooking her handbag under one arm, ready for escape. "Do they explode, or burst into flames?"

"Not so far."

Yasmin's besties linked arms.

"Are you okay, guys?" Yasmin asked.

"It's like I've hit my funny bone all over my body," Nicole said, without fear.

"This feels like I'm dancing to my favourite folk album on rotation," Deborah said, shimmying her shoulders.

"I feel like my muscles have gone to sleep, and they're just waking up with pins and needles," Audrey said.

"You need to make this stop, Yasmin." Felicia's hand hovered over her desk phone. She paused before picking up the receiver. "Who can I call?"

"It's okay," Deborah said. "We're Yasmin's fairy ghost-mothers. Only she knows what comes next."

"I hate it when you say that," Yasmin said, pacing the room, trying to force some cohesion into her thoughts. How had she spirited Audrey from the ghost world, that first time? And how did she invoke Deborah and Nicole after that? How did they become real for everyone else? There must have been a common thread.

"I don't know what to do," Yasmin said. Nobody wanted to hear it.

Felicia started to recover from her initial shock.

"I'm bringing Roger in," she said, stepping tentatively around Audrey.

"This is absolutely the wrong time to call in the fuzz," Deborah said, coming between Felicia and the door, the heat of Deborah's force field crackling between them. Felicia backed up again.

"Do something," Felicia said to Yasmin.

"Let me think. I need to think," Yasmin said, and her besties spread out to give her space. "So I guess I felt sad, right before you all did the shimmery thing."

She peeked hopefully at her friends, but they hadn't changed a bit.

"You're going to have to do a lot better," Nicole said.

"*Reserare se serum tuae*," Yasmin said.

"What?" Nicole said.

"The inscription. Remember it means 'unlock your true self.'"

Yasmin closed her eyes, took a deep breath, and let it out slowly, like a yogi taking control of their very consciousness.

Yasmin held the magical penny in both hands and remembered that first time she saw Nicole, in her lab coat, on the front cover of the magazine, iridescent in whiteness, comforting Yasmin after her dad left. She felt Nicole wrap her arms around her, telling her that everything would be okay. The rest of her family sat quietly in the living room, solidified by shock. Yasmin sat on her bed, feeling so incredibly alone. Nicole patted her shoulder, waited for her to cry. But it was too soon for tears. Yasmin didn't feel anything, except maybe the hole that needed filling. And Nicole reached right in there, until it felt a little better, until it felt like Yasmin could stand up again. And she did, and went downstairs, and sat with her sister.

Back in Felicia's office, Yasmin opened her eyes.

"You helped me be smart, to make the right decisions. You've always been the intelligent one, and I've borrowed your wisdom whenever I needed it."

Nicole smiled at Yasmin.

"You're already intelligent enough for the both of us," Nicole said.

"And I needed you after Dad left," Yasmin said.

That's when a curious thing happened to Nicole.

Her shimmering started to pulsate – brightening and dimming slowly. Electricity sparked off her. Everyone took a step back as her glow grew in intensity. They closed their eyes. They heard a *pop*, and the office fluorescent lights flickered. A short wind of energy buffeted them gently. Then calm descended again. Everyone opened their eyes.

Nicole floated a metre above the floor!

She was translucent, flickering like a strobe light. She squeezed in on herself, folding inwards from a three-dimensional person to a faded image, to a two-dimensional floating entity. Her gloss strobed in and out, and she floated upwards, towards the ceiling. Yasmin could see the cornices between her translucent face.

"Nicole!" Yasmin moved to stand underneath. "Where are you going?"

"It doesn't look like a dimension you'd be able to follow me to," Nicole said, and her voice was small, as if from the other end of a long-distance call.

"Are you okay?" Yasmin said. She didn't notice Felicia, her mouth agape, crouching by her mahogany desk.

"I'm fine," Nicole said. "I think this is meant to be."

"But I need you," Yasmin said, feeling herself choke up.

"You've found your true self," Nicole said, giving two flat thumbs up.

"It's okay, sister," Deborah said, laying a hand on Yasmin's arm. "We don't belong here. We have to go."

Yasmin pulled Deborah closer, and Audrey joined their group hug. Yasmin wanted to hold on forever.

As they disentangled, Yasmin wiped at the tears coursing down her cheeks.

"I don't want you to go, Deborah," she said.

Deborah brushed a tear off Yasmin's chin. "We know."

Yasmin took a steadying breath. "Are you ready?" she asked.

"I'm always ready, sister," Deborah said.

Yasmin closed her eyes.

She thought back to the day she came home from school after her best and only human friend's friendship was a lie. How she lost that friendship, how they never spoke again. How Yasmin tried – and failed – to make other friends, that year or any other. How alone she felt in the world, how she couldn't even tell her sister, because Catina pretended not to care. Yasmin sat in her room, feeling like the only person who felt that way, that nobody else would ever understand what it was like.

And she went to that old box of magazines and found Deborah, fierce on the front cover, her fist in the air. And behind her, a mass of women, all following her! Yasmin wanted to know how to attract people like that, to fight the good fight. How did you get other people on your side? How did you make friends?

"You taught me to be passionate and fight for what I believed in," Yasmin said, back in the office. "I would have never landed this job without you."

"You might have done a better job if I hadn't led you astray all those years," Deborah said.

"You were there for me after I lost my best and only friend," Yasmin said, closing her eyes.

Yasmin opened her eyes, watching Deborah slowly raise her fist in the air as her shimmering started to rotate around her body, growing faster and faster, a whirlwind of red light and heat crackling around the room. The energy increased, reaching the ceiling where it fanned out like a cyclone. It became too bright to see. They turned away.

Then the storm dissipated, and the rumbling stopped.

Deborah floated up to the ceiling, becoming wraith-like as well. She deflated and flattened into a two-dimensional wisp of her former self. She flickered and joined hands with Nicole. They both swirled around the ceiling, whooping as they went.

"I dig this," Deborah said. "You can love me or lump me."

She checked herself out and did a backflip around the fluorescent lights. She turned her attention back to Yasmin.

"You, my friend, are the best reformed liar I know."

"Thanks, Deborah," Yasmin said.

Yasmin nodded to Audrey, who stood taller and placed her handbag on the floor.

And then it hit her. What would she do without Audrey?

"I can't do this to you," Yasmin said.

"Yes you can," Audrey said, picking up both of Yasmin's hands in hers. "But it's okay. You need this, and I need to go. We've outgrown each other."

"No, Audrey," Yasmin said, feeling the fear catching in her throat. "You'll die."

"I'm already dead, remember?" she said, putting her head to the side. "I'm just moving on. But never forgotten, okay?"

Yasmin couldn't in all conscience go ahead. Could she?

"Audrey, you're the best friend I've had in my entire life," Yasmin said, burying her face in Audrey's uniform jacket.

"And I won't be the last," she said kindly, patting Yasmin on the head. "Time to be brave."

Audrey pressed their foreheads together and stood there for a while. It wasn't enough time, but then Yasmin realised it never would be. She knew Audrey was right, but it still took a good minute for Yasmin to pull herself together.

They finally let go.

Yasmin closed her eyes and thought about Audrey – at the top of those boxes of magazines, so bright and fresh in her uniform on the painted cover; the brown watercolours mixing; that carefree expression on her face, as if she could do anything, at any time.

Yasmin remembered feeling so sad that day, the first day she lost someone. She didn't understand how everyone could go back to Grandma's house afterwards, and stand in her kitchen, and make sandwiches and tea as if it was their own home. It was

Grandma's home, and she would never step foot in that kitchen again.

Yasmin felt alone in her grief. She'd never been as close to anyone again after that. And she guessed that's why she needed Audrey.

"You taught me to be courageous, to never give in to fear," Yasmin said. "That there will always be a way through the darkness."

"You always knew that in your own heart," Audrey said.

"You were there for me after Grandma died," Yasmin said.

She opened her eyes and reached up to touch Audrey's face. Yasmin felt the little tickle as her fingers broached the shimmery force field. Audrey took Yasmin's hand and just held it. Yasmin didn't notice her tears or the hiccups that arrived with them. She felt the warmth of Audrey's hand, the electricity coursing through them, that feeling of intense sadness.

"It's time for me to go," Audrey said.

Yasmin felt the intensity of loss of all the people who had left her over the years. And it was too much. She clenched Audrey's hand and lost herself in grief, not wanting to let go.

"I get it now," Yasmin said hoarsely. "It's loss. I needed you all after I lost people. I needed you to fill the pieces of me that were taken away."

Audrey floated upwards, thinning out, losing her shape, until she was as flat as cardboard and as ephemeral as smoke. She smiled at Yasmin as she rose to the ceiling and held Deborah's and Nicole's hands.

There were Yasmin's fairy ghost-mothers, for the last time. They basked in each other's glows as the hotness intensified, growing incredibly bright, like white-hot lightning. Yasmin felt her senses rise to the heat, felt the electrical sizzle, and one last, monumental flash.

She closed her eyes.

A tremor rocked the building, and everyone lost their footing. Yasmin fell to the floor, head bowed, feeling calm. And when she raised her eyes, her three fairy ghost-mothers were gone. And where they had stood: three piles of grey ash, smoke rising like slender fingers from their peaks.

Yasmin stood sadly over the ash pile. Felicia sat at her desk, clearly moved. Then her gaze fell on Yasmin.

"Well," Felicia said, shock playing in her eyes. "I guess I believe you now."

31

*F*elicia ran her fingers through her hair, which flitted about with the latent electricity in the air. Nobody spoke for a while.

Yasmin felt closer to Felicia, as if they were now the sisterhood in the inner circle. Did Felicia feel the same way? Her face was a little hard to read.

A pain caught in Yasmin's chest as she remembered her friends – those shared years, the ups and downs of life.

Felicia's phone rang, stunning Yasmin out of her grief. The ringing reminded her of the normal world that Felicia would soon have to go back to. Back to desks and emails and missed dinners and forgotten friends.

Felicia answered the phone.

"Yes, we had it up here too. I'll check." Felicia hung up the phone, stood, and opened the office door. She poked her head out. "Everyone all right?"

Shocked faces greeted them, but nobody appeared to be hurt. Felicia headed back into her office, closed the door and folded her arms.

"So, what now?" she asked.

And Yasmin knew, more than anything else. This couldn't remain in her memory, her imagination. She'd found Felicia – the most improbable person ever – to share her ghostly friends with. But in sharing, they'd become real to others too. *The Standard* had to honour them.

"We can't forget them," Yasmin said. "We can't forget Audrey, or Nicole or Deborah. We owe it to our readers to remember them for their accomplishments, to honour their lives. Otherwise, it will have all been for nothing."

Felicia picked up Yasmin's research from the top of the box.

"So the research is sound?" she asked, her tone business-like.

"I bet my life on it."

"It's not your life at stake here," Felicia said. Then her eyes flicked, almost apologetically, to the piles of ash on the plush carpet square. Her smile knew pain, too. "I'm going to write the story."

"Oh, thank you, Ms Pine!"

"But I'll need a research assistant, and you're most familiar with the ladies' lives. However, I can't keep you on in the office. It's not a good look for the company."

"I could skype in from home."

"Good. Let's do that." Felicia pointed to the pile of ash on her carpet. "Ah, not to be insensitive, but what are you going to do with...*them*?"

"I'm on it," Yasmin said, rounding on Felicia's desk, grabbing her Lifetime Achievement Award from its display case and scooping the ash inside the cup. Yasmin ran her finger over the grey ash stains on the carpet. She felt each tiny grain, the powder sticking to her skin. She rubbed her forefinger and thumb together. Dusted off her hands.

"I'll bring it back," Yasmin said, holding up the cup.

"Keep it," Felicia said, with the hint of a smile.

Yasmin sat at her desk in her bedroom fact-checking Felicia's story – Audrey, Deborah and Nicole's stories. She pulled documents from the box, fanning them about her bedroom floor, checking and cross-checking until her back ached and her shoulders seemed frozen from hunching over. She felt tense with stress and multiple cups of instant Moccona.

Night crept in, and Yasmin turned on the lights, stretched, and took yet another cold sip of coffee. She made a face and replaced the cup on the desk.

Catina knocked and popped her head inside.

"How much longer?" she asked.

"I'm almost finished marking it all up. Then I'll send it over to Felicia."

There was a pause while Catina considered this.

"So, Felicia gets the glory of writing the feature?" she asked.

"I'm just happy not to have my name smeared through the bog-holes of the publishing world," Yasmin said.

"Who's to say that Felicia won't smear your name. After she's finished using you, I mean?"

Yasmin shook her head.

"You're missing the point. Do you realise how much trouble I was in before she saw my friends transform? My career was over. All of them were doomed to disappear forever and remain forgotten. Now we still get to run the feature – their feature. And I can still work on it, which is a huge honour, even if I don't get credit. Felicia's pretty generous."

Catina remained unconvinced.

"We shared a moment in that office, didn't we?" Yasmin said. "You can't see something like that and not be touched somehow."

She took another sip of cold coffee and placed the cup out of arm's reach, swivelling back to the laptop. She felt the screen hot on her face, she had been that long in front of it. Her eyes felt like they were cramping, if that were possible, and filled with grit. She rubbed them and opened the Word document.

It took Yasmin nearly all night to finish marking up the feature. She saved the document in the Dropbox folder and massaged her fingers. Everything ached, including her head. She felt exhausted, barely able to open her eyelids against the approaching dawn. Everything felt stiff as if *she* had just travelled to the plane beyond, and not her friends.

The croaks of dawn began. Birds began to stir, the sky grew visible with just the promise of light. And on her laptop, she fact-checked the Word doc – her story – called simply, "Beyond the Stereotypes."

She'd done it – she'd finished and was ready to send the edited feature to Felicia.

She peeked at the blanket on the floor where Audrey used to sleep. Yasmin's eyes rested on Felicia's Lifetime Achievement Award, the cup filled to the brim with their ashes. She'd have to find something more permanent to hold them. They could be distributed around Yasmin's bedroom in a slight wind.

Thinking about her friends sapped all Yasmin's energy, but Felicia was on a deadline.

Yasmin emailed the Dropbox link to Felicia. She waited for the email to show up in her sent items, proofread the email again to make sure she hadn't made any mistakes, and snapped her laptop shut. The sound of finality.

She loosened the tension in her body, crinkled down into a tight ball and stretched back up again. She shook out her hands, twisted her torso and flexed her neck.

She flopped onto the bed. She got comfy, put head to pillow, and fell instantly asleep with such force that she would struggle to recall it later.

Audrey flitted along a row of cavorting couples dressed in evening wear, skirts spinning in a wheel of colour. A twenty-piece big band blasted horns and brass from the stage. Tables ringed the dancefloor, their white tablecloths set with candles flickering in tiny crystal vases.

The air smelt of perfumes, cigarettes and boeuf bourguignon.

Audrey paused at a dashing young man dressed in his finest officer's uniform, his hair cut short at the back and sides, standing tall, a head shorter than she. They were both breathless from the dance. He offered her a cigarette from a silver case. She took one with her gloved hand, just like a movie star siren, and he struck a match for her, watching her face as the flame lit her features and glistened off the red of her lipstick. He offered her his arm, and she took it, and he led her out of the room, away from the frenetic energy of the dance floor, away from the big band, and out into the night beyond. At the door, she paused, glanced back. She waved her gloves, winked, and disappeared out into the moonlight.

After an hour's nap, seven a.m. rolled around. Time to skype into the office. Tasha was already seated at her desk, setting up the session. And, behind her, the proofs had been delivered, mocks drawn up by the new designer, copy slashed and reworked and laid on desks. People toiled at keyboards, whiteboards and light boxes. Even the archivist had delivered a set of film negatives. Yasmin waved, and the archivist waved back. She mouthed "thank you" and pointed to Felicia, then to herself, clearly star-struck.

Through it all, Felicia flitted from one person to the next, nodding in agreement or pointing to changes. Nobody stood idle. It felt as if Yasmin were watching the frantic energy of a rugby match – people scurried back and forth, trying not to fall over each other. Yasmin waited for the great Felicia Pine to join them at Tasha's desk for a quick skype.

"You must have been up all night," Felicia said.

"Oh, it was no trouble." Yasmin gave a little laugh.

Yasmin – laughing over some insider joke with Felicia Pine!

"You didn't think the angle on the war was a little over the top?" Felicia asked.

"No, just the right mix of nostalgia, fist fights and espionage."

Tasha leaned into view. "Wouldn't want your Audrey any other way."

"You girls leave it to us," Felicia said. "I'll run the copy past Tasha for one last sub."

"Great, thanks so much, Felicia. I appreciate you keeping me on—"

"I'm not keeping you on," Felicia said lightly. "I'm exploiting my freelancer budget."

Yasmin waved as Felicia moved away. Tasha came back into view.

"I know you want to be here," she said, not unkindly. "So I'm going to leave the Skype session running so you can virtually participate in the office madness. Just be sure to turn your webcam's video off."

"You're the best. Thanks, Tasha."

"Don't thank me. It's to make you feel guilty for leaving," Tasha said. "Now I'm stuck with the coffee order."

Her eyes crinkled and she stepped away, leaving a view of the bustling office in the webcam.

The Skype session ticked over for the rest of the day, right through lunch and into the afternoon. And through it all, Yasmin felt pride, impressed with everyone's stamina, and professionalism, and downright sense of calm.

Yasmin, a worried mess, screwed up tissues and drank endless cups of tea and paced the room as if she was able to transfer her energy into the office. It became excruciating watching from a distance. Tasha was right; Yasmin should be there. But she tried not to get maudlin about it. Instead, she decided to be thankful just for being a part of it all.

Darkness began to drop by the time the energy petered out. People stared at screens without reading, or massaged sore necks, or rotated stiff shoulders. Yasmin felt just as exhausted.

Around eight p.m., Felicia emailed the finalised copy.

"What do you think?" she asked Yasmin.

"It's wonderful, Felicia. Simply outstanding."

"I want your real thoughts, please. Don't stroke my ego. I already know I'm the best editor over the age of thirty in the office."

"You're the only one over thirty in the office," Yasmin said. Then blushed. "What I meant was—"

"It's okay, Yasmin." Felicia grinned. "Tell it to me truthfully now."

"Well, I think you need to define the moment when they stood up and decided to be different from their mothers, and their friends, and to the norms of the time. What made them who they are."

Yasmin's heart edged up the back of her throat. In the safety of her bedroom, rather than Felicia's office, she felt more courage than she actually had. Felicia paused, delaying having to speak again, perhaps reconsidering her choice to keep her on as a freelancer.

"I appreciate your honesty," Felicia said. "Tell me about Nicole; when did she know she wanted to be a climate scientist, when it was unpopular and on the fringes of mainstream science?"

Yasmin thought for a second, recalling the anecdote.

"A friend of hers at the university was working on an early climate model," she said. "He showed her the graph of temperature changes before the Industrial Revolution. It had all been pretty stable. Then he showed her a graph after the Industrial Revolution. It was off the charts. Then he showed her the last twenty years, and she knew it spelled catastrophe. She knew if we kept on like this, it could mean the end of humans. The next big extinction. And nobody was doing anything about it."

"There," Felicia said. "Keep talking."

And soon Felicia had her angle, and she moved on.

"What was the tipping point for Deborah?" Felicia asked.

"The day David Deloitte spat in her face when she asked why she wasn't paid as much as her male colleague. Ron was half as competent and got paid twice as much. I mean, her boss actually spat in her face. As if that was his God-given right as a man. As if Ron could have been forty times less competent and he would still get a raise ahead of her. That day she realised it would always be true unless they did something about it."

Felicia scribbled notes. She finished and addressed the screen.

"Um…what about Audrey?" she asked delicately. "You knew her best."

"The day her dad arrived home from the First World War," Yasmin said, almost in a trance herself. "He was shell-shocked, having lost half his troops. He sank into drink. Audrey saw what war did to people, to good people. And she wanted to be one of the strong ones, for all the people who couldn't be that strong. She wanted to prove that you could go to war and not come home mad. Because, somehow, she wanted her dad to recover, to see that she was all right, and he would be too. And maybe if he had survived the second war, maybe he would have been okay. Maybe Audrey could have saved him."

Felicia stopped taking notes and regarded Yasmin with a newfound respect. Felicia, too, had climbed the rungs in a world dominated by men. And most were not afraid to stamp on her hands from the higher rungs or look up her skirt from further down. Felicia Pine must have some of her own stories to tell.

The workers thinned out as people left to go home, until only Tasha and Felicia remained. Tasha hadn't eased up and was still typing furiously. Felicia scanned mocks in her office.

Felicia gathered up the mocks on her desk and strode out to Tasha.

"What do you think?" Felicia asked, holding up two.

Felicia had addressed Yasmin, not Tasha!

Both mocks were amazing. They were simple – the three women, at thirty, as they had been in the first issue of *The Standard* that they had each appeared in. A call-back to their original articles, and their thirty-year-old selves.

But as Felicia held them up, Audrey's face in the first mock seemed to jump straight off the page. Did a shimmer appear right there, at the photo's edges?

"The one on the left," Yasmin said. "Definitely that one."

32

They'd survived the final hours of D-day – deadline day. Tasha ran the files for the final time and sent them to Production to drop in the ads. Production would then send the magazine to the printer. What passed through these walls tonight would be in print forever: hard copies in people's hands and bookshelves and cardboard boxes left in the garage while their readers grew old. It suddenly hit Yasmin that this was an enduring piece of copy; this feature would be enjoyed by many people for many years to come.

Or it could be used to line the kitty-litter tray, or as cut-out collages for pre-schoolers, or be covered in bacteria in a doctor's waiting room. But it would still be one of the most permanent things of today. It would live on long after Yasmin's laptop had frozen in Motherboard Malfunction Land. It would be as flimsy and as time-tested as anything else that had existed in the world before. And if their cities fell, the new world that would rise up might find the magazine somewhere and consult the annals of humans past, and realise they had a history. Even if these women could live forever in only one person's heart, then they would never be forgotten.

And that was all that mattered to Yasmin. It was the whole point. *The Standard* could change someone's life, or inspire them when they felt hopeless, or encourage them when they thought it wasn't possible. Because today's girls needed real heroes, not badly behaved celebrities or amoral politicians. Real women, who'd lived, and loved, and lost, and won. Real women who had helped humanity realise who they were today.

Today's women were their legacy.

The next morning, Tasha linked Yasmin into the office via Skype. Catina was on school holidays and lounged on the bed.

Yasmin watched Tasha's face as she pushed the approval button, waiting for the files to send and the hourglass cursor to stop spinning.

"That's it," Tasha said. "The magazine has been submitted!"

A thrill shimmied through Yasmin.

Felicia popped some champagne and filled the eagerly held glasses.

"Well done, everyone," Felicia said, flicking her eyes briefly at Yasmin through Tasha's monitor, and raising her glass slightly higher.

Catina popped their own bottle of bubbly – Spumante – and filled their now-empty coffee cups with the cheap sparkling. They clinked mugs and swigged their first taste of victory.

"I want to give a special shout-out to everyone on the fourth floor," Felicia said as the office around her hushed. "You've all pulled out an enormous effort here to achieve something we thought impossible only a few weeks ago. And I think we're well-placed for this to be the issue that defines *The Woman's Standard* in the modern era. You can all be proud of the work we've done here. There is some enormous talent in our editorial team." She turned slightly, and Yasmin swore she stared straight at her, through Tasha's screen.

"She means us! She means us!" Catina said, grabbing Yasmin's arm.

"Shhhhh…" Yasmin hissed, muting the webcam microphone. Felicia seemed amused, and a few other workers turned to see the source of the outburst.

"And, regardless of how this pans out for *The Standard*, I want you to know it was my enormous pleasure to work with, what I have come to regard as, the most gifted editorial team in Australia."

The office burst into applause, at first a little surprised. Felicia was being, for once, generous with her praise. Yasmin saw the deep flush grow on Tasha's neck and up into her face. She turned to the monitor and beamed at Yasmin. Tasha understood Yasmin's joy, even if they did have the webcam's video turned off.

A couple of weeks passed before the magazine was finally printed, and Tasha received advance copies at the office. She skyped in, for what could be the last time.

She flipped through the magazine, showing Yasmin the articles of her ghost-mothers as their real selves.

"I'll slip your copy in the mail," she said. "We're already working on the next issue. You know, just in case we all still have a job this time next week."

"When are the circ figures released?" Yasmin asked.

"Any day now." Tasha sucked in a deep breath.

"So how is everyone?"

"Good, we're much happier. Felicia seems to have made peace with whatever happens next. I know she feels like we gave it our all. We can't influence what comes next. Honestly, I think it's been healthy for her to let go of control like that."

"Have you had any more of those editorial meetings?" Yasmin asked, screwing up her nose.

"Oh sure, but it's more like a brainstorming session. I guess, what do we have to lose?"

"Whatever happened to Buckley?" Yasmin's brow creased. She hoped he was okay.

"He loved it in Archives. He wasn't even that mad when they let him out," Tasha said. "Can you believe he's going to study to be a librarian? You know, so that he can work with dusty shelves and yellowing books all day?"

"I can't believe it. Buckley? That old square?" Yasmin said.

"Of course I'm joking," Tasha said. Yasmin groaned. "He's been spending less time in the foyer and more time in the valet parking area. I guess his boss wasn't too happy with the security breaches."

"Poor man," Yasmin said.

There seemed to be a commotion at the water cooler. People crowded around.

"What's happening?" Yasmin asked.

"It's Oliver Standsfield-Cage," Tasha said.

"Oh, my. The circ numbers."

A crowd gathered around the small man, huddling so close together that Yasmin could barely see his curled and pointed moustache. The pinstripe-suited man from all of those photos in Felicia's office!

Felicia's door opened, and she stepped out.

"Oliver," she said.

"I knew you wouldn't be able to wait for the news," he said. Yasmin could hardly see past the backs of heads. Did his voice sound hopeful, or resigned? Yasmin decided it sounded resigned. Her stomach felt constricted as if she'd overeaten. She started to feel a little nauseous. They absolutely couldn't let Audrey down now.

"I'm not one to stand on ceremony," he began in his clipped, almost-English tones. The office hushed. "So I'll keep it brief. We won't have the official circ numbers for a month or so, so today is just a best-guess kind of situation."

"Did we do it?" Tasha asked.

"If by 'do it,' you mean, did we smash our previous figures for the most new subscriptions ever, then…yes."

The floor let out a collective squeal.

"And if you mean 'did we save *The Woman's Standard*, our jobs, and the whole damn company,' then it's a resounding 'yes, we did!'"

Everyone jumped around, hugging each other. Felicia rushed to fill Oliver's champagne glass. He managed a smile, and shuffled towards Felicia. He held out his arms and the two air-hugged in an approximation of warmth.

"We've bloody done it," Yasmin said, hugging her sister and crying and laughing all in one messy, runny-nosed huddle of happiness.

Tasha approached the screen and asked Yasmin to unmute her microphone.

"Seriously, you gals saved our arses."

"It was a joint effort," Yasmin said. "Congratulations to you as well. It was your rigorous, supportive training strategy that got us here today."

Yasmin smiled cheekily at Tasha, and she grinned back. Someone called to her.

"Got to go," she said, waved, and headed off into the throng of office celebration. One of the workers cranked up the sound of Destiny Child's 'Survivor', and the dancing began.

"Well, that's me out," Yasmin said, shutting the laptop.

She glanced at Catina. Her room suddenly seemed cramped and childish. Totally inadequate for two women of the world.

"Let's take this party on the town," Yasmin said.

"Now you're talking!" Catina said.

33

*A*s Catina was still technically underage, Yasmin found a quiet cafe a few blocks away, a darkened affair with natural wood and brick tones and a plethora of bearded patrons sitting at mismatched tables. The cafe smelt like cinnamon and ground coffee.

Yasmin held a spiced chai latte, and Catina poked at the foam on her mocha.

They both remembered the fairy ghost-mothers.

"My favourite part was when Audrey's wig fell on the floor!" Catina said, smiling.

"My least favourite part was Deborah blowing smoke into Felicia's face," Yasmin said, taking a long sip of her latte. "That was the beginning of my slide into unemployment."

Someone dropped a water glass by the espresso machine. The glass shattered into tiny shards, and the ice dripped in a watery lump to the floor. It dribbled towards them.

"The signalling of the witching hour," Catina said, "when all good women should be tucked up in bed."

"We're not good women," Yasmin laughed.

"No, we're the best," Catina said, roughly patting Yasmin with sisterly warmth. One of the bearded gents at another table noticed and smiled. Yasmin nodded back.

"So what are you going to do now?" Catina asked.

"I…ah…" Yasmin said, evading Catina's gaze.

"It's okay. Whatever you want. You're free now," Catina said.

"Well, I was thinking of finally granting your wish and moving out," Yasmin said.

"Oh." Catina tried to hide her disappointment. "I was just starting to enjoy your company, and it's nice that the household chores are being shared between us."

"I can stay for a little longer," Yasmin said.

"No, it's okay," Catina said, a smile blooming. "It's the right thing."

Yasmin wasn't sure that it was okay and she started to feel sad again, thinking of her besties as a pile of ash. Everything seemed so final. Could she move on without them?

"So who are you moving in with?" Catina asked.

Yasmin's phone buzzed in her pocket. The office number.

"Oh darn…it's Felicia." Yasmin left the noisy cafe for an even noisier street. She answered just as a bus roared past.

"Sorry, can you wait for just a—" She waited until the bus engine died to a distant rumble. "Sorry, a bus just went past."

"You still overuse the word 'sorry,'" Felicia said.

"Sorry…I mean…"

"Have I caught you at a bad time?"

"No, not at all. I'm glad you called. How's life at *The Standard*?" Yasmin asked.

"Fantastic." Felicia paused. "Wait until you hear why I've called."

Yasmin laughed nervously, flattening herself against the wall as a bicycle shot past on the footpath. "We've been sued? By the families or something? I will say it was my idea, and it will get you off the hook; you'll be fine. I mean, I think it works like that. Am I rambling?"

"Yasmin," Felicia said, stopping her. "I can't have you back in the office. Not after what happened."

"Of course," Yasmin said, confused. Is that what she had rung her about?

"And that's why I want to hire you, as a freelance researcher, to help Tasha write a regular column."

"A column?" Yasmin said, in shock. "What's the column about?"

"What it means to be a woman. You know, a real, three-dimensional, human woman."

In her bedroom, Yasmin packed boxes and filled her suitcase with collectibles: the china cat she inherited from her grandmother's display cabinet, the tea infuser from Great Aunt Bessie, the lace hankies from the Salvos store. The various books, trinkets and pictures from her childhood. Everything was wrapped in white-grey packing paper and placed into boxes to be taken away.

Catina helped for a couple of hours, and they chatted and bickered and reminisced.

Yasmin was going to miss her sister.

She found the boxes of *The Woman's Standard* on a high shelf in her wardrobe. She set them on her bed, opening the flaps carefully, dusting off the covers.

"Hey, remember this?" she asked, flipping to the page with Deborah's egg-stained face, at her at the protest march she'd organised.

"Yeah, all those things she accomplished that day, all the things they stood for. And the media reduced it to that stupid egg."

Yasmin found Nicole, the epitome of authority and knowledge, in her white lab coat and a pair of smart specs. She held out her Nobel Peace medal to the camera.

"I would have been so proud of her that day," Yasmin said.

Catina held out another magazine, Audrey's magazine. Neither of them spoke, remembering her – Australia's most-decorated female war hero. Their hero.

Yasmin roused herself and began taking things downstairs to a pile by the door. Her mother, dressed in her nurse's uniform, found her in the hallway.

"Are you off, then?" Susan asked, checking her watch.

Yasmin threw her arms around her mother, taking them both by surprise. Susan leaned into the hug, and Yasmin held tight.

"I'm proud of you," Susan said, stroking Yasmin's hair.

"Thanks for putting up with me," Yasmin said.

They pulled away, and Susan fished the car keys from her handbag. She smiled at her daughter, then headed out the side door to the garage.

Yasmin finished the rest of the packing, carried the boxes of magazines to her car, and carefully set them into the boot.

"Do you need a hand at the other end?" Catina asked.

"I'll be fine," Yasmin said, but walked right up to her and hugged her. "Thanks, Catina."

Catina wrapped her arms tightly around her sister. "You're welcome, sis."

It did feel like the gang was breaking up. Yasmin felt a little nostalgic, as if already contemplating a reunion tour.

Catina and Susan waved Yasmin off – Catina from the front door and her mother from the garage. Yasmin eased the car down the driveway and through the streets she'd grown up in. Past squat houses with neat lawns, which morphed into terrace houses, which finally gave way to blocks of units.

She found a red-brick apartment complex which had been built in the seventies. She idled into the driveway to the back set of parking spots, and deposited her car in a spare residential space.

She sat for a moment, turning her mobile phone in her hands. Then she got out of the car and walked down the path to the security door of the apartment. She opened Skype on her phone. It rang a few times.

"Hello?" a distant voice answered.

"Dad? It's Yasmin."

She unlocked the door and let herself in.

EPILOGUE

*Y*asmin came to realise that she'd never win a war, or start a movement, or save the world. These things were left to better people. However, she helped Tasha write about these feats; she shone a light on women's lives, in a world that seemed so full of darkness. She brought their stories to the women who read *The Standard*, and she showed the readership what was possible. She depicted these women as real people, with real problems, but also with real hopes and dreams for the future.

A future they could all help to make.

Yasmin interviewed politicians and business owners, police detectives and race-car drivers. She interviewed those who used their brains, or their dexterity, or their strength. She spoke to people from backgrounds grand and tiny, those who were educated, and those who were not. She interviewed the real women of Australia.

The Standard became known, not as a bastion of fashion, cooking and tips on keeping house, but as a place for all voices – influential and otherwise, voices that made up the tapestry of life – the life of being, or identifying as, a woman. Yasmin showed their real faces, their unglossed lives, their true struggles. And, above all, she ended the note on a high, to show the good in all, to show that anything was possible. These women could let loose the shackles of the life they thought they had, and live the life they wanted.

Yasmin was allowed back in the office, on occasion, to organise the shoots for the women she interviewed. They were shot in the clothes they arrived in, with few props – stark photos that captured the wrinkles and imperfections of real lives lived, of happiness and heartache. Some came with their kids or their pets. A few brought their partners. But they all had one similarity: they were snapped fresh, clean, and without embellishment.

And *The Standard* was lauded for it. They'd ushered in a new magazine era, one that didn't gloss and primp and objectify. One that told it like it was, by people who were real. One that told the truth and didn't make their readers feel less because they didn't measure up to the glossy version of these people. The women in their magazine were just like the readers at home.

Yasmin packed up the shoot with Australia's first female Prime Minister and heartily shook her hand. Whether or not Yasmin would have voted for her didn't matter. She was real and willing to be honest. The first of any role had to carry the burden of all the people who came before, and give hope for those who came after.

Yasmin thanked the former Prime Minister and watched her leave the studio, her head high, her back straight, and her gait as easy as any who had been here before. She was, at her core, just another woman.

Yasmin rode the train home to her new apartment, and put her key in the front door. She dumped her laptop bag on the kitchen table and dropped her keys in the bowl on the counter. She opened the fridge, sorting through the vegetable tray.

An hour later, Tasha arrived home. Yasmin's flattie had worked out pretty well. They liked the same television shows and had the same taste in food. They pontificated for hours on the brilliant people in the world, and who they would feature next in the magazine.

"Smells good," Tasha said. "I forgot it was your turn to cook."

"I hadn't," Yasmin said, putting a fork at the fifth place setting on the kitchen table.

"Are we expecting someone?" Tasha asked, surprised.

Yasmin set three photos of her fairy ghost-mothers between the place settings. Yasmin touched each frame in turn and took her seat.

The two women sat and shared a meal that Yasmin had prepared, and they laughed and reminisced and told each other stories, tall and true.

Yasmin felt the happiest she'd ever been, and possibly ever would be. She was paid to do something she loved. And she knew, beyond anything else, that they would take care of each other, for now, and for always.

Because they were family.

Want to discover how the ghost-mothers' adventure really began?

As a thank you for reading *The Ghost Mothers*, I've prepared a special bonus just for you!

In this exclusive (spoiler-free) short story, you'll follow the ghost-mothers on their unforgettable last day on Earth—and uncover the magical misadventures that started it all.

Claim your free short story prequel at:

jackiemccarthy.com/free-short-story-prequel

Loved *The Ghost Mothers*?

If you have a moment, I'd be so grateful if you could share your thoughts wherever you love to leave book reviews.

Your feedback helps new readers find their next favourite story—and it means more to me than you know.

Thank you so much for being part of this journey!

ABOUT THE AUTHOR

Jackie lives in Sydney, Australia. She has worked in the magazine and online publishing industry, in both London and Sydney, for more years than she'd like to count.

She loves writing epic female characters, scrappy heroines, and magical mayhem.

The Ghost Mothers is her debut novel, and she's also the author of *The Kaseath Chronicles*, a YA dystopian science fiction series.

More novels, short stories, and novellas are coming soon!

Find out more at: jackiemccarthy.com

Want behind-the-scenes goodies, freebies, and first dibs on new releases? Join the Readers Group: jackiemccarthy.com/sign-up

Thanks for reading!

ALSO BY JACKIE MCCARTHY

The Hybrid Cure

(The Kaseath Chronicles, Book 1)

jackiemccarthy.com/books/the-hybrid-cure

Rebel Conspiracy

(The Kaseath Chronicles, Book 2)

jackiemccarthy.com/books/rebel-conspiracy

For all current and upcoming titles, visit:

jackiemccarthy.com/books

ACKNOWLEDGMENTS

A special shout out to anyone who bought, shared, commented, liked, tweeted, posted or reviewed. You are the best, and I appreciate every one of you, so thank you.

To my incredible family, what can I say, besides I love you guys! You've been my biggest supporters, and for that I am grateful.

To my talented and insightful editors; Roisin Heycock for guidance throughout the entire process; you've championed my book right from that early draft; and Lauren Finger, for consistently over-delivering in the final stages, to a very tight deadline.

Thanks to my generous beta readers – Jennifer Bisset, Judy Lai, Katie Steuerwald, Kristie Montagu, Maggie Connors and Sian Thompson – for helping me to find the final version of the book.

For my Launch Team, who helped those early readers find my book – your support has meant the world to me as a debut novelist, so massive thanks.

Thanks to the eagle-eye proof-readers who picked up things the rest of us had missed.

And finally, but by no means lastly; thanks to my friends for listening to my endless ramblings, and for remaining enthusiastic throughout.

Author Photo by Alessia Francischiello

ISBN (eBook): 978-0-6486942-1-2

ISBN (Paperback): 978-0-6486942-0-5

www.ingramcontent.com/pod-product-compliance
Lightning Source LLC
Chambersburg PA
CBHW020130120726
47903CB00007B/2187